LAST NOCTURNE

LAST NOCTURNE

M.J. Trow

CRÈME de la CRIME

This first world edition published 2020
in Great Britain and 2021 in the USA by
Crème de la Crime an imprint of
SEVERN HOUSE PUBLISHERS LTD of
Eardley House, 4 Uxbridge Street, London W8 7SY.
Trade paperback edition first published
in Great Britain and the USA 2021 by
SEVERN HOUSE PUBLISHERS LTD.

British Library Cataloguing in Publication Data
A CIP catalogue record for this title is available from the British Library.

ISBN-13: 978-1-78029-130-7 (cased)
ISBN-13: 978-1-78029-754-5 (trade paper)
ISBN-13: 978-1-4483-0492-9 (e-book)

All Severn House titles are printed on acid-free paper.

Severn House Publishers support the Forest Stewardship Council™ [FSC™],
the leading international forest certification organisation.
All our titles that are printed on FSC certified paper carry the FSC logo.

Typeset by Palimpsest Book Production Ltd.,
Falkirk, Stirlingshire, Scotland.
Printed and bound in Great Britain by
TJ Books Limited, Padstow, Cornwall.

ONE

The full moon hung over the Cremorne Gardens like a Chinese lantern broken from the strings around the lake. The blossom-laden branches which glowed beneath it swung gently to and fro in the breeze and, looking up through gin-glazed eyes, it wasn't hard to imagine that it was the moon swinging, not the trees. It wasn't often that Clara had a night off from her work – she had told her mother she was a seamstress and it was indeed true that she did occasionally sew on a button, torn off in the general hurly-burly – and technically, she wasn't having a night off now, in that she had already been paid handsomely. She jingled the coins in her pocket as she leaned back on the bench beside the lake; they sounded like the music of distant bells. She smiled and turned her head languidly to look at her gentleman. Everyone was a gentleman to Clara; if she thought of them as anything else, how would she face herself in the tiny square of speckled mirror above the sink on the landing where she washed every evening before she went out?

She smiled and waggled her fingers at the man sitting next to her. He was a cut above her usual, she would give him that. If his hat brim was a tad too wide and his clothes a little passé, she didn't mind. As far as she was concerned, her gentlemen could wear old sacks as long as they had a pocket for her money.

He dipped his head a little and the sharp shadow cast by the moon slid down his face and hid it completely. If she looked hard, Clara could just see his eyes, glimmering in the depths under the exaggerated brim. She lolled her head on one shoulder. Was he young or old? She couldn't tell. She was still new enough at this game to prefer the young ones. She had been recommended to one old fellow of ninety and although she hadn't been kept at her work long, the feel of those papery thighs wouldn't leave her as long as she lived, she knew. So she told herself this one was probably middling, as far as age went. Middling as far as money went; he had paid her more than usual, but in small coins, generally a sign that a man had been foraging down the sides of the sofa to raise the wind; or even worse, saving up for the great day. She looked down his body from his invisible face. Middling as regards build and – so far, at least – she didn't know whether he was middling in the other parts or built like a donkey or a shrew. She reached out with a hand floppy with gin and traced a line up from his knee with a grubby finger-nail. She had almost reached the buttons of his fly when he put his hand over hers.

'Not now,' he said, softly. 'Let's wait a while, enjoy the moon, the blossom, the warm night.'

'I have my usual gentleman in a while,' she said, slurring her words a little. 'He likes to meet me on the bridge at midnight. There's some good shadow under the arches then.'

He clenched his fist with her hand inside it and she flinched. 'You're too good for a quick one under a bridge,' he said, and although he didn't raise his voice from its low register, she could tell he was getting angry.

'I'm as good or as bad as I need to be,' she said, her annoyance breaking through the fog of the gin. 'I'm a working girl with the rent to find.'

'I paid you extra,' he said. 'I didn't know I was on the clock.'

She flexed her fingers and loosened his grip enough for her to be able to make a grab at what she was there for. 'You're not on the clock,' she reassured him, fluttering her fingers to and fro. 'But I need to get something to eat before I see my next gentleman. A girl has to eat, you know.'

The man laughed and pushed her hand away, crossing his legs primly. 'Well, if you had said, I can help you there.' He bent down to the bag at his side. She had wondered about the bag. Not many punters turned up with the weekly groceries in tow.

She leaned forward and the moon swung wildly, so she leaned back again and closed her eyes. 'Help?' she said, weakly, waiting for the world to sit still.

'I have some food here in my bag. Would you like' – there was a sound of rustling paper – 'a sandwich? I've got cheese or I've got ham. Or I have a pie.' There was more rustling and Clara risked opening her eyes.

'What pie?'

'Pork.'

'Do you mean a pork pie, or a pie with pork in it? There's a difference, you know.'

The gentleman clucked his tongue. 'You're a picky one, and no mistake. It's a pie with pork in it, as it happens.'

Clara pulled a face. 'No thank you, then. I'll get something on the way. Speaking of which,' she reached out again and wormed her fingers between his crossed legs. 'If you want your money's worth, we really should . . .'

'I don't really fancy it now, to be honest,' he said. 'I'm just enjoying your company.'

She turned her head sharply and the view swam. 'Are you?' No one had ever said that to her before, not even her regular gentleman.

'You're very lovely,' he said, suddenly, his eyes gleaming in the depths of the black shadow under his hat. 'Like a painting.'

She stared back at him, bemused.

'I just want to watch you sitting there, under the moon.' He leaned back and seemed to scan her face, the eyes flickering in the dark. 'But, where are my manners?' He foraged in the bag again. 'How about a piece of cake?'

Her face lit up. She had always had a weakness for cake. It was why she had a struggle keeping her waist trim and her thighs inviting for her gentlemen. 'What kind of cake?'

'You're a fussy one,' he complained, but not seriously. He reached out, a slice of pale cake in his hand. 'Almond. With marzipan.'

'Marzipan?' She almost cried; it reminded her of her mother, sitting at home back in the village, telling proud tales of her daughter the seamstress up in London. She reached out and took it greedily, biting into the yellow covering with strong white teeth, not yet fallen to the gin.

He sat back and tilted his head slightly, showing a pleasant smile. 'Good girl,' he murmured. 'Eat it up.'

She stopped chewing and looked dubiously at the cake. 'This marzipan is really strong,' she said, stifling a cough.

'All the best marzipan is,' he murmured, reaching into his bag again. 'I wonder, have you read this book?'

'It's dark,' she said, coughing again and holding her chest, and indeed she was right; clouds were scudding from the west and fast obscuring the moon.

'It's a picture book,' he said, opening it on her lap. 'The moon is still just bright enough, I think.'

'I . . . I can't really catch my breath . . . do you have a drink in your bag?' She leant forward, her hands to her throat.

'I'm afraid not,' he said, quietly. 'You had all the gin, if you remember, when you said you would go with me into the park and give me the time of my life.' He looked down at her as she struggled, her face blue in the cold light from the sky. 'And I must say, my dear,' he added, as he watched her eyes grow sightless and her arms slump to her sides, 'you don't disappoint.'

'The what?' Sergeant George Simmons had been up all night and his cape leaked like a sieve. Why did it always rain when there was a body to view? The warm night had turned chillier and had brought rain from the west.

'CID, Sergeant,' the detective said slowly. 'Criminal Investigation Department. Haven't you read the memorandum?'

'Ah, we don't get those in B Division . . . sir.' The last word had come as an afterthought and both men knew it. B Division *did* get every memorandum sent from headquarters at the Yard and Simmons had read it too. But he was too long in the tooth to give it his full attention, having pounded the Cremorne beat since the Year of Revolutions and he wasn't going to sit up and take notice now. Like all other government directives, it would go away if you just ignored it.

'Sir' was clearly a rookie, a fresh-faced detective of the new school, one of Mr Howard Vincent's boys, desperately trying to grow a pair of dundrearies to give his schoolboy cheeks some gravitas. Detective-Constable William Barnes was not long out of uniform himself and, although he would die in a Cremorne ditch rather than let Simmons know it, this was his first murder.

He looked down at the girl on the seat. What with the rain and the darkness, illuminated in flashing beams by Simmons's bullseye, she wasn't going to tell him much. That was because she was dead. That was because, whatever they tell you, dead women tell no tales.

'So, Sergeant,' Barnes stood up to his full height, feeling the drips from the tree bounce off the brim of his wideawake, 'what do you make of it all?'

Simmons had spent years belittling his superiors, stifling giggles at their expense, making them feel ill at ease. And he did it again now. 'Isn't it rather more important what *you* make of it, sir?' he asked. His bullseye was shining right in the lad's face. Barnes moved to one side, delivering his next line with what little bravado he had. 'I like to give my men the chance to improve themselves,' he winced, rather than smiled, probably because he knew what was coming next. 'Increases the likelihood of promotion, you know.'

Simmons knew. He knew that at nearly fifty years old, promotion was for other people. Especially when you've had your fingers in the biscuit barrel as often as Sergeant George Simmons. Even so, he took pity on the lad. Kneeling on the wet grass, he shone the bullseye directly into the dead woman's face. 'What is she?' the sergeant was talking to himself, 'Twenty-one? Twenty-two?' He peered down at the book in her lap and removed it from under her right hand. It was leather-bound and the rain had made a mess of the open pages.

'Page one three eight, sir,' Simmons said. 'Just for the record, you know. You know how Their Lordships at the Bailey like fiddle-faddle like that. And the book is . . . oh, my, this is a naughty one, sir – *The Fruits of Philosophy*.'

'Er . . . I don't think I know it,' Barnes confessed.

'The subtitle is *The Private Companion of Young Married People*. I'm sure I don't have to paint you a picture.'

Barnes was secretly hoping that Simmons would. The sergeant sensed the plainclothesman's confusion. 'It's what that Annie Besant calls birth control, sir. She republished the book last year. Plain filth to you and me, of course.'

'Of course.' Barnes thought it best to agree.

'No, all that sort of stuff is best left to the Lord. That's the line that Mrs Simmons and me have followed all these years. Us and the eleven little Simmonses.'

'Eleven.' Barnes was a little startled. 'Quite the cricket team.' His solitary laugh sounded a little out of place at a cold, dark crime scene not far from the Thames shoreline.

'Which is odd.' Simmons had placed the book, closed, on the bench next to the body.

'What is?' He had lost Barnes already.

'The fact that this lady had this book with her.'

'Really? Why?'

Simmons looked up at him. He placed the back of his hand on the girl's cheek and shook his head. 'If you are of a sensitive disposition, sir,' he said, 'I should look away now.' And he hauled up the girl's skirts, thrusting his hand up her thighs. Barnes gulped. This was 1878. Surely, society had not become so utterly depraved . . .

'She was a lady of the night, sir,' Simmons told him. 'No kecks. It saves time, y'see, with a client. Up with the skirt, legs apart, away we go. I've seen it dozens of times.'

'Really?' Barnes had come to the CID from the horse troughs of Pimlico. It was a bit late now to realize that he should have got out more. 'Didn't you arrest the miscreants?'

'Of course, sir!' Simmons feigned horror that he would have done anything else. 'This is the Cremorne Gardens. It used to be a respectable place, full of tea rooms, genteel young ladies and old besoms walking their dogs. I seen that Elizabeth Barrett Browning here one day, oh yes; walking of her dog, she was, high as a kite on laudanum. We had a standing order to take her home if we seen her.' Simmons chuckled. 'Couldn't tell her apart from the mutt.' He sketched long hair or ears, depending on species. 'Oh, yes, back in its day, the old Cremorne was the place to be seen and no hanky-panky in the shrubbery. But now' – he shook his head – 'you see some sights.' He forbore to tell the detective constable what he did with the miscreants at the various times when Mrs Simmons found herself indisposed.

'Had she been . . . interfered with?' Barnes sketched a rough circle with one hand in the region he was considering.

'Have a heart, sir,' Simmons said. 'If I'd got the tart spread out on a marble slab in some mortuary, I could give you a reasonable stab at that. As it is, in the dark in the park, as it were, it's not possible to tell. Mind you, it goes with the territory, don't it? I mean, interfering's the name of the game, innit? By various other names, of course.'

Barnes nodded, trying to extract the essence of what Simmons had just told him. 'So, she was a prostitute . . .' After that, deduction failed him.

'She was, sir.' Barnes got up, cursing his arthritic knees. 'We know this because of the scarcity of kecks and also . . .'

'Yes?'

'Well, women of this sort – park girls, if you take my meaning – they're not known for their extensive libraries.'

'Quite, quite,' Barnes nodded, suddenly a man of the world.

'But in my experience, pretty much all of 'em can read.'

'Indeed, indeed.' Barnes was following every word of this.

'So, how come, then,' Simmons asked him, 'the book was in her lap upside down?'

Maisie was not the brightest maid that Mrs Rackstraw had ever had under her control, but she was pleasant enough. If only she could stop standing with her mouth open and her eyes like stars whenever Matthew Grand was in the room, she would be almost the ideal servant. This habit tended to make her rather less than coherent when reporting back to Mrs Rackstraw the conversations she overheard while serving at the table, breakfast being the best time to get the gossip which the housekeeper could chew over all day until it came out in a rather different form at her afternoon teas, shared with other housekeepers of homes of distinction just off the Strand.

'He said what?' Mrs Rackstraw asked, not for the first time. Maisie often had to take a couple of runs at it to get all her ducks in a row.

'Master Matthew,' Maisie liked to roll the name out slowly, enjoying the taste on her tongue, 'Master Matthew said that he was going to throw paint over a man.' Maisie's eyes were like gooseberries, both in shade and protuberance.

Mrs Rackstraw looked doubtful. Matthew Grand was

American and he couldn't help that of course, poor soul, but he wasn't the kind of man to resort to random vandalism. She decided to delve. 'Did he say who?'

'What?' Maisie had lost the thread.

Mrs Rackstraw sighed and went back to scrambling the breakfast eggs. Matthew Grand preferred his soft and runny, James Batchelor liked his to be firmer so they sat perkily on the toast. It needed timing and concentration. It was not the moment for trying to get Maisie's brain, as scrambled as the eggs, back on track. The housekeeper knew that if she left her long enough, she would sort it out for herself.

The eggs were cooked, delivered and half eaten before Maisie remembered. 'It was because he was whistling,' she suddenly announced.

By now, Mrs Rackstraw was on another subject in her head – the butcher's boy had been unconscionably rude again the day before and the kidneys more gristle than anything else. She would be going round to the shop later, dressed in her signature black and with her second best bonnet at its most terrifying angle in order to give Mr Juniper a piece of her mind and the fright of his life. She ran through the projected conversation in her mind, and Mr Juniper was certainly getting the worst of it, when Maisie spoke. Mrs Rackstraw jumped visibly and turned on Maisie like a rattler.

'Whistling? Who was whistling?' Whistling went through her head like a knife.

'The man who Master Matthew said he was going to throw paint on.'

The whole thing had seemed rather spurious to Mrs Rackstraw from the beginning but now she knew that Maisie had the wrong end of the stick. Matthew Grand could strip paint with his whistle, especially when he was in the bath. She had seen his partner in the enquiry business sitting in the morning room with rolled-up cotton wool in his ears when it reached a certain level, so she used her logic.

'So, it was Master James who was going to throw the paint?' she checked.

'No.' Maisie didn't have anything against the Englishman

but she hardly heard a word he said when Master Matthew was in the room.

Mrs Rackstraw stood back and looked at Maisie, six stone of stupidity in a frilly cap and an apron which would go round her twice. The stare she got in return didn't help with the solution of what would have to remain a puzzle until, perhaps, the police knocked at the door and told her that her employer had been taken into quod for throwing the contents of a paint-pot in a whistler's face. For now, she had the butcher to look forward to and she couldn't follow every flitter of the maid's mind. Sufficient unto the day, as she believed Shakespeare had once said, unless she missed her guess, was the evil thereof.

Matthew Grand and James Batchelor sat at opposite ends of the breakfast table as they had for over a decade, looking with mild horror at each other's scrambled egg. Batchelor could no more eat a soft egg than sprout wings and fly around the room. Grand, for his part, didn't see the point in eating something which resembled, in almost every respect, a lawn tennis ball. But they had had the conversation many times, and on this particular morning, anyway, they had other subjects to discuss. Their enquiry agency was doing well and they were considering taking on a junior, for the legwork. Not that their own legs were in anything other than fine fettle, but Grand was contemplating marriage and his wife-to-be had let it be known that she would not appreciate the undoubted delights of the marriage bed being interrupted in the wee small hours or – Grand had been delighted to hear – the quieter hours of the afternoon, by lowlife wanting someone to find their lost cat. Grand had told her quite categorically that they had risen above those levels now, but she was adamant; he took on help or the marriage was not going to happen in a hurry.

James Batchelor was not contemplating marriage. Grand's inamorata, Lady Caroline Wentworth, of, it must be stated, the Worcestershire Wentworths, had provided numerous oppor-tunities by wafting friends of hers – mainly ones with a squint or a rather odd disposition – under his nose, but Batchelor had decided that until he wrote the Great British Novel, any kind of relationship was out of the question. He had tried doing both, but ended up writing either mushy drivel, one hundred thousand words of introspective misery, or pornography, depending on the lady of the moment, so he was being strict with himself.

'Do you have anyone in mind?' Batchelor asked, reaching for the marmalade.

'Not really,' Grand admitted. 'I know it's been a while, but I wondered if you could ask around in Fleet Street. See if there's a likely lad who can stick his nose into other people's business and yet not give offence.'

'Why would you think there would be such a lad in Fleet Street?' Batchelor said with a wry smile. 'There's not a reporter born, old or young, who doesn't give offence wherever he goes.'

'True. But perhaps if we snaffle one early, before the old cynicism kicks in. Anyway, that's just something to keep in mind.'

'I thought that Caroline said . . .'

'She did,' Grand said, looking round just to make sure she hadn't crept in under cover of the sound of crunching toast, 'but there's no sense in rushing, is there?'

Batchelor hid a smile. Like Grand, he rather liked the life they led – big changes lay ahead and neither man was dashing to make them happen. 'Anything else?'

Grand shuffled through some letters at the side of his plate and drew one out. It was on flimsy, cream-coloured paper and from his end of the table, Batchelor could see it was covered in florid writing, in deep blue ink.

'I've had this letter from James McNeill Whistler.' He looked up expectantly at Grand. Though he was not dragged through art galleries by a determined fiancée as Grand often was, Batchelor knew who that was and nodded for his friend to continue.

'He's from Massachusetts,' Grand said, by way of background. 'His folks know my folks, the usual sort of thing. He was at West Point as well, I understand, though ten years before my time. They still had some paintings by him on the wall in the mess – he has always been a good hand with a brush.'

'Just catching up, is he?' Batchelor asked, ringing the bell for more coffee. He hoped that this wouldn't mean another trip across any significant seas – he sometimes felt the floor sway, two years after his last voyage.

'Yes, just to be civil. But he wants us to do some digging for him, into the background of John Ruskin.' Grand looked up at Batchelor, to see if he knew more about the man than he did.

Batchelor snorted. 'We'll dig for a long time, then,' he said. 'Ruskin, in my honest opinion and that of most reporters and people who don't make being pretentious a hobby, is a total pain in the backside and as weird as a wagonload of monkeys. You heard about his marriage, of course?'

'This isn't a divorce thing, I don't think. I confess to finding the handwriting a bit tricky towards the end.'

'No, no, the marriage is long over, annulled. His wife has become Mrs Millais now – she seems to make a habit of marrying painters – but she was Effie Gray when she married Ruskin. Before my time, thirty odd years ago, it must be, but the old-timers at the *Telegraph* used to talk about it, usually when they'd had a drink or two. Rumour was that when they got married and she undressed, he saw her' – Batchelor made an all-purpose gesture to his nether regions – 'and was so shocked he couldn't touch her. Never did, so the marriage was annulled. Obviously,' he said, smiling, 'the old-timers were a bit more direct, but I don't make a habit of discussing pudenda at the breakfast table.'

From the hall came a muffled shriek as Mrs Rackstraw left the house for a pleasant hour shouting at Mr Juniper, the pork butcher.

The men glanced round and then Batchelor continued. 'That's not all, of course. There's lots of rather dubious gossip about Ruskin, if you know who to ask.'

'Well,' Grand folded the letter into a complex shape and sent it flying down the table. 'Have a look at that and see if it's something for us. I have to say, poets and painters and such aren't really my cup of tea, but as you know so much already, it could be some easy money.'

Batchelor unfolded the paper and looked at the contents.

Then he turned it the other way up, which didn't help much. 'His writing is . . .' He was stuck for the right word.

'A bit like his art, these days,' Grand said for him. 'Back in his West Point days, you could tell what things were and apparently, he was a whizz at maps. But now, well, it's a bit less comprehensible, to put it mildly. Caroline and I went to the Grosvenor last month and saw one of his. I don't know much about art, but I do know what I like. And a nice Lady Butler is what I like. Lots of fine, upright chaps from the Limey Army with no chins below their stiff upper lips. Whistler's stuff is a bit speckly for my taste.'

'The only one I know of his is that one of his mother. That isn't speckly, as I recall it.'

'Well, no. She isn't a speckly woman. I only met her once, but she seemed a clean old broad. No, this one that seems to have got Ruskin riled up is a *Nocturne*, though I admit I thought that was music.' Grand looked around. 'Did you ring for some more coffee about a day ago?'

'Yes,' Batchelor told him. 'But Mrs Rackstraw has gone out. You know how Maisie is. She'll bring us some tea in a minute. She can never remember how to make coffee. She gets all confused about the beans.'

'Tea will do, I suppose. As long as it comes before dinner. Meanwhile, do your best with that handwriting and I'll have a look through the paper, see if there are any cases hidden in the small columns.'

The two men read their respective material, both jotting down the odd note as things came to them. Grand noticed something murky going on in the Cremorne Gardens, then Maisie came in with something hot in a pot which, even after tasting, might have been either tea or coffee. Pencils whispered over paper and all was calm around the post-breakfast table.

TWO

The memories came flooding back for James Batchelor as he stepped out of the growler into the nightmare that was Fleet Street. Years ago, as it seemed to him now, he had hurtled along those hardest of pavements, the dome of St Paul's watching his every move like a giant editor. The night of rain had turned into a morning of spring sunshine and the shopkeepers of the sunny side had winched their awnings down.

He could already hear the thud and grind of the *Telegraph*'s great ten-feed printer, a monster of steel and traction six times taller than a man. He brushed aside the shoe-blacks and winced at the discordant Italian hurdy-gurdy man. A black-coated woman from the Christian Mission touched him for a few coppers at more or less the same time as two real coppers – marching at their stately two and a half miles an hour tread – ignored her completely. So, the boys in blue were patrolling in pairs in Fleet Street now; that didn't surprise Batchelor one jot.

Inside the double doors of the *Telegraph*, he paused and took in the smell. Newsprint, ink, cigar smoke, strong tea and the sweating fear of hundreds of hacks, all of them slaving away to meet the Deadline, that most fated of words that every newspaperman repeats as a mantra, day after day. On the wall above the great staircase, the even greater George Augustus Sala frowned down on Batchelor in an orgy of treacly oils, the famous nose only a little smaller than the gilt frame surrounding it.

A journalist of rather less stature lounged in an anteroom halfway up the curve of the stairs, along a little corridor that Batchelor remembered as leading to a privy.

'Johnny Lawson,' Batchelor's grin was wide. The journalist leapt to his feet, whipping the cigar out of his mouth and gripping his visitor's hand.

'James Batchelor, you old newshound. It's been a while.'

'It has, it has,' Batchelor agreed and sat himself down. 'How's the old trade?'

'Mad as ever,' Lawson told him, 'There's a kettle here somewhere. Can I offer you some tea?'

Batchelor looked at the tiny, barely glowing fire and the chipped mug and suddenly longed for Mrs Rackstraw's finery. 'A little early for me,' he smiled.

'Ah,' Lawson slid open a drawer in his desk, 'Scotch, then?' He produced two glasses, both moderately clean, along with the bottle.

Batchelor winked. 'Lord Beaconsfield keeping you busy?' he asked.

Lawson groaned. 'International diplomacy's all very well,' he said, pouring a pair of sizeable snifters, 'but there are limits. I'll be a happy man when this bloody Congress is over and we all forget what a treaty is.'

'You should have voted for Gladstone,' Batchelor wagged a finger at him.

'Wash your mouth out,' Lawson said, straight-faced. 'The day I give my support to old Glad-eye is the day they'll put me in a box. The Queen – God bless her!'

'The Queen!' Batchelor toasted and they raised their glasses. 'Good God, Johnny,' he rasped, 'the last time I tasted something like this I was stripping paint with it.'

Lawson chuckled. 'You didn't come all this way just to compliment me on the quality of my whisky,' he said. 'To what do I owe the etcetera?'

'Well – and don't take this the wrong way, pet – I'm looking for a young man.'

'Ah, aren't we all? Dare I ask the purpose?'

'You know Matthew Grand and I are in the private enquiry business?'

'That's what you did here, wasn't it? Back in the day?'

'More or less.'

'So . . .?'

'The snooping business is expanding and we need to expand our staff accordingly. We're' – Batchelor looked left and right and behind him, checking for eavesdroppers – 'we're looking into John Ruskin as we speak.'

Lawson chuckled. 'Well, the very best of luck with that,' he said. 'The man's as squeaky clean as they come.'

'But . . . the stories . . .'

'Precisely,' Lawson said. 'Stories, to ginger up the young and inexperienced lads in the office. Ruskin made one mistake in his life, if you want to call it a mistake, and that was marrying Effie Gray and expecting her to be' – he waved a generic hand – 'a little tidier down below than turned out to be the case. And even then, if he had just shrugged and got on with it, no one would know about that, even. I expect it's this Whistler thing, is it?'

Batchelor nodded. He had already said too much.

'Well, if you're being paid by the scandal,' Lawson said, 'you've backed the wrong horse. Whistler may love his mother, but that's about the only thing about him that's fit for mixed company.'

Batchelor decided it was time to change the subject and waved his arm to the office. 'I'm not wrong, am I, this *did* use to be a privy?'

'Convenience, James, please,' Lawson scolded. 'This *is* the *Telegraph*.'

'Quite. Quite.'

'Yes, it did. Ironically, I now have to go down two flights of stairs for a piss. They call that progress. The young man?'

'Ah, yes. The young man. Grand and I need an amanuensis.'

'Dogsbody.'

'Yes, that's right. Must have a brain, though. And a present-able appearance – meeting clients, that sort of thing. Can't have someone with an eye in the middle of their forehead, knuckles on the ground, like that lad we had . . . what was his name?'

Lawson chuckled. 'I can't remember. He's making big money on the Halls now, I believe. Apart from not looking like something out of the zoo, anything physical required? Fisticuffs?'

'Lord, no. I keep Grand for that sort of thing. I was wondering whether you know of anybody. You do *know* everybody, of course, I realize that.'

'Well,' Lawson become conspiratorial, 'as a matter of fact . . .'

Batchelor leaned forward too, both men's elbows on the table. 'Yes?'

'I may have just the lad. Here in this very office, as we speak.'

Batchelor withdrew his elbow. 'Ah, that's a bit *too* pat, Johnny.'

'No, no, hear me out. He's the son of a friend of mine, just come down from Oxford.'

'Age?'

'Twenty-one, twenty-two. Anybody under thirty these days all look alike to me.'

'Which college?'

'Magdalen, I think.'

'What did he read?'

'Books, probably.'

'I'll do the jokes, Johnny,' Batchelor said, straight-faced.

'*Literae Humaniores*,' Lawson told him. 'That's Greats to you and me.'

'It may be Greats to you, my lad,' Batchelor sneered, 'I call it Classics. Latin and Greek and the cultures thereof. Essential, I'd say, for a career in Fleet Street.'

'Yes, well, that's as maybe. He's at a bit of a loss to know what to do with himself, vocationally speaking. I suggested a month or two at the *Telegraph*.'

'And?'

Lawson grimaced and shook his head. 'It's not really working out, to be honest. I can't give him anything meaningful, send him to Berlin or anything like that. There is a murder on my books at the moment, but with no experience—'

'What murder?' Batchelor's ears pricked up.

'In the Cremorne, a couple of nights ago.'

'Oh, yes, *The Times* had a piece on it.'

'Don't you come round here admitting you read other establishment's journals, James Batchelor. This one's got the *Telegraph* written all over it.'

'Lady of the night, wasn't she?' Batchelor asked.

'She was. Name of . . . er . . .' Lawson shuffled through the mountain of jottings on his desk. 'Clara Jenkins. Twenty-one.'

'Little young for a park girl,' Batchelor commented. Both men knew that park girls were at the bottom of the heap. Nobody started out that way.

'Agreed. She used to be at a rather nice establishment in Chelsea – Turks Row. A Mrs Arbuthnot runs it. I gather there was something of a falling out.'

'Disgruntled client?' Batchelor asked. 'The murderer, I mean.'

'Probably,' Lawson said. 'The book's odd, though.'

'Book?'

'Found open in the dead girl's lap. She was sitting on a park bench, just as though she was reading.'

'That *is* odd,' Batchelor nodded.

'Yes, particularly so since there was a similar case eighteen months ago.'

'There was?'

Lawson looked oddly at Batchelor. 'You do live in this city, do you, James?'

'Ah, no . . . well, yes, of course I do, but eighteen months ago, Grand and I were pursuing our enquiries in America.' Batchelor gripped the edge of the table in case a spot of reminiscent seasickness overwhelmed him.

'Ah, the colonies,' Lawson smiled. 'How lovely.'

'In what way was the earlier case similar?'

'Er . . . let me see, now.' Lawson topped up his glass, but Batchelor held a hand over his; there was only so much paint-stripper a man could take. 'Unsolved, of course, as I suspect this one will be. It was in the Cremorne, further away from the King's Road than Miss Jenkins was found.'

'Near the river?'

'That's right. I seem to remember the usual argy-bargy between B Division and Daddy Bliss of the River Police over whose jurisdiction it all was. Of course, that was before the shake-up at the Met and the arrival of St Howard Vincent. Have you met him?'

'No.'

'Keep it that way,' was Lawson's advice. 'The day we have to go cap in hand to the French to learn how to organize a police force . . . well, don't get me started. The first dead girl had a book with her too. All right, she was lying on the ground, not sitting on a bench, but it's the book that tells me our friend is back.'

'Do you remember who handled the case?' Batchelor asked, 'from B Division, I mean.'

'No,' Lawson bit his lip trying to remember. 'Useless bugger, whoever he was. Couldn't catch a cold as it turned out.' The door swung wide and a dapper young man stood there, an eye-shade strapped round his head and a pencil behind one ear. 'Ah, Gan, we were just talking about you.'

'You were?' the young man said. 'How jolly!'

'This is James Batchelor,' Lawson said, 'an old *Telegraph* man from the days of my distant youth. James, meet Alexander Martin.'

'My friends call me Gan,' Martin said, extending a hand.

'Do they, now?' Batchelor shook it. The grip was firm enough, in a Magdalen sort of way. 'John here tells me you have recently graduated, Mr Martin.'

'That's right,' the boy beamed. 'But I must say, Oxford seems a long time ago now.'

'And how are you enjoying Fleet Street?'

'Top hole,' Martin said, a smile frozen on his face.

'Hmm,' Batchelor murmured. 'Enjoying the cut and thrust of snooping, eh?'

'Rather!' Martin's smile had not faded.

'I should tell you, Gan,' Lawson said, 'that Mr Batchelor here is a private detective these days.'

'Enquiry agent,' Batchelor corrected him.

'Really?' Now, the smile was genuine. 'How fascinating. I've never met one before. I couldn't . . . er . . . do a story on you, could I?' Martin was reaching for the pencil stub and ferreting in his pocket for a notebook.

'No,' Batchelor said, flatly. He caught the look of disappointment on the lad's face. 'Discretion, you see,' he said by way of explanation. 'Vital in my line of work. Wouldn't do to have my Agency all over the front page of the *Telegraph*.'

'Don't flatter yourself,' Lawson said. 'You'll have to wait in line behind the Treaty of San Stefano and whatever the Iron Chancellor had for breakfast this morning.'

'Bratwurst and American coffee,' Martin said. Both men looked at him. 'The Iron Chancellor,' the boy went on. 'Otto von Bismarck. It's what he always has for breakfast. Ever since—'

'The Cremorne Gardens murder,' Lawson cut in. 'What was the book found with the body?'

'*The Fruits of Philosophy*,' Martin told him. 'An American publication initially, but it was republished last year by Mrs Annie Besant.'

'I don't suppose you happen to know the name of the book found near another body in the Cremorne eighteen months ago, do you?' Batchelor asked.

'Oh, let me see.' Martin closed his eyes tight. 'Yes, if I remember the file correctly, it was *Moby Dick* by Herman Melville.'

'The dead girl's name?' Lawson asked.

'Mabel Glossop,' Martin said. 'Aged seventeen. Cause of death, believed poisoning.'

'And the detective who worked the case?' Batchelor asked. 'Out of B Division.' Martin didn't seem to need clues, but Batchelor wanted to play fair.

'Ah,' Martin smiled broadly. 'I couldn't forget that. Meiklejohn. Inspector John Meiklejohn.'

There was a silence. 'You don't know who the murderer is, do you?' Batchelor asked, almost expecting an answer. It would have saved a lot of time.

Martin's eyes flickered open. 'Er . . . sorry. No.'

'Never mind, young man,' Batchelor said. 'Some miracles take a little longer. In the meantime . . . Gan, can I buy you a cherry bun at the Cheshire Cheese?'

Matthew Grand was not usually that at home with artists. He justified it to himself, whenever justification seemed necessary, by saying that as James Batchelor was a writer of sorts, it was more his milieu. But this time, the artist in question had got in touch with him personally, as an ex-West Pointer, so he had little choice. He had dressed particularly conservatively for this interview, though; he had had an unfortunate experience in Chelsea before when inadvertently wearing a cravat and wasn't really ready to repeat the experience.

Despite the Chelsea address, Whistler's house looked quite normal on the outside. Someone had hung some window boxes from the ledges which clearly led into the hall and from the basement area came the sounds of rug-beating and an untrained voice raised in song. The smell of toasting muffins wafted up as well and he could hear the crying of a child coming from an upstairs window. He was beginning to wonder whether he had the wrong house when a window flew up above his head and a maid's face appeared, draped in a net curtain flapping in the spring breeze.

'Yes?'

'Is this Mr Whistler's house?'

'It depends who's asking.'

'I'll take that as a yes, then.'

'I never said it was.' The maid was testy, as people often are when caught unaware.

'No, but . . .' Grand was getting a crick in his neck. 'Look, my dear, I had a letter from Mr Whistler and I have come to discuss it.'

'He ain't . . .' The maid was suddenly whisked from sight and a petulant argument echoed down to Grand, still standing on the step. The voices overhead stopped and the sound of light feet running downstairs and across the hall culminated in the door being flung open so sharply that the man holding the handle almost flung himself back up the stairs.

'And who might you be?' he said, in fluting tones. Even in those few words, he gave away his Massachusetts birthplace.

Grand, used to damping his accent down in general company, racked up his native Boston. 'I'm Matthew Grand, Mr Whistler, sir,' he said, dragging out the a's and swallowing the consonants. 'I believe you wrote me . . .'

'Matthew Grand!' The artist grabbed him by the arm and whisked him inside. 'It surely is good of you to call.' He slammed the door behind the enquiry agent and the house seemed to shake. The crying baby overhead seemed to redouble its volume. Whistler went to the foot of the stairs. 'Maud!'

Silence, save for the baby and the distant singing from the basement.

'Maud!'

This time, a female voice answered, almost drowned out by the baby. 'Yes, James? What is it? I'm trying to quieten little Ione.'

'Yes, well,' Whistler looked over his shoulder at Grand and grimaced. 'Any children, Mr Grand?'

Grand shook his head.

'A blessing, a blessing I do declare, but sometimes a tad loud.' He turned his face upwards again. 'Maud!'

This time the woman appeared on the landing. She was tall, slim and elegant and held the screaming child to her breast, which gleamed white in the shadows. 'James.' She sounded at the end of her tether. 'As you see, I am trying to feed your child.' There was a wealth of meaning in the single word 'your', which even Grand did not miss. 'If you will give me a moment, I will be down to' – she saw Grand for the first time and smiled a smile of fake welcome – 'greet your guest, if that is what you are yelling about.'

Whistler was a little downcast. 'No, no, my dear,' he said, above the noise. 'I was just asking that perhaps you could keep her . . .'

At this moment, the child seemed to realize what was expected of her and, with a last yell, latched onto her mother's breast and all was peace.

'Quiet.' Whistler's voice screamed out in the silence and the voice downstairs stopped with a startled squeak.

The woman on the landing hitched the child more comfortably into the crook of her arm and with a magnificent sweeping gesture, disappeared into the shadows.

Whistler stood for a moment, with one foot on the lower stair, the other on the Turkey rug which took the coldness from the black and white tiles of the hall. There were pictures on every wall, some of recognizable subjects, others not, and Grand found that some made his eyes go funny, so he tried not to stare. He was trying to place Whistler from back home;

Mrs Grand was an inveterate soirée hostess and he was sure
their paths would have crossed at least once, but he couldn't
bring an occasion to mind. Whistler was clearly thinking the
same.

In their own ways, each man was easy to remember, Grand
for his broad-shouldered physique and profile tending to the
Grecian, Whistler for his wild, tousled black hair and a figure
so slim and willowy he could hide behind Grand simply by
turning sideways. He was tanned to a shade impossible to
obtain in the thin spring London sunshine, and had a flashing
eye and a ready smile; though when he released it, his mouth
was petulant and surly. Grand, looking at him as he posed
blatantly in a shaft of light coming through the hall window,
was very much afraid that this man would be joining the long
list of clients that neither he nor James Batchelor could really
stomach.

'As I said,' Whistler said, finally relinquishing his pose and
leading the way into an over-furnished sitting room, 'thank
you so much for calling. I have a little . . . problem with John
Ruskin which you may know about . . .'

Grand shrugged. He had found over the years that a well-
timed shrug could speak volumes, especially when the other
person liked the sound of their own voice as much as Whistler
clearly did.

'Exactly.' The artist cast his eyes up to the ceiling. 'The
whole art world,' he swung his head down and round, setting
his curls bouncing, 'the *whole art world and beyond* knows
what that animal, that monster, said about me and my
painting. I shall sue, of course. *Am* suing, I should say, as it
is in the hands of my attorneys' – he chuckled and corrected
himself – 'I mean *solicitors* – when in Rome, Matthew, when
in Rome – as we speak. But what I need from you, if you
would be so good as to take the case, is for all the dirt on
Ruskin you can find.'

Grand had been thinking while Whistler had been playing
to a non-existent gallery. This man was not a natural for
currying favour with a judge or jury, should it come to that.
Many of the paintings in the hall seemed to have been done
by a crazed baboon who had got into the paintbox. He kept

a house where half-naked women shouted at him in front of guests. The little he had been able to find out about Whistler had not mentioned a wife, and yet there was clearly a wife-equivalent on the premises, unless he had guests who were unusually relaxed under his roof. So, Ruskin would have to be extremely louche and unusual to be worse. Yes, yes, Batchelor had told him all about the pubic hair or lack thereof incident, but did that make a man a bad critic? Was this a job that Grand and Batchelor, enquiry agents to the gentry, really needed? They were taking on staff. They were going up in the world. But there again, his mother and Whistler's mother, before she moved to England to look after her darling boy, had been friends, in a going-to-the-same-soirées kind of way.

'You look doubtful, Matthew,' Whistler suddenly remarked, leaning forward and scanning Grand's face minutely. 'A painter knows every thought in your head, did you know that? You have millions of tiny muscles which all have a tale to tell. For example, at this moment, you are wondering how anyone who is sane could possibly say anything untoward about a painter as wonderful as myself. You are thinking, would it be fair to investigate Ruskin when he is so clearly unbalanced?' He leaned back with a wild gesture of his arms and knocked several silver vases over, which crashed into the hearth and rolled irritatingly to and fro. 'Am I right? Or am I right?'

Grand smiled indeterminately. 'Partially,' he said and indeed, that wasn't a lie. Some of the words had featured in his thoughts, just not in that order.

'And of course, our mothers were friends, back in the day. I believe they still correspond.'

'Oh.' Grand was crestfallen. 'I didn't know that.'

'Oh, yes. Still firm friends.' Whistler looked at Grand, lifting his rather hooded lids and staring intently.

Grand wanted to say that his mother didn't choose his clients for him, that a whole Atlantic sat between the two women and then some, but somehow, his heart wasn't in it. He had intended all along to shift this one to James, to the lad who they would hopefully have employed before the day was out, at a pinch. So he smiled again and nodded.

'We'd be delighted to help, Mr Whistler . . .'

'Oh, please, James.'

'If we might keep this on a professional footing, I think we will do better,' Grand said, on his dignity.

Whistler tossed his head and his curls bobbed theatrically. 'As you wish. Anyhow, you'll have no problem finding the dirt on Ruskin . . .'

'We're not looking for dirt,' Grand reminded him. 'We are investigating Mr Ruskin, no more, no less.'

'As I said,' Whistler continued as though Grand had not spoken, 'you'll have no problem finding the dirt on Ruskin. The man is as mad as a tree and he can't keep his tongue behind his teeth for ready money, so you'll find scads of people he has vilified already. We could all sue him, perhaps!' Again, the hooded lids opened and the eyes flashed fire. 'Imagine. We could ruin the little—'

The door was barged open by the woman from the landing, a baby on her hip. 'Not still going on about Ruskin, James, surely?' she asked. 'I do apologize, Mr . . .?'

'Grand.' Grand had bobbed to his feet at her entrance and she waved him back to his seat.

'Mr Grand. I am afraid my . . .' She paused, glancing at the painter.

'Say it, say it, my dear!' he carolled in his odd, high voice. 'You are with like-minded people, don't forget.' He turned to Grand. 'Maud here is my mistress, Matthew, my inamorata, my helpmeet, my *querida*, if you will. But though she has honoured me by harbouring in her body my children, the fruits of our love, she is a little shy over what to call me. One day, she may be honoured to call me husband, but . . . I am sorry, my heart's delight, what did you say?'

Grand, who had heard the woman's muttered epithet, was too much of a gentleman to say and Whistler's mistress shook her head, gesturing generally at the sleeping child.

'Where was I?' Whistler asked the pair, the room, the street, the city, the cosmos, his arms above his head and his voice fluting into almost impossible registers.

'We were agreeing terms,' Grand said, quickly, and couldn't help but notice the desperate look of gratitude on the woman's face.

'Were we?' Whistler was puzzled. He had no memory of that part of the conversation at all.

Grand put his hand into the inside pocket of his coat and drew out a folded paper. 'These are our standard terms,' he said. 'The minimum we work for is one week, but after that you can cancel at no notice. Terms are strictly cash, one week in advance and then on invoice. I do appreciate that you won't have that kind of money on you today' – and indeed, Whistler's eyebrows had shot up a little as he unfolded the paper – 'but by the end of business today to the address on the letterhead will ensure our prompt attention from first thing tomorrow morning. Should you decide not to go ahead I do understand, and a note to that effect before the start of business tomorrow will mean that no monies will be owing.' Grand reached for his hat from where he had stowed it under the chair. 'I hope that is all in order.' He stood and bowed slightly to Whistler, raising his hat to his inamorata. 'Good day.'

'My, you're your father's son right enough,' Whistler said. 'Heredity's a wonderful thing, sure enough.' He was reminded of his mother's Southern heritage and it showed in his speech. Maud sighed and hefted her daughter to a more comfortable position on her hip. This would mean biscuits and gravy for dinner and she would have to be prepared to repel not just her lover but the entire Army of West Virginia tonight, unless she missed her guess.

Grand stepped gratefully out into the fresh air of Chelsea with misgiving; he wasn't sure this was going to end well. Apart from anything else, he didn't have the first clue what Ruskin was supposed to have done. He had better pop round and see Caroline.

James Batchelor had been to Newgate before. It was a grim, grey, flat-roofed building under the dome of the Old Bailey and he hadn't had to walk far from the Cheshire Cheese to get there. Gan Martin, with his Fox Talbot lens memory, was going to prove useful, but he was still a lad from Eton and Oxford and Batchelor wasn't sure he was ready for the lowlife of the ancient prison, so he had sent him on his way, at least for now. William Penn, the Quaker, had done time here for preaching in the street. So had the playwright Ben Jonson, for killing somebody in a duel. The difference in these men's crimes spoke volumes for the fads and prejudices of the society that put them there. Jonson had, bizarrely, pleaded benefit of clergy and got away with it; John Meiklejohn had no such excuses.

'Tell me why I should talk to you at all,' he said to Batchelor, sitting on the narrow iron bed-frame in Cell 312, the one with the rather desirable view of a grey stone wall, just like all the others.

'Because, before the events of last year,' Batchelor told him, 'you used to be an inspector of the Detective Branch at Scotland Yard.'

'And?' Meiklejohn's face showed no sign of regret, or remorse, or indeed, any emotion at all.

'And I need to know about the Cremorne case – Mabel Glossop.'

Meiklejohn looked again at the *carte de visite* that Batchelor had given him. '"Grand and Batchelor",' he read aloud, '"Enquiry Agents". Good money in that, is there?'

'We get by,' Batchelor told him. He knew perfectly well that money was everything to Meiklejohn. That was why he was here, serving his two years with hard labour. And *that* was why he had agreed to see Batchelor in the first place. Spending half an hour with some nosy bastard was at least a break from the creaking grind of the treadmill, hands on the bar, knees buckling under the strain of kicking down the planks for fifteen minutes, climbing a thousand stairs to nowhere. Then, the pause. Two minutes to sit, to flex the fingers, to ease the back, unlock the elbows. And, just when you have, the whole thing starts all over again.

Batchelor didn't know John Meiklejohn, but he knew the type. A tall, upright Scotsman with a heavy beard and a lived-in face, he had a kid brother in H Division, a beat copper who must have been highly embarrassed by his big brother's fall from grace. The 'Turf Frauds' the papers called it, 'The Trial of the Detectives' and four of them – Meiklejohn, Druscovitch, Palmer and Clarke – had fallen for the lure of quick cash from conmen and a titled lady. Scotland Yard had fallen apart and an unknown busybody called Howard Vincent had set up the new Criminal Investigation Department to shore it up. And now, Meiklejohn had lost none of his arrogance. To him, everybody, even an honest enquiry agent, was little more than the shit on his shoe.

'What's in this for me?' the jailbird asked, his arrowed grey jacket a sorry replacement for the fancy duds he used to wear at the Yard.

'A chance to do some good,' Batchelor told him, 'to redeem yourself.'

Meiklejohn chuckled. 'I'm not one of your tambourine brigade, Mr Batchelor,' he said. 'If General Booth himself had been on my patch back in the day, I'd have felt his Methodist collar. What else?'

Batchelor looked from side to side. The walls were green, running with damp, and Meiklejohn's blanket was wriggling with bugs. Behind him, the green door was locked steel, a small grille at the top kept open or closed at the whim of the turnkey. Today, it was closed. 'I wouldn't insult you by offering you a bribe,' he said.

'Oh, I wouldn't be insulted, Mr Batchelor,' he said. 'Contrary to what Superintendent Dolly Williamson would have you believe, folding stuff is what oils the wheels at Scotland Yard. My former associates and I were the ones unlucky enough to be caught, that's all. But we are, believe me, the tip of the iceberg.'

'So' – Batchelor rummaged for his wallet – 'a pound note . . .?'

'. . . would be missing the other four,' Meiklejohn said.

'You don't come cheap, sir,' Batchelor said.

'No,' Meiklejohn leaned back, his head against the trickling wall. 'No, I don't. Mabel Glossop'll cost you five pounds. But not here. And not now. Give it to my sister Margaret – I'll give you her address before you leave.'

'Fair enough,' Batchelor said. 'Mabel Glossop.'

Meiklejohn looked at him through narrowed eyes. 'I don't want to deprive my Maggie of five quid,' he said, 'but why don't you just go to the Yard? They wouldn't have the nerve to charge you for the information up front – after all, you might go to the papers.'

'Times have changed, Mr Meiklejohn,' Batchelor said. 'Even in the short time you've been here, the Yard has closed ranks.'

'You astonish me,' Meiklejohn said flatly.

'I didn't see much point in wasting my time with monkeys when I have the organ-grinder right here at Her Majesty's Pleasure.'

'Colourfully put, Mr Batchelor,' the ex-inspector said, 'but true enough. What's your interest in Mabel Glossop?'

'None, specifically,' Batchelor shrugged, 'although even ladies of the night are God's creatures, aren't they?'

'There are people who wouldn't agree with you on that one,' Meiklejohn nodded, 'and you haven't answered my question.'

'Mabel Glossop is one of at least two,' Batchelor told him. 'Another girl, of the same calling, was found in the Cremorne a few nights ago. Her method of dispatch is similar, if not identical.'

'Cyanide,' Meiklejohn remembered, 'artfully administered, I seem to remember. Tell me, was there a book with the body?'

'There was,' Batchelor said. '*The Fruits of Philosophy.* Yours?'

'*Moby Dick*. Strange.'

'*Moby Dick*?'

'Don't know,' Meiklejohn shrugged. 'Never read it. *The Fruits of Philosophy*?'

'Advice to married couples,' Batchelor said, 'and I haven't read that.'

'Filth,' Meiklejohn said. 'The sort of thing they sell under the Adelphi arches. No, the strange thing is the books at all. Tarts out on the game don't go in for reading much, not in my experience.'

'Tell me about the cyanide.' Batchelor was making notes.

'Tricky stuff, apparently.' Meiklejohn was getting into his stride. 'Old Doc Holliday was sure that was what killed Glossop. He could smell it on her. Bitter almonds. His post mortem found traces of cake in her stomach.'

'The poison was in the cake?'

'Or the marzipan thereof.'

'Which is made from almonds, isn't it?'

'Precisely,' Meiklejohn smiled. 'That's where the killer was so clever. I couldn't smell a damned thing, by the way, and I was standing alongside Holliday and the girl in the mortuary.'

'Could you trace any of her clients?' Batchelor asked.

'Do me a favour!' Meiklejohn chuckled. 'The park coppers reckon there are, on average, forty to fifty men in the Cremorne every night, paying good money to play the beast with two backs or various other parts of their anatomy at any given time. Not one of these came forward and the three we *know* were there were monkeys made of brass, if you catch my drift.'

'Did she work alone or was she part of an establishment?' was Batchelor's next question.

'On and off with Mrs Arbuthnot, Turks Row.'

'Any joy there?'

'Not a dickie bird. Old school, Mrs Arbuthnot. Rather cut her own throat than talk to a copper. You might do better. Undercover, maybe. That is, if you haven't got a problem with the Contagious Diseases Act 1864 and the Amendments thereto. We closed the old besom down for a while, but it didn't last. There'll always be a demand for finishing schools in the West End.'

'And you got nowhere near a suspect?'

Meiklejohn sighed. 'No, not really. There was an old clergyman, said he was carrying out research for a forthcoming book.'

'And was he?'

'I couldn't see how having his flies unbuttoned was helping him with his enquiries. He did, however, help us with ours.'

'Did you get anywhere with the *Moby Dick*?'

'Well, I did *start* it, to be frank. Load of tosh, as it turns out.'

'No, I mean, why Mabel Glossop should have had it with her.'

'Nah. Mrs Arbuthnot had never seen it before, although she did have a copy of *The Lustful Turk*, if I was interested. None of the other girls knew anything about it either.'

There was a thud and a rattle and the steel door swung open. 'Right, Meiklejohn, back to work. Sorry, sir, but I'm going to have to end this interview.'

The turnkey, a solid, brick-privy of a man, looked as though he meant business, so Batchelor took his leave.

'Thank you, Mr Meiklejohn,' he said. 'It's been.'

'It certainly has,' the prisoner agreed. 'That's Margaret Meiklejohn, Twenty-five, Eastern Court, Islington. You *will* give her my regards?'

'Of course I will,' Batchelor promised.

'When I get out,' Meiklejohn said, 'I might turn my hand to your line of work. Bit like being a copper, really, only getting paid for it.'

THREE

Matthew Grand had made the short journey from the Whistler ménage to the London home of his fiancée on foot. He liked exercise anyway, but he needed to get the whiff of domesticity gone bad out of his nostrils before meeting his intended. With luck, her parents would have gone back to their country place; he didn't dislike them, but he always had the feeling that they were watching for some social gaffe, such as using an imaginary spittoon in the corner, or drinking whisky from the bottle and wiping his nose on his sleeve. He was too well brought up to tell them that some of the behaviour he had witnessed in their houses would give his mother the vapours; it wasn't for him to come between an old English family and their preconceived bigotry. He bounced up the steps to the front door and rapped on the knocker. The door was flung open almost immediately by a girl with a cloth round her head and a duster apron swathing her dress.

'Hello, Eleanor,' he said, brightly, doffing his hat. His policy was to be polite to the servants and they would always know when to turn a blind eye when he and Caroline wanted some privacy. It was a policy which had not let him down yet.

'Mr Grand,' the maid said, stepping aside. 'I'm afraid the master and mistress have gone back to the country.' She gave him a broad wink.

'Oh, dear,' he pulled a clown's sad face. 'But Lady Caroline is here, I assume?'

'She's still in her boudoir,' the maid said, shutting the door. 'I would go up and tell her you're here, but . . . I am rather busy.' Another wink.

'What say I go up for you?' Grand said, as if it was a new and original idea.

'That would be helpful, sir,' the girl said, smothering a giggle. 'Shall I tell Cook to put the kettle on for some tea?'

Grand consulted his pocket watch. 'Give me half an hour?' he suggested and bounded up the stairs.

Lady Caroline Wentworth was at her toilette when he stuck his head around her bedroom door and she met his eyes in the mirror. She didn't flinch or bridle that her fiancé had invaded her boudoir in this unseemly manner. In fact, her lazy smile said something that she didn't have the words for. 'Matthew,' she murmured. 'I'm afraid Mama and Papa are not At Home.'

He went up behind her and laid his hands lightly on her shoulders. 'I'm sorry to have missed them.' He bent down and nibbled her ear. 'Are they expected back shortly?'

'Not for about six weeks,' she said, reaching up and caressing his cheek.

He straightened up. 'Six weeks is a feat I fear may be beyond me,' he said, budging her along the stool in front of the mirror and perching on the edge. 'Especially as I am in fact here to ask a favour rather than to . . .'

She pouted. 'Rather than to? Matthew, you disappoint me.'

'When we have run the little errand I have in mind, I would be at your disposal, of course,' he told her.

'In that case,' she flapped at him with her powder puff, 'off you go and annoy Eleanor and Cook. I need to get dressed.'

'I'll help,' he said, smiling brightly.

'Go.' She smiled as she said it and stood up, her silk night-gown skimming her body seductively. 'A lady must keep some secrets.'

He pulled down a shoulder strap. 'You have secrets under there?' he asked, doubtfully.

'A few, dear. A few,' she said, kissing him on the cheek. 'Give me ten minutes. Oh, Matthew?'

'Yes?'

'Where are we going?'

'The Grosvenor Gallery.'

She looked amazed, one elegant eyebrow lifted in a perfect arc. 'Again? Don't tell me that you have decided you like art after all, Mr Grand?'

'Indeed I have not, Lady Caroline,' he assured her with a bow. 'It's work.'

'Ooh!' She clapped her hands. 'You're taking me sleuthing with you? Shall I wear a disguise?' She lifted a swathe of silk and held it over the lower half of her face, her eyes dancing.

He glanced down at what the lifted nightgown had revealed. 'If you like,' he said, with a straight face. 'But perhaps not that one. Not at the Grosvenor, in any event.'

She dropped the nightgown hem and pointed at the door. 'Out. Ten minutes.'

Eleanor was still polishing in the hall. Though not quite in Maisie's league, she did find Matthew Grand rather appealing, if a touch old for her. She had eyes on the grocer's boy, a lad of keen enthusiasm for both herself and business. She was convinced he would go far and, as she polished, she dreamed of a little shop somewhere affluent, with a queue down the street and counters stretching back as far as the eye could see. But for now, she turned a beaming smile on Grand.

'Are you ready for your tea, now, sir?' she asked. If she thought he hadn't been up there long, she kept the thought to herself.

'Don't worry about that now, Eleanor,' he said. 'Lady Caroline said she would be ten minutes.'

This time, Eleanor's smile was the sort one gave to a child, or an idiot. 'Ten minutes?' she said. 'I think perhaps Cook ought to put the kettle on. You'll have plenty of time for a cuppa.' Eleanor had been helping Lady Caroline get dressed for a year or more now and she knew the woman could no more dress in ten minutes than fly.

Grand cast his mind back to other occasions where he had waited for Lady Caroline and nodded.

'I'll wait in the drawing room, shall I?' he said, pushing open a door.

'A good idea, sir,' Eleanor agreed. 'I'll bring the tea when it's ready.'

After a while, Matthew Grand slept.

An elegant sign swung in the May sunshine outside the columns of 138, Turks Row. The house looked just like all the others in the street, with a basement, steps leading up to the glossy front door and two storeys reaching up to an attic above them.

The sign was painted with two entwined capital As and all the windows were shuttered.

A knife grinder was trudging away from the premises, muttering darkly. He looked for all the world as if he had been rebuffed by the downstairs maid. As it turned out, the downstairs maid was rather pretty, as she opened the door to James Batchelor's ringing of the doorbell.

'Good afternoon,' he tipped his hat to her. 'Is Mrs Arbuthnot at home?'

'Who wants to know?' The voice, out of such pretty lips, sounded not unlike something Batchelor had occasionally heard at Billingsgate Fish Market.

A large, matronly woman batted the girl aside. 'Thank you, Dorcas,' she purred. 'Aunt Alice will handle this.' The girl with the unlikely name scowled at her and flounced away. 'She's new.' Aunt Alice smiled at Batchelor. 'How may I help you, sir?'

'I was hoping to talk to Mrs Arbuthnot,' Batchelor said.

'Every man lives in hope, I hope,' she beamed. 'I am Alice Arbuthnot. And you are . . .?'

Nearly out my depth, thought Batchelor. He had visited bordellos before, always in the line of enquiry, of course, and each time he never knew what to expect: fluttering fingers over his folderols or a stiletto slightly higher up. He fished out his card.

Alice Arbuthnot raised an eyebrow. '"Enquiry agent",' she read aloud, as most people did. 'And which of these enquiry agents are you, Mr Grand or Mr Batchelor?'

'James Batchelor, madam.' He took off his hat. Grovelling, he had found, was a sure way of getting across a threshold. He had, after all, business to discuss that he was fairly sure Alice Arbuthnot would not want bellowed all the way down Turks Row.

'Come in, Mr Batchelor,' she smiled. 'To your right,' she ushered him in. 'The parlour.'

Batchelor was glad that Mrs Arbuthnot had explained the room's function because it looked to him like a tart's boudoir. The shutters cut out the daylight and the oil lamps were fringed and shaded. Aspidistrae gleamed in every corner and there were rather risqué paintings on every wall.

'I see you're admiring my art,' she said, looking proudly at the oils. 'Gifts from admirers.'

'Really?'

'*The Rape of the Sabine Women*,' she pointed at a huge canvas over the fireplace. 'Not so much rape as everyone having a jolly good time, wouldn't you agree?'

Judging by the rapturous glee on the Sabine women's faces, Batchelor would. The Romans seemed to be enjoying themselves, too.

'When Antony met Cleopatra,' she pointed to another one.

'Ah.' Batchelor knew a thing or two about classical history, though probably not as much as Gan Martin. 'I thought she turned up in a barge,' he said. 'At Ephesus, wasn't it? Everybody else dashed off to gawp at the queen in the harbour, leaving Antony all by himself in the marketplace. They seem to be a little . . . adjacent . . . for that.'

The famous ancient lovers were naked, rolling on a gilded bed.

'This was a few minutes later,' Mrs Arbuthnot explained, 'allowing for artistic licence. But you haven't come to admire my gallery, Mr Batchelor. If you know of Ephesus, you will know that there was an establishment rather like mine behind the library. The oldest profession. Nothing like a good book, eh? Would you take tea?'

'Thank you.'

She rang a little silver bell on the table beside her and ushered Batchelor to a chair. It was wider than most, covered in plush crimson velvet, and he sank into it. From nowhere, a maid appeared, not the foghorn-mouthed Dorcas but an equally lovely girl with dark hair and eyes. She was wearing an apron and a dolly cap and she was carrying a cake stand. Call Batchelor a suspicious git, but he found himself checking the stand for marzipan goodies; he wasn't sure he'd be able to smell much, especially as the potpourri in the parlour was filling his nostrils as Mrs Arbuthnot spoke.

'Thank you, Tilly,' she trilled. The maid bobbed and left, causing Batchelor to jump out of his skin. From the front, the girl looked as demure as any other West London maid. From the back, she was completely naked, except for the apron tie around her waist. Mrs Arbuthnot said nothing until the girl had pulled the door shut behind her.

'Langue du chat, Mr Batchelor?' she purred. 'Some of our guests *love* those.'

Gingerly, the enquiry agent took one and, before it reached his lips, the girl was back.

'Ah, Tilly,' Mrs Arbuthnot said. 'Speed of light, eh?' She was carrying a silver teapot and two cups on a tray. 'Tea, Mr Batchelor?'

'Thank you.' He waited until the girl had poured and added the milk and desperately tried not to let his eyes wander as she left the room again.

'Do you like that?' Mrs Arbuthnot asked.

'Delicious,' he mumbled through the crumbs.

'Not the cake, Mr Batchelor,' she tutted patronizingly, 'the girl, Tilly. Is she to your taste? Or perhaps Priscilla? She is of the Chinese persuasion. Skin like a peach. I could ring for her.'

'No, I . . .' Was it suddenly hot in the parlour that James Batchelor was loosening his collar?

'Dorcas,' Mrs Arbuthnot clicked her fingers. 'A bit of rough, eh? Not exactly a choirgirl, our Dorcas. She assures me she often had three farmhands at once back in her Dorset village. I have no reason to disbelieve her.'

'I am an enquiry agent, madam,' he thought he ought to remind her.

'And I am a madam, enquiry agent,' she replied. 'What's your point?'

'My point is that I have no interest in your girls.'

'Really?' She widened her eyes. Alice Arbuthnot had been devastatingly beautiful in her day; she was no slouch now. 'Not as other enquiry agents, eh?'

'No, I . . . Yes. Look,' Batchelor put down his tea cup and made sure he knew where the exit was. 'I am pursuing a murder enquiry,' he said, 'or, rather, two to be precise.'

'Ah,' Mrs Arbuthnot was suddenly serious. 'Clara Jenkins. Yes, dreadful business. Dreadful. The police have been here already – in pursuit of their enquiries, of course, not as regulars. I told them I hadn't seen the girl for months, which is true.'

'And Mabel Glossop?'

'Mabel?' Mrs Arbuthnot frowned. 'That must have been . . . what? Two years ago?'

'Eighteen months,' Batchelor told her. 'Can you have forgotten?'

Mrs Arbuthnot put her cup down. 'No,' she said, solemnly. 'No, of course not. While they are under this roof, these girls are mine. I am their Aunt Alice and I am responsible for them. If they leave, as Clara did, I am powerless; I'm sure you understand.'

'And Mabel?'

Mrs Arbuthnot got up and swept towards the fireplace, looking down at the phallic symbols painted on the screen. 'Mabel was different. She was only seventeen and still, I have to admit, in my employ. I don't know what happened.'

'The police enquired about her too?' Batchelor asked.

'They did. A pig of a man named Meiklejohn. He made me an offer for another of my gels before he left. I turned him down.'

'Did Mabel have any regulars?' Batchelor asked.

She turned to face him. 'Mr Batchelor, my profession has certain similarities to a priest or a doctor.'

'If you say so,' he said.

'In the confessional and in the surgery, conversations take place that are between a man and his God and a man and his physician. It is like that here. What goes on under this roof stays under this roof. It must be so.'

'But two women are dead, Mrs Arbuthnot.'

She chewed her lip for a while. Then she crossed the room and refreshed his tea cup before refilling hers. 'You're right, of course. Clara and I had words, I regret to say. I am a businesswoman, Mr Batchelor. I give my gels smart clothes, good food and an education of sorts. In return, I expect them to work, mostly horizontally, and to give me two thirds of their takings. I found that Clara was conning me.' She stood impressively. 'And I will not be short-changed.'

'So she had to go?'

'She did. As it turned out, to the parks.' Mrs Arbuthnot sighed. 'These are hard times, Mr Batchelor, as I'm sure you know. I read in the *Pink 'Un* only the other day that a Great Depression is on the horizon. There are few enough trades for women and these newfangled gadgets – what are they, typewriting machines? – they'll never catch on. A girl must find work where she can. And if that has to be with her legs open, so be it.'

There was silence for a moment.

'Mabel did have her regulars, yes. Three of them, as I recall.'

'Do you have the names?' he asked her.

She laughed. 'If you mean, do I have a little black book full of addresses of the great and good that I can make a little money out of on the other side, the answer is no.' She tapped a finger to her temple, 'It's all in here.'

Batchelor waited, his notepad still in his pocket.

'As to the others, one was a Mr Keen, of Keen, Griswold in the Inner Temple.'

'A lawyer?' Batchelor wanted to make sure he understood.

'Of the worst sort,' she bridled. 'A Queen's Counsel, no less.'

'And the other?'

'Lieutenant Anstruther Peebles, Twenty-First Hussars. Rather peculiar, that one.'

'Oh, in what way?'

For the moment, Mrs Arbuthnot opened her mouth to say something, then she thought better of it and stooped to whisper in Batchelor's ear. The enquiry agent's eyes widened as he heard of Lieutenant Peebles's peculiarities and the room grew hotter still.

'Have you told all this to the police?' he asked her.

'Lord, no,' she said, 'I hardly ever talk to them.'

Matthew Grand had woken up with a start. Lady Caroline Wentworth usually got her own way and could charm the birds from the trees, but this time, she had pushed Grand perhaps a tad too far.

They travelled in silence, until, 'Don't sulk, Matthew, please,' she said, smoothing her gloves as she stepped down from the growler.

'I'm not sulking, Caroline,' he said, sulkily, checking his watch. 'But two and a half hours. Two and a half *hours*! Really, it's not much like ten minutes, is it?'

Lady Caroline snorted and marched across the pavement towards the doors of the Grosvenor Gallery. 'How long have you known me, Matthew?' she asked, knowing he didn't know the answer.

He didn't know *that* answer, but he knew what came next, so answered that one instead. 'Long enough to know you can't get dressed in ten minutes.'

'Correct,' she said, shutting her parasol with a snap. She stood by the door and a flunkey, seeing her waiting, rushed to open it. 'Why are we here again?'

Grand had to work quickly. 'Our latest client is James Whistler. He's suing John Ruskin.'

Lady Caroline's eyes popped open on stalks. 'Suing? Ruskin? But why?'

'He was rude about one of his paintings, apparently.' Even as he said it, Grand knew it sounded weak.

'Well, really, Matthew,' she said, flapping her hand at a scurrying assistant to keep their distance. 'That's hardly a *case*, is it?' She swept off down the left-hand wall of the gallery. 'Look at some of this stuff. I know that the models often have faces only a mother could love, but even given that, is this art, as such?' She stood in front of a particularly gloomy daub. 'What is that, even?'

'That, madam,' a slender floorwalker had appeared at her elbow, 'is an allegory on . . .'

Lady Caroline turned her head as though on ball bearings, and looked down her nose at the assistant. 'An allegory?' she asked in tones that could etch steel.

'It's the fash—'

'I do under*stand*,' she said, 'that there must *be* fashions in art, but when it looks like this, one can only hope that it isn't one that lasts long. Actually, you may be able to help. My fiancé Mr Grand – that is, Mr Grand of the Massachusetts Grands – and I are particularly interested in any works you may have by Mr Whistler.'

Grand loved Caroline when she was imperious. To other

people, that was. He could see that she might need watching, down the line. But for now, he let her have her head. There was nothing art gallery staff liked better than a British aristocrat with a rich American in tow. The way she said he was one of the Grands of Massachusetts even convinced him, and he had no idea who they were. He knew his father, for one, would be flummoxed.

The assistant led them down the room and through a door at the end. He turned to speak over his shoulder. 'Since the' – he cleared his throat – 'the hoo-ha, as you might say, we have moved the painting into the second gallery. Not that it isn't simply *wonderful*, of course,' he added quickly, 'but it was attracting adverse attention, you see. Terence Saunders,' he introduced himself belatedly and Grand shook his hand.

He crossed the room and let up a blind which was covering a large window. Sunlight flooded in and picked out the picture opposite. Grand, whose art taste usually ran to military themes or some of Frederic Leighton's more esoteric works, depending on mood, had to admit he rather liked it. Shadowy figures in the foreground to the left were clearly looking up into the sky, despite being mere sketches against the dark grass. They led the viewer to look up too and there, against the London night over the Cremorne, fireworks sparkled and spat their magic and reflected in the lake. You could almost hear the bangs and whistles as they shot up and exploded above the city.

'I really like that,' Grand said, stepping back to look from a distance.

'You didn't like it when we were here before,' his fiancée pointed out.

'That might be because it was crowded with people when we were here before,' Grand said. 'I couldn't step back and watch it.'

Saunders drew closer. 'Do you see that too, sir?' he asked, in an awed whisper. 'The fireworks seem to be going off, don't they? Do you see them change?'

Grand nodded, turning his head this way and that.

'Whenever I come in here in the morning and check things, adjust the blind and so on, I would swear they are different from the day before. Mr Whistler is a genius, no more, no less.'

The two men stood side by side, gazing in admiration at
the painting. Lady Caroline, on the other hand, had other
views. She glanced at the picture and then leaned in close to
examine the figures in the foreground.

'Shoddy,' she said, standing back again. 'Shoddy work.
These figures here,' she twirled her finger round in a vague
circle, 'aren't even painted properly. I mean, Matthew, look
. . .' She looked around to see the men still gazing deep into
the picture, lost in firework displays of their youth, when every
spark was a thing of magic, owing nothing to sulphur or charcoal; when they didn't even know that aluminium, titanium
and tin existed. She opened her mouth to speak, then shut it
again with a smile. Perhaps it was a man thing. She allowed
herself a little giggle. Perhaps that was why Mr Ruskin didn't
like the painting much. She looked at it again. There was
something about it, as long as you let your eyes wander about
and not concentrate on one spot or another.

Leaving the men to their memories, she wandered away,
through another door in the corner. More paintings stretched
away, lining the walls. These were less challenging, still lifes
of roses, dropped petals artfully reflected on shiny table tops.
This was more like art, to her mind, though at her mother's
soirées, she would rather die than admit it. She settled herself
in front of a rather winsome child, holding a puppy. She made
a face – even for her, this was just too sugary for words.

'Surely, you don't like this, do you?' a voice said, from
behind her.

She spun round. An artist, in full rig, stood behind her, a
brush behind his ear and a palette on one thumb.

'Umm . . . not, *this* one,' she said, hastily. 'Some of them,
though. That one with the petals. It's very' – she was stuck
for a suitably artsy word – 'realistic, isn't it?'

The artist tutted and strode off down the room and stood
in front of a painting in a dark corner.

'What about this one?' He raised his voice, so she knew he
was talking to her and she went to join him. 'Is this realistic
enough for you?'

Lady Caroline looked at the picture as she approached it
and couldn't really make it out. It looked like . . . well, she

really wasn't sure. She went closer and closer and then suddenly recoiled. 'Is . . . Is that woman . . . dead?'

The artist was silent and she turned round to check he had heard. He had looked a little elderly. Perhaps he was deaf.

But he wasn't deaf – or, if he was, she might never know. He had gone. Lady Caroline was not given to unladylike movements. Numerous governesses and a couple of finishing schools in elegant locations had taught her that. But nevertheless, she found herself spinning round on the spot. Wherever could the man have gone?

Back in the middle room, Grand and the assistant were no longer lost in the Cremorne fireworks but were looking for her, in an aimless kind of way.

'Oh, there you are, darling,' Grand said, then looked again. He was not used to seeing his fiancée out of countenance, but she clearly was now. 'Are you well?'

'I've had a bit of a shock,' she said. 'A man . . .'

'A man?' Grand was ready to punch the man's lights out, whoever he might be. 'What man?'

'Average build,' she waved a hand around the top of her own head, allowing for the hat. 'Average height. Not sure how old . . . oldish. Not *really* old, but not young. Dressed' – she let go of a nervous laugh – 'well, dressed as an artist, as it happens. The full fig, you know, like that self-portrait of Rembrandt, you know the one. The hat. The floppy clothes. Like someone in fancy dress as an artist.' She looked at Saunders. 'You know these things.' A little more of the imperious Lady Caroline was coming to the surface. 'Artists don't dress like that, do they?'

The man shook his head. 'Mostly they wear tweeds,' he said. 'Except Frederic Leighton . . . but I don't think you should believe all you hear on that score.'

Caroline gave him a withering glance. 'And another thing,' she said, before she forgot. 'That rather nasty picture. The one in the corner of the next room. I think you should remove it. It's very disturbing.'

Saunders looked crestfallen. 'Is it that one with the puppy? I don't know why we even have that on the wall. But the artist is . . . titled, and you know how they can be.'

'I most certainly do,' snapped Lady Caroline and the man blenched. 'But I don't mean that one. I mean the one in the corner.'

Saunders looked puzzled. 'Would you show it to me?' he said, and led the way through the door at the end of the room.

Caroline pushed past him and swept down the room, talking over her shoulder to explain what had gone on. She reached the end of the room and turned, with a theatrical gesture which would have made Lillie Langtry proud. 'There,' she said. 'Isn't it appalling? The woman is clearly dead!'

Neither man spoke and she looked to where she had pointed. The wall was now host to a picture of a reclining nude, but clearly perkily alive if her stare was anything to go by, piercing its way out of the canvas and into any man's libido.

'As I said,' Saunders gushed, 'you really shouldn't believe all you hear about Frederic Leighton . . .'

'But this isn't *it*!' Lady Caroline's voice was rising into hysteria. 'This isn't *it*! It was dark, the painting, with a woman sprawled across it, clearly dead.' She rushed up to Grand and grabbed his lapels and shook him like a dog shakes a rabbit. 'There was *blood*, Matthew. *Blood*.' And she burst into a storm of tears, half angry, half frightened.

Grand gathered her into his arms and spoke over her head to Saunders. 'I'll take her home,' he said, half mouthing the words. 'She's a bit overwrought.'

The assistant nodded and followed them to the door, where he stood until they had been taken away in a passing growler. Only then did he turn away, shrugging to the doorman.

'A bit overwrought,' he said, with a smile and a toss of the head.

'Overwrought,' the man replied, 'or' – and he mimed tossing off a glass – 'overwrought?'

'No, just a bit overwrought,' Saunders said, and laughed. 'I was about to tell her about the ghost as well. But I didn't get around to it.' And he went off chuckling, to change the price tag on the Leighton. He reckoned that American would be back as soon as he could ditch Miss Hysteria there.

*   *   *

The firelight shone on Mrs Rackstraw's well-polished brass and threw rainbows off the cut glass of the decanter. Grand and Batchelor, Enquiry Agents of the Strand, stretched their legs across the hearthrug and took their ease. One way and another, the day had been a little unusual for them both.

'So,' Batchelor said, drawing on his cigar, 'Caroline thought she saw a ghost.'

'No, Caroline *did* see a ghost. She never thinks she saw or heard anything – life for her is a series of blacks and whites.'

'A little like Mr Whistler, then,' Batchelor chuckled.

'Indeed. Actually, I rather liked what I suppose we should call The Painting in Question. It's very atmospheric.'

'This case isn't going anywhere,' Batchelor observed, 'but it pays its way while we look into this other thing. The Cremorne Case, I've called it in the ledger. Although, once Mr Martin starts, we won't need a ledger as such. The man has the most phenomenal memory. Never forgets anything, or so I'm told.'

'He must forget some things, though,' Grand said, dubiously. 'Wouldn't he go mad, otherwise?'

'Well, he could well be stark staring as far as we know. I only have John Lawson's word that he's sound. But he seems quite pleasant, has his own rooms, so we don't have to find him lodgings, and he can make tea, I suppose. He's only a dogsbody, when all is said and done.'

'We're paying him, though?' Grand didn't like to take advantage.

'Of course. But he is of private means, as far as I could tell. He's just working for the experience.'

Grand chuckled. 'Well, we can certainly give him plenty of that. It's a shame you didn't have him with you when you went to the brothel . . .'

'I'm not sure Mrs Arbuthnot uses that term,' Batchelor corrected him. 'She even has her own letterhead – Alice's Academy, if I remember rightly.'

'Wherever it was. But you found out some good information, so worth a little embarrassment.'

'I wasn't embarrassed.'

'You're blushing now.'

Batchelor loosened his collar and sipped his drink. 'Good leads, though, from Aunt Alice. I'm going round to the Temple tomorrow.'

'I don't remember deciding that.' Sometimes, Grand liked to remind Batchelor whose name came first on *their* letterhead.

'Well, naturally, Matthew, I thought you'd go for the soldier.'

'Did that once,' Grand nodded, blowing his cigar smoke to the ceiling. 'Not sure I liked it.'

'Don't give me that.' Batchelor topped up the brandy. 'The Civil War made you the man you are today.'

'Amen, brother!' Grand raised his glass in a toast. 'Do you really think any of this is going to produce a murderer?'

Batchelor thought for a moment. 'I don't know,' he said, 'but it's all we've got at the moment. The Yard are being particularly tight-lipped about this latest case and if I read Meiklejohn aright, he had other things on his mind when he was supposed to be investigating Mabel Glossop.'

'Like lining his own pockets,' Grand murmured.

'The same. How will you handle it?'

'The soldier?' Grand flicked his ash onto the tray. 'Didn't Meiklejohn suggest you might get into Mrs Arbuthnot's undercover – as a john, I mean?'

'He did, but I decided against that as being altogether too slow and too risky.'

'Contagious diseases,' Grand nodded.

'The same again,' Batchelor said.

'I thought I might try it, though. With the army, I mean. Cavalryman to cavalryman, that sort of thing.'

'Yes,' Batchelor nodded. 'Yes, that might work.'

'You?' Grand asked. 'How will you handle the lawyer?'

'With my customary charm and bonhomie,' Batchelor said.

'I beg your pardon?' Perceval Keen, QC, was the wrong side of sixty and he could smell an ex-newspaperman a courtroom away.

'I said,' Batchelor spoke a little louder, 'as Shakespeare once said, "Let's kill all the lawyers".'

'I heard you,' Keen snapped. 'And that, by the way, is a well-known misquotation. I think you'll find, if you consult the First Folio, that the line is "First, kill all the lawyer's clerks". There is a world of difference and in terms of the correct quotation, I would probably agree with him. What did you say you wanted?'

'I was enquiring about a mutual friend of ours,' Batchelor said. 'Miss Mabel Glossop.'

The QC looked at him blankly. 'I don't know that name,' he said. He was sitting in his palatial chambers in a particularly blossom-laden corner of the Inner Temple, the clash and carry of Fleet Street metaphorically miles rather than yards from his door. Legal tomes surrounded him. The cigar-cutter on his desk took the form of a guillotine.

'You seem very sure of that,' Batchelor said, 'Not a moment's hesitation.'

'Hesitation is for the defence, Mr Batchelor,' he sneered. '*I* prosecute.'

'That's exactly what I would like to see happen here, Mr Keen,' Batchelor said, 'in the case of Miss Glossop.'

'It is a case, then?' Keen asked.

'Oh, very definitely,' Batchelor assured him, 'in that the lady was murdered.'

'Oh dear,' Keen said, as if he had just narrowly missed stubbing his toe.

'You were a client of hers.'

There were times in his life when James Batchelor cut to the chase; this was one of them.

'You must be confused, sir,' Keen bridled. 'I *have* clients. I am not one of them.'

'In this case, sir,' Batchelor countered, 'You are. Or rather, were. I had hoped not to have to be direct, Mr Keen, but you leave me no choice. Miss Mabel Glossop was a prostitute and you were her regular client. I assume you have moved on, to pastures new, as it were?'

Keen leaned forward in his leather-padded chair, fixing Batchelor with a deadly smile, the sort he used on men facing the gallows. 'Are you familiar,' he asked, 'with the laws of slander in this country?'

'On slander, I'm shaky,' Batchelor admitted, 'but after several years in Fleet Street, I'm no slouch at libel.'

'Take it from me,' Keen thundered, leaning back, 'that I am an expert on both. The only lady with whom I have had carnal relations is Mrs Keen, my good lady wife. If you repeat what you have just said outside these doors, I shall not hesitate to bring an action against you.' He picked up the *carte de visite* that Batchelor had just given him and tossed it into the nearest bin. 'And after that, you and your partner-in-crime can certainly kiss goodbye to your dubious calling and the property from which you operate.'

'Mabel Glossop was murdered, Mr Keen,' Batchelor repeated. 'Did I not say that?'

'You did, sir,' Keen was on his feet, 'and while that is undoubtedly tragic and a blot on the moral compass of this great country of ours, it has nothing whatever to do with me. Good morning.'

James Batchelor knew the bum's rush when he got it. Mrs Arbuthnot seemed very sure of Keen's identity, but in the cut-and-thrust world of the criminal underclass, it was her word against that of Perceval Keen, QC, and everybody knew how *that* would go in court.

'Until we meet again,' Batchelor said, making for the door.

'That will be when Hell freezes over,' Keen assured him, and slammed the door behind his retreating figure.

FOUR

T he Rag was busy as usual that night. The brightest of all clubs along the Mall, the lights flared from its windows and carriages came and went in what seemed an endless stream. Liveried flunkies and uniformed privates stood rigidly to attention, saluting anyone whose face or uniform they recognized. No one recognized the undress frock coat of the Army of the Potomac, nor the distinctive scarlet scarf of its Third Cavalry draped around the body and neck of Matthew Grand. It was just as well that everybody recognized the colour of money, especially the sergeant-major on the front door who, after some whispering to an underling, led Grand to the newly refurbished billiard room.

'Good evening, gentlemen,' he said to the two officers at the table. 'Any chance of a game?'

They both looked at him past the glare of the lamps, both upright officers a few years Grand's junior, both wearing the glittering mess dress of the 21st Hussars.

'Who are you?' one of them asked.

'Matthew Grand,' the American extended a hand. 'Army of the Potomac. Third Cavalry.'

'Mr Grand,' the taller of the two said.

'Captain,' Grand thought it best to assert. He knew from the single stars on the men's shoulder cords that he outranked them both.

'Captain Grand,' the tall man shook his hand. 'I am Anstruther Peebles, Lieutenant, Twenty-First Hussars.' He pointed to the shorter man, altogether more weaselly. 'This is Willoughby Inverarity. Are you over here on army business, Captain?'

'Snooping, I'm afraid,' Grand smiled. 'My bosses at the War Office back in Washington want to know what effect your Mr Cardwell's reforms have had on the British army.'

'That was a while ago,' Peebles said. 'Neither of us had taken the shilling at that point.'

'Came up the hard way,' Inverarity chipped in. 'Written examinations! I ask you, what sort of world is it where cavalry officers have to pass written examinations?'

'You have a point there, Mr Inverarity.'

'Brandy, old boy?' Peebles had reached for the decanter on the sideboard.

'Very kind,' Grand smiled. 'To be honest, my fact-finding is almost over. I'm looking for some relaxation.'

'Ah, well, the Rag's the best place for that,' Peebles told him. 'You've missed dinner, I'm afraid, but there's some excellent port in the smoking room. Your very good health, Captain Grand.' Peebles handed the American his glass and raised his.

'And yours, Lieutenant Peebles.' They clinked glasses. 'No, I was hoping for something else. Female company, for instance.'

The hussars looked at each other. 'Ladies' night was last night,' Inverarity told him.

Grand laughed. 'They're not exactly the kind of lady I was talking about,' he said. 'Not so much the colonel's lady, but Judy O'Grady.'

'I don't follow,' Peebles said.

'Well, I don't know about you fellows,' Grand became confidential, 'but in the Army of the Potomac and indeed, since, we let our hair down a little.'

Peebles frowned. 'Are you talking about ladies of the night?' he asked a little tensely.

'Got it in one!' Grand clicked his fingers. 'I heard tell of a little place in Chelsea . . . where was it, now? Turks Row, that's it. Run by a madam called Arbuthnot. You fellers heard of it?'

Peebles stood up squarely, the lamplight glancing off the buttons of his fancy mess vest. 'Clearly, Captain Grand, the habits of the officer class in the American army differ from ours. I'd be happy to drink with you and to beat you hollow at billiards, but anything more than that . . .'

'How about you, Lieutenant?' Grand turned his attention to Inverarity. 'Come across a lady by the name of Mabel Glossop?'

Inverarity said nothing, but Peebles took the brandy balloon out of Grand's hand. 'I think it's time you left, Captain,' he said.

'Are you going to make me, Lieutenant?' Grand asked him.

'Hah!' sneered Inverarity. 'Can't even pronounce the word properly.'

Grand's hand snaked out and he slapped Peebles across the face. The man staggered backward, then he retaliated, his left hand stinging across Grand's cheek.

'Gentlemen!' Inverarity stepped in, his billiard cue in his hand. 'This sordid discussion has developed into an affair of honour. Contrary to what we've just heard from you, Captain Grand, are you a man of honour?'

'What are you getting at?' Grand felt obliged to ask.

'Sabres, Grand. Sabres. You and me,' Peebles snapped. 'You've insulted me, by your foul innuendo and a physical assault. Time for the reckoning, I think.'

'Are you challenging me to a duel?' Grand couldn't believe it.

'I am. We've done the exchange of slaps. Do you have a second?'

'All the time in the world,' said Grand.

The hussars looked at each other.

'What Lieutenant Peebles means . . .' Inverarity began.

'I know what he means,' Grand said. 'And no, I don't, not at the moment.' Where *was* Batchelor when you needed him? 'But I can manage without. Where's this going to happen? At dawn on some misty meadow?'

'Dawn be buggered,' Peebles said. 'It's going to happen here and now.'

He led the way through corridors without number, where fierce red-faced and red-coated generals glared down at them from their canvases. As they marched through the bowels of the building, interested club members followed them. Word was getting around of an altercation, and it was a rare member of the Rag who could stand idly by when steel was going to clash, and perhaps, who knew, blood was to be spilled. Grand found himself standing in a gymnasium, with galleries at both ends, crammed with club members, smoking and drinking, trying to see what was going on. He noticed cash changing hands.

'Dymock,' Peebles beckoned an infantry officer over. 'Will you act as Captain Grand's second?'

'I should be honoured, er . . . Captain Grand,' the officer said. 'Henry Dymock, Twenty-Fourth Foot.' He extended a hand.

'Matthew Grand,' the American shook it, 'Third Cavalry of the Potomac.'

'May I hold your coat?'

'Be my guest.'

Grand unbuttoned his uniform and passed it to Dymock. Peebles stripped off his shell jacket and stood in his mess vest, flexing his knees and loosening his wrists. From nowhere, another officer arrived, carrying a sword case. He placed it on the floor and flipped open the lid.

'Three-bar hilt all right for you, Grand?' Peebles asked.

'Three-bar hilt is just fine,' Grand said, taking up the nearest weapon to him. It was a little heavier than his own sword that had been on his hip throughout the Wilderness campaign, but it was a finely balanced weapon with etching all the way along the blade.

Dymock crossed the floor and checked Peebles's sword. Inverarity did the same to Grand's.

Yet another officer took centre stage and the noise in the galleries stopped. 'As President of the Mess Committee,' he said in a long drawl, 'I must point out to you both that duelling is explicitly against the law of the land and, as such, you both have the right to withdraw with honour intact.'

'Honour be buggered!' Peebles said darkly. 'Let's get on with it.'

'*En garde!*' shouted the President, and the sword tips slid together. He held both points at shoulder height, then he brought his swagger stick upwards, banging them apart and stepped back. There was a deafening roar from the galleries as the two men faced each other, blades circling in the dim light. At either end, Inverarity and Dymock dodged in and out of the duellists' unmarked piste, watching intently.

Peebles struck first, clashing with Grand's blade and driving him back. Parry in sixte. Parry in quarte. Riposte. Peebles's lunge wasn't his best. He missed his footing slightly and the blade point hissed high above Grand's shoulder. The American banged the blade aside and sliced against thin air. Peebles jerked upright, steadying himself. This damned colonial knew his onions.

Now it was Grand's turn. He feinted not once, but twice, trying the same move to throw his opponent. Peebles expected it and their blades slid together, locking momentarily at the hilts. Grand pushed Peebles back but the hussar was strong and he slashed to the right, catching Grand's left hand, and he swung to avoid the blow. Blood spattered over the American's shirt cuff but it didn't slow him down and he hacked to his right, pinging a couple of buttons off Peebles's mess vest, ripping the lace and cutting the French grey cloth.

'Enough!' a voice bellowed, echoing round the gymnasium like cannon fire. The bellows and catcalls from the galleries stopped at once and a pot-bellied general strode into the centre of it all, a glass of brandy in one hand, a cigar in the other. Grand had no idea who this man was, although he recognized the rank insignia on his collar. It was clear from their reaction, however, that everybody else knew exactly who he was.

'Hamilton,' the old man barked, and the officiating officer stepped forward. Grand expected the men to salute, then he remembered that the British didn't do that unless they were wearing caps, and the officer merely stood to attention. 'You are President of the Mess Committee, man. What do you mean, allowing this tomfoolery to go on? Someone could have been killed.'

'Yessir. Sorry, sir,' was the best Hamilton could do.

'You, sir,' the general rounded on Grand. 'Who the devil are you?'

'Matthew Grand, General,' he told him. 'Third Cavalry of the Potomac.'

'Huh!' the old man grunted. 'McClellan's lot, eh? I might have known. What are you doing here?'

'Making rather a fool of myself, I suspect,' Grand was sheepish enough to admit.

'You got that right,' the general said. 'Now, get another thing right and get out. Dymock,' the officer clicked to attention, 'give this man his coat and see him off the premises.

And make sure he doesn't walk off with that sword.' The general scowled at Grand. 'Pretty dodgy lot, McClellan's outfit, if memory serves.'

Grand stood open-mouthed, but there wasn't a lot he could do. He had already insulted one officer tonight; starting a duel with another, especially an overweight old man, was not a good idea. The general whirled to face Peebles. 'And as for you, Inverarity, what were you thinking? There will be consequences, sir, you can mark my words. And you lot,' he snarled at the spectators, 'get back to whatever shady rocks you crawled out from and pray I don't remember any of your faces. Bloody overgrown schoolboys, the lot of you.'

There was a first-day-of-term feeling in the offices of Grand and Batchelor, Enquiry Agents, the next morning. Grand was keeping the typewriter who came in every other day to cope with the letters agog with the tale of his duel, complete with actions, using the furniture to stand in for Peebles when Batchelor refused to play. The woman was about to resort to smelling salts when a light tap on the door heralded the arrival of Alexander Martin, dogsbody extraordinaire.

Miss Wolstenholme, the typewriter, had become rather anxious when told that Grand and Batchelor were taking on more staff. She was a single lady of straitened means and needed all the typewriting she could get; if they were going to get some young whippersnapper wet behind the ears to do her out of her hard-earned crust, she would . . . she would . . .

As it turned out, she would sit there with her mouth open like a goldfish, making indeterminate noises in the back of her throat. Batchelor gave her a nudge and she gave a little start and remembered to blink and swallow again. She had never, in all her life, seen a man as handsome as the one who had just walked in. Matthew Grand could turn heads, it was true, and James Batchelor had a certain weaselly charm, but Alexander Martin simply left them floundering in his wake. Miss Wolstenholme, when regaling the ladies in the sitting room of her lodgings – Mrs Newark; Rooms to Rent, Quiet Ladies Only Considered, Strictly No Callers – found it hard to explain quite what made him so unutterably gorgeous, and it was a problem she shared with many who came within his aura. His hair was . . . hair, but the best there could be. His teeth were not at all like pearls, as better poets than she had pointed out about others, but they were perfect nonetheless. His nose was like something from a Grecian urn, but much more human. His mouth, when he smiled, made it seem as if the sun had come out. She didn't go into his chest, shoulders and legs; Miss Manifold had recently come out of a Home and still couldn't take too much excitement. Suffice it to say, she concluded as the ladies hung on her every word, he was, in short, just perfect.

He parted his perfect lips to speak and Miss Wolstenholme held her breath; if his voice was a squeak, her disappointment would be terminal. But no. In measured tones, not too deep, not too shrill, not too hurried, not drawling, the vision spoke.

'Oh, I *am* in the right place! Thank goodness for that. I don't have a very good sense of direction, I'm afraid.'

Grand's heart sank. So much for the *wunderkind* with the perfect memory!

'Except when I have been somewhere before, of course. Then, I'm all right. I have been using any spare moments from the *Telegraph* to visit new parts of London and learn my way about.' He smiled at the small company. 'I hadn't got round to these streets yet, but I was grateful for the opportunity.'

He stepped into the room and closed the door.

'In fact, I am grateful for the opportunity full stop, sirs.'

Miss Wolstenholme's heart gave a little flutter. And polite as well; perfection.

'I was not sure that the newspaper business was quite right for me. But enquiring, now, that *is* something I think I could enjoy.' He looked around the room, his smile dying as he did so. 'What happened?' he asked, his melodious voice full of concern.

'What happened where?' Grand shook himself free of the almost soporific atmosphere which Martin seemed to engender.

The dogsbody waved a languid arm. 'Well,' his eyes were wide, '*here*! Those papers everywhere.' He looked more closely at a pile in the corner. 'Is that a *chair* under that one? And the ink-stains on the floor. The blind at the window, all caught up in its strings. The wastepaper basket overflowing.' He suddenly stopped and laughed. 'Oh, I *see*. You set up this whole scene to test my enquiry agent skills. I should have known, as soon as I saw the stuffed parrot on the shelf.'

Grand glanced behind him. 'I thought I asked you to dispose of the parrot, Miss Wolstenholme,' he said, frostily.

'I don't like touching it, Mr Grand,' she complained. 'The feathers make my fingers feel all funny.'

Batchelor turned to Martin to explain. He was worried that the lad would be back to the *Telegraph* if he didn't make the office seem at least passingly normal. 'The parrot is part of a divorce case we worked on,' he said. 'There was an issue regarding custody and, while it was being thrashed out, we looked after it.'

Martin gave a nervous laugh. 'You do know it's dead, though,' he said, as one breaking bad news.

'It's dead *now*,' Grand said, testily. 'Parrots get like that when they don't get any food.' He looked at Miss Wolstenholme, who began to sniff into her hankie.

'It could have happened to anyone, Mr Grand,' she snuffled.

'Long story cut short,' Batchelor said hurriedly, 'we had the parrot stuffed . . .'

'. . . it was the least we could do,' Grand said.

'. . . and the gentleman and lady involved didn't get divorced after all. They decided we could keep the parrot. But I'll get rid of it, if it offends you. I know not everyone is keen on taxidermy.'

'Don't worry on my account,' Martin said. 'My father has an extensive collection at our country house. He is trying to bag every known species of antelope before he dies. Mother isn't so keen, but I don't really mind one way or another. Perhaps if it wasn't hanging from its perch like that . . .'

A silence fell, broken only by an occasional sniff from Miss Wolstenholme.

'But . . .' Martin said, looking round the room again, 'if all this paper isn't to test my powers of observation, what *is* it for, may I ask?'

Grand and Batchelor looked at each other. Miss Wolstenholme refused to meet anyone's eye. Eventually, Batchelor tried to answer.

'It's not . . . for anything, really. It's old bills, invoices, notes taken of interviews, surveillance records, that kind of thing.'

'So,' Martin brightened up a little, 'that pile is invoices,' he pointed to another, 'and that one is interviews. Is that it?'

'Nooo . . .' Batchelor looked hard at Grand and Miss Wolstenholme, but they had their eyes firmly elsewhere. 'They are *all* those things. Mixed. Um . . . random.'

'*Random?*' Martin could hardly force the word through lips gone suddenly pale and dry. '*Random?* You mean . . .' He put a hand to his forehead and took a deep breath. 'You don't know where anything *is?*' He looked from one of his new employers to another, desperate to be told that it was otherwise.

Grand spoke with the voice of authority. 'Of course we know where everything is,' he said. 'It's in these piles. It has never stopped us from closing a case, I can assure you.'

'There was that one . . .' Miss Wolstenholme was a child of the manse and was honest to a fault.

'That was never going to be solved,' snapped Grand.

In the ensuing silence, Martin had an idea. 'While I'm new,' he suggested, 'perhaps I could do some filing. Where are your filing cabinets?'

Telling him they didn't have any was a little like kicking a puppy, but Matthew Grand could think as fast as the next man. 'Miss Wolstenholme,' he said, 'nip down to Tottenham Court Road – better take a cab – and see what Heal and Son have in the way of filing cabinets. Immediate delivery. Put it on my account.'

Miss Wolstenholme was on her feet and donning her walking cape like lightning. The atmosphere in the office was getting a little edgy.

'May I go?' Martin asked, politely. 'Only, I bought some for the *Telegraph* offices the other day and if you're not careful,' he looked at Miss Wolstenholme and smiled kindly, 'they'll fob you off with inferior rubbish. Mr Lebus of Hull builds the only filing cabinets worth having, though they do cost a *little* more.'

James sighed and nodded to Miss Wolstenholme. 'You can both go,' he said, pulling out his chair from under his desk. 'Miss Wolstenholme because she deserves some fresh air and you because . . . well, just because. We'll see you both later. Have some lunch, why not? Get to know each other. Talk office stuff. We may not be here when you get back.'

When the sound of clattering feet died away from the landing outside the office, Grand looked at Batchelor. 'James,' he said, shaking his head. 'What have you done?'

Mrs Rackstraw was surprised to see her gentlemen home in the middle of the morning, but also, relieved. The peculiar gentleman in the drawing room was beginning to get on her wick and Maisie had been in the kitchen in hysterics ever since she had opened the door to him. He had refused to give his name or his business, but when Mrs Rackstraw had been appealed to, he had offered, in very cultured but rather definite tones, to fetch a constable if he was refused entry. Mrs Rackstraw was almost certain that refusing someone entry to your home wasn't a crime within the meaning of any Act she had ever heard of, but the gentleman was very smartly dressed – over-dressed, if anything – and what with one thing and another, it was just easier to let him in. He had given a little cry of distress when he had seen the décor of the drawing room, and had shied like a spooked horse when she had offered him coffee in the best *famille rose* cups, but apart from that, he had been no trouble. Even so, she had to keep coming up from the kitchen to check he wasn't stealing the silver, and tripe pie didn't cook itself. She was all behind like the cow's tail, as she told her gentlemen as she encountered them in the hall, and she was relying on them to get rid of the annoying thing as soon as they could. Apart from anything else, his perfume was making her sneeze.

'Perfume?' Grand was ready to take this as a bit of Rackstrawian hyperbole, but Batchelor's nose was twitching.

'She's right, there is a funny smell in here.' He looked like a bloodhound, testing the air. 'Lilies, is it?'

'I think it must be,' the housekeeper said. 'The flowers make me sneeze and I have been snuffling all morning since he arrived. I'll have to air the room once he's gone.'

Despite their conversation having been largely sotto voce, the ears of the sensitive gentleman must have matched their owner, because the door was flung open and he stood there, quivering with annoyance.

'*Must* you?' he cried. 'If there is one thing that *shreds* my nerves it is people talking behind doors. I can hardly *bear* these curtains as it is, and now you mutter. Either go away, or speak up.' He leaned forward and peered at the two men. 'Are you Grand and Batchelor, by any remote chance?'

The enquiry agents looked at their uninvited visitor. He was a distinguished-looking gent with swooping hair and, indeed, a penchant for lilies. The smell seemed to be emanating from the luxurious, if greying, locks which were swept back from an intellectual brow. His full lips were set in a sneer of distaste below a nose which seemed to dominate the room, and his spade-shaped beard was combed to perfection. His clothes were immaculate, though not in the highest fashion. He leaned heavily on a stick.

Grand took a wild guess.

'Mr Ruskin?'

The man smiled, which transformed his face. 'So you *are* an enquiry agent,' he said. 'But which?'

'I am Matthew Grand,' Grand said, extending a hand, which Ruskin took for just the briefest moment.

'And so you,' Ruskin said, turning to Batchelor, 'must be Mr Batchelor.' Again, the merest touch of the fingers into the palm. He looked at Mrs Rackstraw in a way that made her feel superfluous, so she scurried off back to the kitchen and the now almost catatonic Maisie.

'I don't really think we should be talking to you, Mr Ruskin,' Grand said, as they went back into the drawing room, heavy as an undertaker's with the scent of lily. 'Conflict of interest.'

'I see no conflict,' Ruskin said.

'Well, we *are* being instructed by James Whistler,' Batchelor offered. 'I believe that you and he are—'

'At *war*, Mr Batchelor,' Ruskin said. 'At *war*! I merely

expressed my opinion of his ghastly daub and he took offence. So now, lines have been drawn, solicitors appointed; the whole thing has gone completely too far. All I said was—'

'We know,' Grand said. 'But really, Mr Ruskin, we can't—'

'Have you *seen* the daub?' Ruskin leant forward on his stick, his nose like the prow of a Viking dragon ship.

'I haven't,' Batchelor said, 'but I know Mr Grand has seen it several times.' He glanced at his partner. 'I believe he rather likes it.'

Grand nodded. 'I do,' he said. 'It has a certain . . . something.'

Ruskin straightened up and rapped his stick several times on the floor. 'I suppose I should not be surprised,' he said. 'Any man who can live in equanimity with these drapes cannot be completely in his right mind.' He sighed. 'I am not a well man, you know. The strain of this is . . .' He sat down heavily in a chair, glancing only briefly to assess the pattern of the fabric and finding it just passing muster to receive his buttocks. 'The strain is taking its toll. I wondered . . . could you ask Mr Whistler,' he forced the name out through clenched teeth, 'to perhaps withdraw his suit?'

'That isn't for us to do,' Grand said politely. 'Have you approached his lawyers? Perhaps that would be a better place to start.'

Ruskin gave a grimace of distaste. 'Approach his lawyers? Keen and Griswold? God, no. I barely approach my own. I just thought . . .' He leaned heavily on his stick and the arm of his chair and hauled himself upright. 'I just hoped that common sense could be made to prevail.'

Batchelor had a ground-breaking idea, leaving aside that he had already met Mr Keen on another matter. 'Have you considered apologizing?' he asked, with a diffident shrug.

Ruskin's eyes nearly fell out of his head. 'Apologize?' His voice sounded like that of a choirboy on the turn from the bottom of a well. 'Never! I stand by what I said.'

'Then we must bid you good day, Mr Ruskin,' Grand said, ushering him out. Over his shoulder, he added to Batchelor, 'Open a window, for heaven's sake. It smells like a tart's boudoir in here.'

Batchelor, who had more recent experience of the same, couldn't agree, but opened the window anyway.

Out on the street, Ruskin looked a little older, a little greyer, a little more likely to attract the sympathy of a jury. Grand was not at all sure how any lawsuit between him and Whistler would turn out. It wasn't as if Ruskin had taken a soapbox at Speakers' Corner and told the world through a megaphone that Whistler couldn't paint, that he lived in sin with a woman called Maud, that he called his children by rather bizarre names . . . his comment had been criticism for the sake of criticism, words for their own sake rather than an honest opinion. How would a jury of twelve solid Londoners pick the bones out? It was in the lap of the gods, as far as Grand could tell. He looked back at the house, where Batchelor was wafting the curtains to and fro at the open window, sending gusts of lily down the street to follow Ruskin as he made his slow way west, towards Chelsea, where curtains and upholstery fabric in general were not so upsetting. Taking a deep breath of fresh spring air, Grand bounded back up the steps and shut the door with a resounding bang.

It seemed only minutes before a rather flustered Maisie scuttled into the drawing room with a *carte de visite*.

'There's a soljer at the door,' she said, and although, clearly, the visitor wasn't a patch on the soljer who was already inside, he did tend to make a maid's heart flutter a little.

'Willoughby Inverarity,' Grand read aloud. 'This is intriguing, James. My opponent's second at the Army and Navy Club the other night. Show him in, Maisie. But check for weapons first.'

'Sir?' Maisie's eyes were wide. She rarely understood what he was talking about at first go, what with the accent and the all-round gorgeousness. And sometimes, as now, it didn't make any sense anyway.

'Never mind,' chuckled Grand. 'Show him in anyway.'

She bobbed and left.

'Think he wants to carry on where Peebles left off?' Batchelor asked.

'Time will tell,' Grand said, and Maisie was back, with a

large, square lieutenant of hussars, sombre in cavalry frock coat, his French grey pillbox at a jaunty angle on his head.

'Lieutenant Peebles,' Grand stood up, looking beyond him to find somebody else. 'I was expecting Lieutenant Inverarity.'

'I know.' The officer swept off his cap. 'That's why I'm here. My comrade and I were guilty of a little subterfuge the other night. *I* am Willoughby Inverarity. *He* is Anstruther Peebles.'

'I don't understand,' Grand said. 'And, by the way, how did you find me?'

Inverarity smiled. 'You are not the only one able to sleuth when push comes to shove. I asked around. This must be Mr Batchelor.'

'If you say so,' Batchelor said. 'I'm beginning to wonder who anybody is.'

'My sleuthing,' Inverarity explained, 'led me to your office around the corner where, in a scene of unbelievable chaos, a rather cultured young man told me where to find you.'

'Alexander Martin,' Grand said. 'Known to his friends as Gan, for some unknown reason. He's our gofer, as I think you guys have it.'

'Guys?' Inverarity frowned.

'Men,' Batchelor translated, jerking his thumb in Grand's direction, 'as his guys have it.'

'I hope Mr Martin didn't exceed his authority,' Inverarity said, 'sending me to your domicile.'

'House,' Batchelor muttered to Grand from the side of his mouth.

'Thank you, James,' the American said. 'I have been living in this blasted country for thirteen years now, on and off. I think I can manage. Have a seat, Lieutenant.'

Inverarity did. 'This is highly embarrassing,' he said, not quite able to look Grand in the face. 'You remember the sarn't major, the one at the door of the Rag who showed you in?'

'Vaguely,' Grand nodded.

'Well, he had a word with a corporal who brought word to Anstruther that an American officer wanted to see him.'

'Go on.'

'I've known Peebles for a couple of years now and I've

never seen him so flustered. He told me he'd lost money in a game of baccarat and that he still owed a certain amount to an American officer. He asked me to change places with him.'

'Wouldn't the American officer in question have known Peebles by sight,' Batchelor asked, 'having played cards with him?'

Inverarity shrugged. 'Drink had been taken, as I understand it, and baccarat is never played in broad daylight. So, comrade and all that, the honour of the regiment, I agreed. The rest you know, Captain Grand.'

'Yes and no,' Grand said. 'I've never knowingly played baccarat in my life and I'd certainly never met either of you gentlemen before. You know why I came calling.'

Inverarity looked suitably shamefaced. 'I do,' he nodded, 'and believe me, I am disgusted. After the general stepped in, before I was blackballed from the Club, of course, I had it out with Peebles. He admitted the baccarat story was a fabrication and that he knew this girl . . . what was her name?'

'Mabel Glossop,' Grand reminded him.

'Quite. It appals me that an officer of the Twenty-First Hussars should stoop so low as to entertain a lady of ill-repute.'

'It was his peculiarities that appalled me,' Batchelor said.

'I don't follow,' Inverarity frowned.

Batchelor glanced at them both. Men of the world all, but Maisie may have chosen that moment to glide past on some domestic business, and it would never do for her to hear such things. He got up and stooped, whispering in the officer's ear. Inverarity's eyes widened and his jaw dropped. 'Good God!' he said. 'That makes it ten times worse!'

'At least,' Grand nodded.

'For what it's worth,' Inverarity said, 'I have officially sent Peebles to Coventry.'

Batchelor opened his mouth to explain, but Grand held up his hand. 'I'm all right, thank you, James,' he said.

'And also, for what it's worth, he assures me that he had nothing to do with the girl's death. I am inclined to believe him, despite his obfuscation over baccarat.' He stood up, extending a hand. 'Captain Grand, I behaved badly the other night and I can only apologize, as one officer to another. May I at least pay the doctor's bill for your cut hand and the cost of a new shirt.'

Grand stood up and took the man's hand and his apology. 'I believe it was I who struck the first blow,' he smiled. 'As for the cut, just a scratch; and the shirt . . . well, the maid who showed you in works wonders with starch.'

'We will have to talk to Mr Peebles again,' Batchelor said.

'Do what you like with him,' Inverarity clapped on the pillbox. 'He's dead to me.'

It was business as usual for Sergeant Simmons of the Park Police. He was patrolling in a westerly direction as the Chinese lanterns of the Cremorne swung above his head. The breeze was stiffening from the river and a skein of geese honked its way across the deepening purple of the sky. Night was coming to Chelsea as it did every twenty-four hours or so and all was right with the world.

Wonderful things, rhododendron bushes. They rose to unprecedented heights if unchecked, produced a plethora of brightly painted blooms and, from time to time, concealed dead bodies. To be fair to Sergeant Simmons, he hadn't actually found the last one – Constable McIndoe had – but Simmons was damned if he was going to let a rookie of the Scottish persuasion steal his thunder. After Clara Jenkins, however, things were a little different. Newshounds had arrived at the Cremorne in gigs, barouches, hansoms and cabriolets. Notepads had emerged from pockets, pencil stubs scurried across paper. Every now and then, there had been the flash of a camera and Fleet Street's finest artists, when not caricaturing Lord Beaconsfield and Otto von Bismarck, were busy sketching trees and shrubs, jotting down notes like 'Where the Dead Woman Lay'.

Because of the press hoo-ha, there had been talk of locking the gates at night, but the League for the Right to Wander had threatened to glue themselves to railings if such draconian measures were introduced, so the Cremorne authorities had backed down. What *had* happened, however, was that Detective Constable Barnes, backed by no less an authority than Chief

Inspector Dolly Williamson, had insisted that should, horror upon horrors, *another* victim appear, *no one* was to touch said body until a detective arrived; a detective with at least five years' experience.

So, when Simmons literally stumbled over the feet sticking out from under a rhododendron bush, he bit back the urge to investigate by himself, straightened up and shook his rattle high over his head. The noise was such that the dead woman herself might have got up to complain. As it was, a sash window overlooking the Gardens slid upward and an angry head poked out. 'Oi. You! What d'you think you're doing?'

'Making sure that citizens like you can sleep safe in your beds, you bloody ingrate!' and he rattled some more. The noise was added to by the familiar pounding of beat feet; not one, but two coppers coming at the gallop, truncheons at the ready, bullseyes' beams darting in all directions.

'What kept you, Mitchell?' Simmons snapped. 'I've been rattling here for minutes.'

'Sorry, Sarge.' Mitchell was humility itself.

'Get yourself over to the station,' the sergeant growled. 'It'll be raining soon, no doubt, and Mr Latimer will want to see this.'

And the constable was gone.

As it happened, Detective Sergeant Latimer, he of the necessary five years' experience, was out on another case, so that nice Mr Barnes came back with Mitchell, apologizing profusely to Simmons for not having enough years under his belt. Even so, Barnes had grown up considerably since his encounter with Clara Jenkins, and he immediately asserted his authority on this case.

'Well, haul her out, Mitchell and . . . you.' He'd forgotten the other constable's name. 'Let's see what we've got.'

The men obliged, one at one ankle, the other at the other, and they slid the body out onto the grass. 'Hold that light steady,' Barnes said, and watched as the bullseye beam trailed up to the head and down again. The boy detective was no happier about being so close to death than he had been a week ago, but there were standards and he knew he needed to impress.

'Height,' he cleared his throat, 'five foot nine. Hm, tall for a tart. Don't write that down, Mitchell,' he snapped. 'Just the height. Blonde. Too much mascara.' He peered at the heavy eyelids and the sightless eyes stared back at him. 'Overdone the lipstick, too.'

'Sir . . .' Sergeant Simmons began, but Barnes raised a forefinger.

'Not now, Simmons,' he said, 'I'm concentrating.'

'I think . . .'

'I'm sure you do,' Barnes said, 'but this is one for the detective branch, I'm afraid. Constable,' he barked at the one who wasn't Mitchell, 'form a cordon or something around those bushes, will you? We don't want members of the public trampling all over the place.'

For the life of him, the one who wasn't Mitchell couldn't see how he could form a cordon all by himself with no rope of any kind, but he saluted and made himself scarce.

'No signs of strangulation,' Barnes said, checking the neck. 'Neckline unruffled. No sign of . . . interference with the breasts.'

'That's because . . .' Simmons was trying to make life easier for the detective, but Barnes wasn't having any.

'No blood.' Barnes held up the fingers. 'No broken nails, so perhaps the lady didn't put up much of a fight. Aha!' He clicked his fingers. 'She knew her attacker. So, she was a lady of the night and he was a regular client. Mitchell,' he glanced up at the man furiously writing in his notepad with the aid of the darting beam, 'how can we prove that this was a lady of the night?'

'Er . . .' Mitchell wasn't sure.

'Detective Constable Barnes,' Simmons tried to cut in.

'Don't worry, Sergeant,' Barnes grinned, pride in his work growing by the second. 'I've got this.' He reached down and hauled up the victim's skirts, sliding his hands up her right thigh. 'We know that she was a lady of the night because she's not wearing any . . . oh, my God!' Barnes whipped his hand away and stood upright, shaking with disbelief.

'Because,' Simmons at last had a chance to say something, 'this particular lady of the night is . . . was . . . a man.' He held up a leather wallet. 'As is obvious from the calling card I found in this, neatly tucked into the deceased's waistband. Difficult to read in this light,' he focused his bullseye on it, 'ah, yes, here we go,' and he read the name aloud. 'Lieutenant Anstruther Peebles, Twenty-First Hussars.'

The other two policemen looked at each other.

'Now, of course,' Simmons went on, 'it may be that our "lady" here found or purloined the wallet of said Lieutenant Peebles along with the wad of cash it also contains. But I assume, sir, that your ejaculation of a moment ago when rummaging in the deceased's folderols was evinced by the fact that she has rather unusual wedding tackle.'

Barnes nodded, swallowing hard. 'It's a man,' he said, 'without any doubt.'

'So,' Simmons said, 'all we need to do now is to discover why Lieutenant Anstruther Peebles is not as other officers of the Twenty-First Hussars. When we've done that, Mr Barnes, we may have our killer.'

The policemen looked down at the wreck of a human being at their feet. Now, Anstruther Peebles was not merely dead to Willoughby Inverarity; he was dead to everybody.

FIVE

The 21st Hussars were the newest cavalry regiment in the British army. Grand and Batchelor went together to find Lieutenant Peebles, in Grand's case to continue a conversation he had begun with Inverarity. The regiment's insignia shone in burnished brass on the barracks gatepost, and under it some wag had daubed, in black paint, the unofficial motto of a regiment that had yet to see active service, 'Thou shalt not kill'. Cruel, but not unjustified in the world of inter-regimental rivalry.

The adjutant, all shoulder-chains and attitude, was unimpressed by the pair's calling card.

'May I ask why you wish to see Lieutenant Peebles?' he said.

'You may,' Grand conceded, but went no further than that.

'Is there a problem?' Batchelor asked.

'Indeed there is,' the adjutant bridled. 'I have to tell you, gentlemen, that Lieutenant Peebles is no longer on the regimental roll.'

'Really?' Grand was not too surprised to hear that. 'Resigned his commission?'

'Resigned his life,' the adjutant said. 'He's dead.'

Grand and Batchelor looked at each other. 'Suicide?' Batchelor queried.

'Foul play,' the adjutant said. 'It's all over the papers. I wonder you gentlemen, as' – he read the card again – '*enquiry agents* . . . missed it.'

Grand and Batchelor metaphorically kicked themselves. Of all mornings not to have read the newspapers, beautifully ironed as they always were. But the imperative to get on the trail of Anstruther Peebles had made them rush off without even a bite of toast. It was annoying to think of the vital news still waiting, folded and immaculate, on their abandoned breakfast table.

'What happened?' Grand asked.

'I am not at liberty to divulge anything, gentlemen. As I have already made clear to umpteen gentlemen of the press. Good morning.'

Out on the pavement, Grand and Batchelor were at a loss. They were used to their plans for any day of the week going awry, but not normally by nine o'clock or thereabouts in the morning. Fleet Street seemed the next rational choice, but between where they stood and the newspaper capital lay the office, and so they decided to drop in. 'A scene of unbeliev-able chaos' was how Inverarity had described it and so they were ready for anything. It was not Miss Wolstenholme's day today, so she at least would not be added to the mess, losing her temper and her will to live in equal measure. It was tempting to leave Alexander Martin to his own devices, but that seemed somehow not in the spirit of being caring employers. So they bent their path towards the Strand and were soon standing, open-mouthed, in the open doorway.

The surprises had begun on the pavement. Someone had polished the brass plate by the door until it was almost blind-ingly bright in the spring sunshine. The letterbox and doorknob were similarly glowing, and the dust of a million passing cabs had been brushed off the panels of the door. But nothing could have prepared them for the scene inside the office.

Along the wall facing the door were ranks of light oak drawers, small square ones to the left, larger, deeper ones to the right. Between the windows looking out onto the street, two desks, with two layers of glass-fronted bookcases above them, stood side by side, their flaps discreetly closed and a leather chair pulled up to each. Against the opposite wall, a desk bearing Miss Wolstenholme's typewriting machine, decently sheathed in a fitted oilcloth cover, was otherwise clear, save for five pencils, sharpened and exactly the same length and aligned with the edge of the desk, alongside a notepad, turned back to a clean page, ready for notes to be taken.

The mismatched Turkey rugs had gone and had been replaced by a precise square of coconut matting. Perfectly in line with its edges, in the middle of the room, stood a kneehole desk, with an open diary, a closed ledger and an inkwell its only adornment. Screwed neatly and in perfect symmetry on the front of the desk was a brass sign that read, 'A. Martin, Assistant'. And behind the desk, was none other than A. Martin himself, slotting the last card into a drawer taken from the bank on the far wall. He looked up when he felt their eyes on him.

'Mr Grand,' he cried, with delight, 'Mr Batchelor! How lovely to see you! Your housekeeper said you were out all day, but I didn't realize that meant you would be coming in to the office!'

'Um . . . no,' Grand said, looking round and dreading his next account from Heal and Son of Tottenham Court Road. 'We thought we would pop in, you know, just to see if you needed any help.'

Martin's beam could have lit a forest fire. 'No, no, as you see, it is all done. Miss Wolstenholme was a great help.'

Batchelor blessed the boy for his kindness. Miss Wolstenholme was many things, no doubt, but a great help was not an attribute they had yet experienced.

Martin came out from behind his desk and took Grand by the elbow. 'May I explain my methodology?' he said, excitedly. 'I have to say, both of you, that I have never been given carte blanche before. It was so invigorating to be able to plan a system from the ground up, as it were. I did have to get rid of some things – well, not get *rid*, as such. The caretaker of the building found me some space in the basement so if you want any of the old fittings, you will find them there.'

Grand felt the wind leave his sails. Although he had to admit that the room looked a million times better, he was going to be a little sniffy about the desk of his great-uncle Dick having disappeared, which would have surprised Batchelor a good deal as they had bought it second-hand in Middlesex Street. It was no good letting the help think they could throw things out, willy-nilly.

'So,' Martin said, flinging out an arm. 'Let me explain my *raison d'être*. I'll start over here. Miss Wolstenholme's desk is over here, as you can see. She has just one drawer in her desk – I don't know whether you had noticed,' he leaned in, conspiratorially, as if the woman might be hiding somewhere in the scrupulously neat room, 'but she does tend to be a little untidy. The more drawers she has, the more rubbish she will accumulate. Hence, just the one.' He smiled happily. 'Actually, Heal and Son's gave me a very good price on her desk, as one drawer is not common.' He drummed a little tattoo on the typewriter's desk and moved across the rooms to the two desks beside the window. 'These are your desks,' he said. 'I know you shared one before, but I think it looks better for clients if you are seen to be both autonomous and discreet. Hence, the drop front which can be raised to conceal contents which might be confidential.'

He dropped one flap with a flourish. Two inkwells sat squarely in the integral holder, one filled with red ink, one with blue. Above, recessed into the depths of the desk were a series of pigeonholes and two drawers, all empty and waiting. The middle row of pigeonholes was raised above the rest and, in the resulting vaulted space, a silver frame held a portrait of Lady Caroline Wentworth, smiling coquettishly over one shoulder.

Grand was astonished. 'Wherever did you get that from?' he asked, amazed.

'It was stuck to a file from a case just before Christmas last year. Mango chutney, I think it was.'

'I don't remember a case involving mango chutney,' Batchelor remarked.

'No, that's not what I mean,' Martin explained, making a mental note to self not to make any remarks that may be a little equivocal. Obviously, enquiry agents or not, these two were a little behind the door when the brains were being doled out and could never have coped with Greats at Oxford. 'I mean, it was stuck with mango chutney.'

Grand clicked his fingers. 'I remember now,' he said. 'Mrs Rackstraw made us some goose curry, do you remember, to use up the leftovers.'

Batchelor blanched. He did remember it. He had been belching curry for days – he had told the woman at the time that Brussels sprouts didn't belong in a dish like that. The mango chutney had been the only way to get it down.

'So,' Martin said, to get the conversation back on track, 'I cleaned it off and here it is. A very beautiful lady, Mr Grand, if I may say so.'

Batchelor decided to take a bit of umbrage. 'How did you know it didn't belong in my desk?' he said, archly.

Martin blushed. 'There was quite a . . . personal message on the back,' he said. 'So I naturally assumed . . .' He looked anxiously at his employers. 'If I have made a faux pas . . .'

'Not at all,' Grand said, clapping him on the shoulder. 'It was a very thoughtful gesture.'

'This,' Martin said, flipping down the next desk lid, 'is yours, Mr Batchelor. I have added a file there, as you can see, for your notes for your novel.'

'How did . . .?' Batchelor had started to speak before he realized it was pointless.

'Notes inserted into the case file of the Duchess of Wolverhampton, as she liked to be known. You had her real name on the front, as you may remember.'

'Oh, yes,' chuckled Batchelor, 'I do remember that. One of the best con-women of the century, unless I miss my guess.'

'Precisely.' Martin waved a hand over his own desk. 'This is in this position merely so I can deal with clients. If you would prefer . . .'

'No, no, it's all perfect where it is,' Grand said. 'But the drawers . . .' He narrowed his eyes to count them. This was going to be really, *really* expensive, he knew. He hoped it would be worthwhile.

Martin grinned again. He was so happy with his System that he knew his bosses would be too. 'It's very simple,' he said. 'The large drawers contain notes and invoices as discussed yesterday. They are not in any particular order . . .'

Batchelor's eyebrows nearly disappeared into his hair. He hadn't expected that at all.

'. . . but they do all have a code number which is unique to their placement. So, taking the first drawer here, you will see that it is numbered 1.' He pointed to the label, for the avoidance of doubt. 'Inside, the sections are labelled in Roman numerals from front to back. Thus.' He pulled out a file from the middle of the drawer which was labelled 1/VIII/1873. 'The date is specific to the year in which the case was taken on. Inside the file, the contents are labelled with letters of the alphabet. So, in this one, you will see that the letter of instruction is now labelled 1/VIII/1873/a.' He slotted the file back neatly into place. 'And so on.' He slid the drawer shut on runners as smooth as Messrs Harris Lebus could provide.

Grand was puzzled. 'But how does this help us find anything, if it is all random?'

'Ah!' Martin brought up his right forefinger with so much enthusiasm he nearly had his own eye out. 'This is the beauty of my System. In these drawers here – designed for libraries, but, if I may say so, put to far better use here – I have the cases all in alphabetical order, but entered in as many places as may be required. To take one example, some years ago you investigated the sad passing of that wonderful author, Charles Dickens.'

His bosses nodded. Wonderful was in the eye of the beholder, but in general terms, the description could stand.

'But depending on how you think of the case, different people might think of looking up different words. In this case, I have filed it under Author, subset Dickens, Charles, second subset, Charles Dickens; Charles Dickens; Dickens, Charles; Gad's Hill; Hill, Gad's . . .'

'I think I get the general gist,' Batchelor said. 'So, when you have found the card, it has the code on it and you can find it in the relevant drawer.'

Martin clapped his hands. 'Yes!' he cried. 'That's it!'

'So,' Grand said, looking around, 'when will it be finished?'

Martin looked puzzled. 'What are you saying?' he said, after a pause.

Grand was puzzled now. 'I'm saying, when will it be finished?' he said, a little more slowly.

'It *is* finished,' Martin said. 'I was just filling in the last card when you came in. Of course, some of the small drawers will seem a little sparsely filled and the last column and a half of the big ones are completely empty, but that is to leave room for new cases which, of course, are coming in daily.'

'May I check?' Batchelor asked. 'Oh, just to see if I understand, of course. I am sure you have done a simply perfect job.'

'Please,' Martin said. 'It's important that you know how it works.'

Batchelor opened a random drawer and took out a card.

Martin gave a small shriek. 'Oh, please, Mr Batchelor, when you take out a card, put a place holder in so you know where it came from.'

'But . . . it's in alphabetical order . . .'

'Even so.' Martin had gone several shades paler and was shaking his hands in distress. 'It's just something I need you to do . . .'

'All right,' Batchelor said, and slotted a bright blue card from a holder on top of the cabinets into the place. Grand meanwhile was making a mental list of all the jobs they would not be able to send Martin out on. In a few moments, his list was complete, and short. None of them.

Batchelor consulted his card and went across to the larger drawers, opened one and walked his fingers down the files. He lifted one out and compared it with the card. He turned to Grand. 'It does work,' he said. 'Look at that!' He tried to keep the amazement out of his voice.

Martin shrugged. 'It's what I do,' he said. 'You should see my sock drawer.'

Grand and Batchelor would rather not.

'I suggest,' Grand said, 'that you take the rest of the day off. We'll have another case for you to sort out tomorrow and Miss Wolstenholme will need to be trained.' The three men looked at each other, all wearing the expressions of those who want to believe in the triumph of hope over experience.

'If you're sure that's all right,' Martin said. 'I do have a lunch appointment tomorrow, though; I had said my friend could meet me here . . . I should have asked first, perhaps . . .'

'Don't be silly,' Batchelor said. 'You're an assistant, not a slave. Look,' he pointed to the sign on the desk, 'it says so, here, so it must be true!'

'Thank you so much, Mr Grand, Mr Batchelor,' Martin said, slipping on his coat and making for the door. Then he paused, came back in and lined up his pencils, just that bit straighter. 'Thank you,' and he was finally gone.

'Mad as a hatter,' Grand said, 'but you have to hand it to the guy. He sure is neat.'

Fleet Street was next. While Batchelor grabbed the *Advertiser* and the *Telegraph*, Grand hailed a cab and they rattled east. In the Strand, with the traffic as usual at a standstill, they bundled out and continued on foot, past the solid spire of St Clement Danes, crossing into the City where, until a few weeks ago, Temple Bar had stood. The City of London Corporation, anxious to widen the street, had taken it down, all 2,700 stones of it over an eleven-day period. Had it improved the flow of traffic? Of course not.

'Why wasn't I told, Johnny?' Batchelor wanted to know, hurtling into the *Telegraph*'s inner sanctum.

John Lawson looked up at him, 'Told what, James?'

'About Anstruther Peebles. *Another* body in the Cremorne.'

Lawson nodded, 'They'll shut it down now, for sure,' he said. 'There's only so much bad publicity a garden can take. Oh, and, sorry, was I supposed to be keeping you informed about every fart that flies?' He looked at Grand, blocking the doorway. 'You must be Captain Grand,' he got to his feet for the first time. 'My condolences, sir,' he shook the man's hand, 'to be working with this reprobate. I know what that's like!' He glowered at Batchelor.

'My apologies, Johnny,' Batchelor had the grace to say. 'The late Mr Peebles was part of an ongoing enquiry of ours.'

'Was he, now?' Lawson reached for his notepad.

'Put that away, you stew-stick. We saw him first.'

Lawson laughed.

'The *Telegraph* was a little coy, Mr Lawson,' Grand said.

'Johnny, please. Yes, I know. The editor's of the Methodist persuasion, prepared to believe good about everybody, you know the sort of thing.'

'How odd,' Grand said, 'in Fleet Street, I mean.'

'Tell me about it,' Lawson muttered.

'We were hoping *you'd* tell *us* about it, Johnny,' Batchelor said. The thud-thud of the ten-feed printer was already pounding in his temples. 'Peebles.'

Lawson leaned back in his chair. 'Cause of death still

undetermined,' he said, waving vaguely to other seats for his guests. 'Body was found by the park police, as per, stuffed under some bushes. The dress was odd, of course.'

'Mess?' Batchelor guessed.

'Walking out?' Grand threw in. 'Stable?'

'Cross,' Lawson said. 'The late Lieutenant Peebles was wearing women's attire.'

'We've met that before,' Batchelor said, 'the Boulton and Park case.'

'It seemed to be all the rage here a couple of years back,' Grand reminded everybody.

'Yes, but this is different,' Lawson said. 'The impression I get – and it is only an impression, mind you, since officially the Yard aren't talking – is that Peebles used the disguise as a lure to have his wicked way with ladies.'

'How would that work, though?' Batchelor asked. 'I mean, if a chap turns up in his three-piece tweeds, jingling a few bob and does a deal with a girl, fair enough – although your editor might not approve, Johnny, it's the way of the world. But if a chap ditches his three piece and dons ladies' kecks, what then? Wouldn't the girl in question be a little surprised? Along the lines of screaming blue murder, attracting a whole station-house of coppers. So it wouldn't work, would it?'

'The ways of the Cremorne are strange, James,' Lawson said. 'It's not for us to delve into a man's inner demons – and it's certainly not anything I can print in a family newspaper. Some people even allow their servants to read it, apparently. That's why we didn't mention the women's clothing bit.'

'We know he was a regular in the Gardens,' Grand said. 'A fellow officer in his regiment confirmed it. We also know that one of *his* regulars was the same Mabel Glossop whose body was found there, not eighteen months ago.'

'I did not know that,' Lawson said, but his movement towards his pad was thwarted by an acid glance from Batchelor.

'You *can* use that, Johnny,' he said, 'on condition that you keep us posted with anything else that breaks.'

'I'd appreciate your insight into all this,' Lawson said. 'It appears that all roads lead to the Cremorne at the moment.'

'More than you know,' Grand said, thinking of the Whistler painting he had rather liked in the Grosvenor gallery.

'Isn't that the whole point of this conversation?' Lawson spread his arms wide. 'There's a lot, apparently, that I don't know, and that'll never improve unless you tell me. See your conversation of seconds ago.'

'It's nothing, Johnny,' Grand said. 'Just a coincidence, is all.'

Neither Grand nor Batchelor believed in coincidences, but Lawson didn't know that.

'We have three deaths.' Batchelor tried to make sense of it all. 'Two at least are related. First, Mabel Glossop, poisoned and found in the Gardens eighteen months ago.'

'Third,' Grand had leapt forward to make the link, 'Anstruther Peebles, found days ago not yards from where Mabel Glossop's body had been left, he being a client of hers.'

'And second,' Batchelor went on, 'Clara Jenkins, ditto ditto the Cremorne. And here we have to differ, Matthew; I think all three are related. After all, Clara and Mabel are out of the same stable, Mrs Arbuthnot's in Turks Row.'

'But no known links between Peebles and Clara?' Lawson checked.

'My point exactly,' Grand said.

'Tight-lipped though they are,' Batchelor looked at Lawson, 'do we know who's on this at the Yard?'

'B Division?' Lawson scratched his head. 'The superintendent there is Hendricks. He'll have passed it down to . . .'

'Metcalfe,' the square-jawed man said, 'Inspector. How can I help you gentlemen?'

Grand and Batchelor knew Scotland Yard well, but they hadn't expected to be allowed across its portals. Instead, they were in the snug of the Clarence, with Whitehall rattling away between the squares, Parliament and Trafalgar, feet from them. The air was thick with cigar and pipe smoke and the planks on the floor crowded with dozens of the largest feet in the Metropolis. A green-looking detective constable sat next to Metcalfe. He had just been despatched to buy the drinks.

'We were hoping you could help us,' Grand said.

'Moses' Metcalfe didn't get out of his Division often. This was a rare visit to the holy of holies, the headquarters of the Metropolitan Police, or at least its drinking den. He smiled, as though chewing a wasp. 'I didn't realize you were from the colonies, Mr Grand,' he said. 'Your coppers over there still shooting people at random?'

'No more than fall down stairs in your lock-ups, Inspector,' Grand countered. This was not going well.

'The Cremorne case . . .' Batchelor thought he ought to focus on the here and now.

'Which one?' Metcalfe asked.

This was progress, Batchelor thought – an acknowledgement of reality.

'Both ladies of the night,' Grand said, 'and Lieutenant Peebles.'

'It's in the paper,' Metcalfe shrugged, dipping his moustache into his beer.

'We all know that's only ever part of the story,' Batchelor said.

'That's right,' Metcalfe smiled. 'You used to work in Fleet Street, didn't you, Mr Batchelor?'

'You're well informed,' Batchelor said.

'Of course I am.' Metcalfe leaned back, folding his arms. 'I'm a detective. And for the record, Mr Grand, I know perfectly well that you are an American. Formerly of the Union army, I believe, Third Cavalry of the Potomac.'

'You've done your homework, sir,' Grand nodded.

'When so-called private detectives ask to see me,' Metcalfe said, 'I make it my business to find out all I can about them. I suspect there's rather more than I can uncover.'

'It would serve all our purposes better,' Batchelor said, 'if we co-operated. After all, we are on the same side.'

Metcalfe roared with laughter. 'Are we, Mr Batchelor? Are we really? I can tell you nothing about the Cremorne case, as you call it, as per a recent directive from the Home Office via Mr Howard Vincent. Scotland Yard's – and B Division's – lips are sealed. But it's been very pleasant sharing a pint with you gentlemen. Don't worry about expenses. Barnes here is paying.'

And that was it. The police clearly weren't helping anybody

with their enquiries. 'Why is he called Moses again?' Grand asked Batchelor as they jostled their way out past Black Marias crowding the archway that led to Whitehall.

''Cos it took him forty years to get out of the wilderness,' Batchelor said.

Back in the snug, Metcalfe finished his pint. 'Busy getting the people of London out of the bondage of crime as I am, Barnes,' he said, smugly, 'I haven't got time for lowlifes like those two. Who's paying them, eh? Who'd engage a pair of privates to look into the deaths of harlots? The only people who catch criminals for nothing is us. There's something going on here, something fishy. They know you now, so put somebody else on them – Twisleton, that university bloke, he's good at undercover. I want to know what they know.'

'So, where are we, James?' Grand was sampling the latest bourbon, sent from Boston care of his mama and sister. The colour was pure Liberty Bell with a hint of Minuteman, all those flavours and hues that the manufacturers claimed to have been mixed into their alcoholic creation. It was all rather rebellious, and decidedly anti-British, so he hadn't offered one to Batchelor.

The ex-Fleet Street man was perfectly happy sipping his Scotch, redolent of the mists of the Highlands and glowing with haggis and sheep-shit. All of it was a part of the advertisement-writers' art and it put hair on your chest.

'The Cremorne or the Grosvenor?' Batchelor asked.

'Let's start with the Cremorne,' Grand said. 'I need to clear my head.'

'Right,' Batchelor cleared his throat. 'Two prostitutes, both working for the same madam, found murdered in close proximity eighteen months apart.'

'Method of dispatch?' Grand asked.

'Cyanide poisoning,' Batchelor answered.

'Administered how?'

Batchelor shook his head. 'Absolutely no idea.'

'But it must go something like this,' Grand reasoned. 'Mabel and Clara, like so many before and since, go into the Gardens looking to relieve a guy of part of his wallet.'

'They give him the eye – "Are you good-natured, dearie?"'

Grand frowned. 'Do they always say that?'

'Oh, yes,' Batchelor assured him. 'Vital part of the training.'

'Right,' Grand nodded. 'So our friend is feeling good-natured, or so he claims.'

'So, he flashes coin of the realm . . .'

'Or does he? We don't know that.'

'He'd have to,' Batchelor observed. 'All right, we don't know either of the deceased, but working girls don't work for nothing. No cash, no how's-your-father.'

'And we don't know how much cash, if any, the women had on them.'

'Thanks to Scotland Yard, no.'

'What next?' Grand asked.

'How's your father,' Batchelor reasoned. 'Or not, as the case may be. The accounts, of course, don't make that clear. This is 1878; there are certain newspaper reports for which the world is not yet ready.'

'And we can't get our hands on any police reports. What about that number two of Metcalfe's?' Grand asked. 'The guy in the Clarence. Seemed kinda wet behind the ears. Could he be prevailed upon, do you think?'

'Worth trying,' Batchelor nodded.

'Okay, so how's your father or not, our friend gets the girls to eat something . . . er . . . currant bun, roast beef sandwich, cyanide salad . . .'

'. . . to which she says "Ta" and wallop.'

Grand frowned. 'Are we being a little trivial here, James?' he asked. 'The women are, after all, dead. Are we being flippant?'

'Flip away, old-timer,' Batchelor said. If his American accent was supposed to be Midwest, it lost Grand completely. Batchelor was serious again. 'We've got a job to do, Matthew,' he said. 'If we can't use gallows humour between the two of us, what's the point?'

'What indeed?' Grand swirled the bourbon around his tonsils. 'What then?'

'Well, this is where it gets interesting. There is no suggestion in the papers of mutilation or anything like that.'

'Not even, as far as we know, disarrangement of the clothes . . .'

'. . . implying that sex is not the motive.'

'So, what is?' Grand had to ask.

'Somebody doesn't approve of prostitution,' Batchelor proffered. 'Takes it out on two unfortunates.'

'Well, that only leaves us with the Church of England and every other denomination, the entire upper and middle class and the vast majority of the workers. Any hope of cutting that down at all?'

Batchelor sighed. 'If only,' he said.

'What about cyanide?' Grand was thinking aloud. 'Who has access to that?'

'Doctors,' Batchelor was making a mental list, 'chemists. The problem is the stuff's cheaper than starch. Anybody can go to a pharmacy and pick up a little without having to say what it's for.'

'Not that they'd admit to intending to poison somebody anyway.'

'Exactly. No.' Batchelor was topping up his Scotch. 'It would take too much shoe-leather to do the rounds of cyanide purveyors, even using the wonder-boy with the Oxford degree. It wouldn't achieve anything.'

'All right,' Grand was topping up too. 'Let's get to the big one. Anstruther Peebles.'

'Anstruther Peebles,' Batchelor passed Grand a cigar. 'You met him. Could he pass for a woman, do you think?'

Grand screwed up his face, trying to remember the billiard room and the gymnasium at the Rag. 'Clean-shaven,' he said.

'That helps,' Batchelor nodded.

'Difficult to picture it. Feller's wearing his regimentals, you naturally assume . . . I mean, it's difficult to picture him in a dress.'

'The issue is,' Batchelor said, 'why did he wear one?'

'Not to lure the ladies,' Grand said. 'We established that with your friend Lawson. If a lady of the night meets another lady of the night, they don't sit down and swap john stories. They both assume the other is trying to steal her patch.'

'And the Cremorne's not that big,' Batchelor nodded. 'So,

what is this with Peebles? Another peccadillo to go with his other peculiarities?'

'Seems like,' Grand said. 'I don't suppose Mrs Arbuthnot shed any light.'

'As far as I know,' Batchelor said, 'she only had the name – and the peculiarities we already know about.'

'Of course,' Grand took another sip. 'Peebles could be one almighty red herring. We're forgetting the Queen's Counsel in all this.'

'Keen? Yes,' Batchelor agreed, 'yes, we are. Or . . .'

'Or?'

'Person or persons unknown. Just because Mrs Arbuthnot had a shortlist of Mabel Glossop's regulars doesn't mean that either of them killed her. And we don't even have a list, short or otherwise, for Clara Jenkins.'

'No,' Grand sighed. 'No, we don't. Let's face it, James, we're getting nowhere fast on this one. What about the Grosvenor? A case, may I remind you, for which we are actually getting paid.'

'Whistler,' Batchelor grunted. 'What do you make of him, man-to-man, I mean?'

'I'm biased,' Grand said. 'He flunked West Point – and not even George Custer did that.'

'What happened?' Batchelor asked.

'They took him in because his daddy taught drawing there. They called him Curly, 'cos of his silly hair – the son, that is, not the father.'

'Still got it,' Batchelor remembered.

'Indeed. Didn't know one end of a rifle from another, but bucked authority every chance he got. Got more demerits than Ulysses S. Grant. In the end, Robert E. Lee kicked him out.'

'Because he was a pain in the arse?'

'Specifically because he wrote that silicon was a gas in a Chemistry exam. Actually, it *was* because he was a pain in the ass, but Lee was too much of a gentleman to say so.'

'What then?'

'Went to Paris, like they all do. Joined the Bohemian set and discovered women and booze. He'd already discovered the noxious weed. Artistically – and I'd be the first to admit,

James, that I'm out of my depth here – the guy goes for what he calls tonal harmony. Hence, the *Nocturnes*; his night paint-ings are like concertos. Black, apparently, is the new black. And it's not only Ruskin who can't stand him. Ask any of his models. He makes them sit – or rather, stand – for hours. His little white girl passed out with exhaustion. He only let his study in grey sit down with her feet up because she was his mother.'

'Why have we taken him on, again?' Batchelor asked.

Grand rubbed his fingers together.

'Oh, yes, I forgot.'

'Your turn,' Grand said. 'Tell me about Ruskin. Apart from the pubic hair bit – I haven't quite got over that yet.'

'He's pushing sixty now,' Batchelor said. 'His father was a failed businessman, his mother an Evangelical Christian.'

'Fatal combination, I should think,' Grand said.

'I'm trying to see him through Whistler's eyes,' Batchelor said. 'A lot of people see him as an Old Testament prophet . . .'

'. . . hmm, the hair and the beard.'

'And, of course, the blue eyes,' Batchelor threw in. 'When did you last see an English painting that *didn't* have a biblical figure with blue eyes?'

'Point taken.'

'When he went up to Oxford, his mama and papa went with him.'

'Of course they did,' Grand nodded.

'As a very young man, bearing in mind his insult to Whistler, he spent time and money defending J.M.W. Turner. From what I know of that bloke, he was worse than Whistler, painting-wise.'

'It's in the eye of the beholder, I guess,' Grand shrugged.

'Ruskin lost God, then found him again. He moves in pretty well-known circles – artists and academics all love him, but I'm not quite sure why. I think where Whistler has the edge is that his nemesis is just a threat deranged. First went mad in Matlock . . . er . . . seven years ago.'

Grand had been there once. 'Not much else to do in Matlock, is there?' he asked.

'I don't really like either of these two, Matthew, if I'm

honest. Best they stand in a field somewhere and take pot shots, as opposed to paint pots, at each other.'

'Ruskin would win,' Grand said, downing his drink. 'Whistler's eyes are awful – hence the *Nocturne* – and he'd probably be holding the pistol the wrong way round anyway, if his West Point record is anything to go by!'

SIX

After the debacle with the unread papers of the previous morning, Grand and Batchelor spent longer even than usual poring over every inch of newsprint that London could produce over breakfast. Maisie was kept especially busy with filling up the coffee pot, often with tea, but, search and scour as they might, there was nothing of even tangential interest to be found. London University was threatening to offer degrees to women and there were all sorts of objections to putting up the Cleopatra obelisk on the Embankment. But that was all rather by the by. Finally, they came up for air and Grand stood up and stretched, going over to the window and looking out on a perfect spring morning. He peered this way and that up their quiet road and tutted.

Batchelor had just had a good idea for the Great British Novel and was jotting it down, so didn't respond.

Grand tutted again, but louder.

Batchelor concluded his train of thought and looked up. 'What is it, Matthew?' he asked, patiently. He didn't know if he would ever have children, but if he did, then he would have had plenty of practice.

'This street. It used to be really quiet. But now, some mornings, it's like Piccadilly Circus out there.'

'Really?' Batchelor went to the other window and looked out. He turned back into the room. 'Unless my counting skills are considerably worse than I thought, there's only one person out there,' he said.

'Exactly,' Grand whined. 'At one time, the only people you ever saw were people coming here, but now, there's all kinds of traffic.'

'One man.'

'Yes, for now, I grant you. One man today, hordes tomorrow. And,' Grand peered round the curtains again, 'he is very big.'

Batchelor took another look. 'He's tallish, yes. But he has

every right to be out there, surely? You seem a little grumpy today, Matthew – is it anything I can help with?'

'No. Yes. No. Oh, I don't know. We need to get back to the Grosvenor gallery, don't we, get a second opinion on that painting of Whistler's. I also need to take Lady Caroline out for lunch. It's been days since I wined or dined her, or anything else come to that, and Lady Caroline needs a lot of . . .' Grand left a gap but Batchelor wasn't playing that game. 'Anyhow, it's going to be a difficult day to manage.'

'It's easy,' Batchelor said, scooping up some marmalade on the last piece of toast and sitting back down. 'You don't even need Martin to work this one out. We go to the office, get Martin to come with us to the gallery. You can take Caroline to lunch, we'll meet you there afterwards. How's that?'

'Sounds simple.' Grand sat down as well. 'But isn't Martin off with his friend for lunch?'

'Still no problem. We give Martin a time to finish lunch, and then we still all meet.'

'Is that done?' Grand might be a colonial, but he wasn't an animal. 'Giving a man a specific time to have had his lunch by?'

'He does work for us, Matthew,' Batchelor pointed out. 'We can tell him to do whatever we like.'

'I suppose so . . . we don't tell Miss Wolstenholme, though.'

'That's because she brings an apple, a ham sandwich and a flask of cold tea every mortal day. It's hardly Simpson's, is it?'

'I suppose so . . . well, let's leave it at that, then. We'll have lunch in our various places – actually, we *are* lunching at Simpson's, apparently; Lady Caroline wants to discuss brides-maid numbers for some reason – and then meet at the Grosvenor.' Nodding to himself, Grand went up to dress for the day. Batchelor was left feeling a little confused. He had no idea men had bridesmaids, not even at society weddings.

If anything, the brass plate outside the offices of Grand and Batchelor, enquiry agents, was even more shiny and sparkling than it had been the day before. The two men walked into the office with trepidation; neither was quite sure that Martin knew when to call it a day. But everything was as before, with the addition of Miss Wolstenholme, sitting at her pristine desk, typing a letter, under Martin's instruction.

'No, no, *no*, Miss Wolstenholme,' Martin was saying in the tones of one at the end of his tether. 'You *never* cross your hands when typing. That's why the keys keep locking together. Look, watch me.' He leaned over her from behind, hitching his cuffs back and making her almost pass out with unknown bliss. 'You go like *this* and like *this*. See? See how much better that feels. Try it.' He stepped back and saw Grand and Batchelor for the first time. 'I'm sorry, sirs,' he said. 'I didn't hear you come in.'

Miss Wolstenholme turned in her chair but seemed to have temporarily lost the power of speech.

'Don't let us interrupt,' Batchelor said. 'We're just popping in to plan the rest of the day, if that's convenient.' If there was any irony intended, no one spotted it. 'Essentially and long story short, we need to revisit the Grosvenor gallery this afternoon and we thought that it would be helpful if you could meet us there after your lunch, Alexander.'

Miss Wolstenholme turned back to her typing. This was clearly not a conversation in which she needed to join.

'Do you know the Grosvenor at all?' Grand asked their assistant.

'*Know* it?' a voice came from the doorway, 'we *adore* it, don't we, Gan? Especially that simply *wonderful* Whistler in the second gallery!'

Everyone turned. Martin sprang forward and towed his friend into the room. The man was much taller than he was and, if anything, he made Martin look even more handsome than usual. He was at least six two, having to duck his head to be sure not to hit it on the doorframe. His shoulders, though tending to slope, were wide, and his flowing coat only increased the impression of bulk. His curly hair was giving his bowler hat a challenge as to how it was to stay on his head. His sleepy eyes ranged over the people in the room and Grand was reminded of nothing so much as a James Whistler, grown large by some mad alchemy. Martin shook his arm as if to bring him to everyone's attention.

'Mr Grand, Mr Batchelor, Miss Wolstenholme, allow me to introduce my friend from university, soon to be down from Oxford and hoping to make his home in London, Mr Oscar Wilde.'

Wilde stood there, looking at his feet. He shrugged a shoulder. It seemed his outburst about the Grosvenor gallery was caused by natural excitement – in fact, he appeared to be quite shy and retiring, difficult for one of his build as he would never be able to hide in a crowd.

Grand, Batchelor and Miss Wolstenholme all nodded and muttered their hellos and then everything went silent.

'Well,' cried Martin, into the void. 'Time for lunch, I think. Where do you have in mind, Oscar?'

'I thought . . . well, I thought Simpson's, Gan, if that suits you?'

'Simpson's sounds splendid,' Martin agreed. 'Would you care to join us, Mr Grand, Mr Batchelor?' Polite to the last, he invited Miss Wolstenholme with a glance and a raised eyebrow, but she gestured to her ham sandwich and her apple and no one was embarrassed.

Batchelor looked at Grand, who nodded. Why not all eat at Simpson's? Grand had a private room booked anyway, far too small for five. It would be more convenient than anything, in fact, if only they could ditch Wilde somewhere along the way, always assuming he was let in in the first place; surely, Simpson's wasn't ready for anyone in a check suit *that* loud.

The Grosvenor gallery, except on exhibition days, rarely had five people through the doors at once. Lady Caroline Wentworth of course was a regular, as was her gentleman friend – disappointingly close-fisted for an American. Two of the others Saunders had seen before, usually talking in loud and pretentious voices to each other in front of some of the more impenetrable canvases. The other one, he hadn't seen before. He looked worryingly like a newspaperman and the gallery preferred to know when anyone from Fleet Street was within its walls. However, Lady Caroline Wentworth was a hard card to trump, so Saunders wandered back to the front desk to stack brochures and straighten piles of price labels, against the day. He kept

an ear cocked for any shouting though – last time, Lady
Caroline had had some kind of turn and had to be helped to
a cab. Perhaps that enormous geezer . . . Saunders corrected
himself, it had been ages since he made a slip like that, even
in the privacy of his own head . . . gentleman, was her minder.

Caroline clung to Grand's arm for several reasons. One was
that she was already finding Oscar Wilde rather trying company.
His strange mixture of intense shyness and wild enthusiasms
were hard to keep up with and his views on art bordered on
the bizarre. He ought to choose uglier friends, was another
thought that she couldn't dismiss. Alexander Martin was
stupidly good-looking, more so than any of the supposedly
beautiful boys in any of the more esoteric paintings in the
gallery. Next to him, Wilde looked like something which
belonged in a zoo. At least, Lady Caroline thought she had
heard him introduced as Alexander. But Wilde kept calling
him Gan. This was one thing she could check and make it
sound as if she was making light conversation, which was
something very lacking in their little group.

'Mr Wilde,' she trilled, looking round at him past Grand's
protecting chest. 'I can't help noticing that you call Mr Martin
"Gan" and I wonder what it is short for. The only name I can
think of is Ganymede, but that can't be right, surely?' She
gave one of her best cascading laughs, copied from the Jersey
Lily herself.

Wilde shuffled his feet and mumbled, but Martin took up
the tale. 'It is *indeed* short for Ganymede, Lady Caroline, and
you may be the only person to have ever guessed it. It was
my nickname at Oxford.'

'Why?' Grand asked, bluntly. Classical mythology was never
given much time in the Grand household when he was a child,
and he had had no real need for it since.

Caroline laid a gentle hand on his arm. 'Why, Matthew,'
she said, in the voice that promised there would be trouble
when she got him home, 'I would imagine it is because
Ganymede is so beautiful.'

Grand and Batchelor looked at her blankly, and Batchelor
even went so far as to raise a shoulder and grunt.

'He was cup-bearer to the gods?' she said, a query creeping

into her voice. 'Mount Olympus. Zeus. Aphrodite.' They remained blank. She sighed. 'Well, I imagine it is because Mr Martin is unusually good-looking, and if you say you hadn't noticed, I really will fell you with my parasol, Matthew Grand.' Without turning her head, she added, 'And you too, James, so there's no need to look so smug.'

Alexander Martin laughed and gave her a bow. 'Thank you, Lady Caroline,' he said. 'It certainly is refreshing to have someone guess the origin. And to precis the story so well.'

'There's far more, of course,' Wilde began, with a strange look at Martin. Batchelor, ever the watcher of men and picker-up of unconsidered expressions, noted it with interest but let the subject change by itself. It was quite a sudden change of subject, as these things go, because the air was suddenly rent by a scream from Lady Caroline which would strip paint.

All eyes turned to her and Saunders came dashing in at the gallop, followed by the doorman. He had known that first time that the woman was as drunk as a lord and was pleased to be proved right. He had smelled the liquor as he had opened the door.

She was standing at bay, holding onto Grand's arm still and bracing her back against the wall, making a picture of a rather gloomy dead-looking animal by Landseer go all wonky and threaten to fall off its hook. Saunders didn't know whether to save it or her, because he could tell one of them was going to hit the deck, any minute now.

Grand's eyes were wide, as would be any man's who had had one of Lady Caroline's best screams an inch from his ear. 'Whatever is it?' he asked, rather loudly as he was temporarily deaf and a little disoriented.

His answer was another scream, but more muted. She let go of his arm and pointed to the door at the end of the gallery, which framed a man in a brown coat made of light material and obviously made for a much larger person. He was holding a broom and was caught like a badger at bay, head down and eyes wide.

'It's him!' she squealed. 'It's the artist from the other time. The one with the paints. And the dead woman. It's him.' She looked round wildly. 'Don't you see, you idiots? It's him.

Look!' Her finger was trembling and her parasol, clenched under her other arm, was poking holes into Landseer's best heather-clad hillside. Saunders was of two minds. He was pleased that Landseer was far too dead to mind. But also concerned that he would have to have it mended by someone without his skills with mist-wreathed ling. But for now, he just needed to move that idiot caretaker. If he had told him once, he had told him twenty times, not to enter the gallery in opening hours. The man really would have to go. And of course, Sir Coutts Lindsay would have to be informed.

By now, Lady Caroline was sliding down the wall to land in a muddle of silk and lace on the floor. Grand and Batchelor hauled her up into a sitting position and Grand put her head between her knees; as a fiancé, it was just barely allowable. Wilde looked towards the caretaker being ushered out of the room.

'Shame it wasn't the ghost,' he remarked, suddenly. 'That *would* have been something.'

Caroline, coming to, heard the word and fainted once again.

In a flurry of running, shouting, cold compresses and hansom cabs, the gallery was finally at peace again.

Saunders turned to the doorman. 'If any of that lot – and I mean *any* – try to come in here again, call the police.'

'But, Mr Saunders, sir . . . Lady Caroline . . .'

'Especially Lady Caroline. Overwrought once is one thing. Twice is just being a gin-soaked trollop and I won't put up with it. I shudder to think what Mr Lindsay will make of it all.'

The doorman was a little more worried about Mrs Lindsay, the definite power behind the throne. She had once caught him a nasty one upside the head because he didn't bow quite low enough to a visiting minor royal, so having one of the aristocracy carried out raving not once but twice was not going to be music to her ears. 'And what about old Joe, sir? He caused it, after all.'

Saunders thought for a moment. 'No, let's leave Joe out of it. He's cheap and generally all right at keeping the place clean. Who else would you get to look after a building like he does for breakfast and dinner and ten pounds paid on New

Year's Day? Let's leave it. I'm sure he won't do that again. Did you see his face? He was as scared as she was. Ghost, indeed? Bloody students. Need horsewhipping.' He remembered the damage to the painting in the gallery. 'Shoot the bolt a minute and help me move this Landseer. Bloody thing weighs a ton.' They strolled through into the gallery and he looked again at the damage.

'Do you know,' he said, 'I'm not sure if it doesn't look better with these holes.'

Matthew Grand had difficulty fending off the female contingent among the servants at the Wentworths' London residence. Yes, Lady Caroline was in a fainting condition, but she was much better now and the less fuss the better. Yes, her stays had been loosened and no, not by him, by the lady herself, in the back of a cab. When the housekeeper had been restored with some sal volatile on hearing that news, Grand managed to shoo the other, lesser, females away, and finally, the affianced two were alone.

For a while, she lay prostrate, but very picturesque, on the chaise longue in the big bow window facing out into the street. Swagged nets preserved her modesty from the people parading up and down, for this was Cheyne Walk, and people who wanted to be seen by the right people, loved to walk between Cremorne Gardens at its end and the Physic Garden up the road, wearing *just* the right hats at *just* the right angle. On other days, Grand and Caroline had sat on this very chaise and laughed at their pretentions, but for now, she just wanted to lie down.

Grand pulled up a small stool and sat beside her, patting her hand and replacing handkerchiefs as hers became too sodden. He found it rather soporific and was in danger of dropping off as his own quiet murmurs became too much to withstand. Then, as he had hoped she would, Lady Caroline Wentworth rediscovered her backbone of old, Norman stock which had come over with the Conqueror and sat up. She gave a final sniff and a wipe of the eye and smiled at Grand, sitting there like a gnome on a toadstool.

'Matthew,' she said, 'do let's sit somewhere else. You look most uncomfortable.'

'No, no,' he said. 'Once my left leg joined my right in sleep, I was fine. It was a bit uncomfy before that, I'll agree.' He struggled to his feet and was immediately assailed by pins and needles and leaped around the room like something being electrocuted. Finally, they subsided enough to allow him to sit down, opposite his light o' love, opposite a small fire which, this still being May, the housekeeper refused to do without.

For a while, they sat in silence, broken finally by Grand.

'Are you sure you recognized that man, Caro?' he asked, gently.

'Of course I am,' she retorted. 'I'm sorry I reacted like a fool, but it gave me a shock. There was something in the light behind him, it looked . . . well, it was a little sinister.'

'He seemed to be the janitor,' Grand pointed out.

'Speak English, Matthew, do.'

'The caretaker, then. Saunders knew who he was instantly.'

'That makes no difference. It was clearly the same man. Without the beard. And the long hair.' She looked at him, certainty becoming less certain. 'And the hat. But *apart* from that, he was the living image.'

'By that, you mean he was a man of indeterminate age and average build. That could be a hundred people. Look,' he strode to the window and pulled back the curtain. 'Look, there's one. And there. And there. There's even one out here who looks like that imbecile Wilde, and I would never have said that was possible, would you? And there's one . . . and . . .'

'Yes, Matthew,' she said, coldly. 'While you're on your feet, ring for some tea, will you? Then sit down. Pulling at the curtains is so common.'

'Yes, ma'am.' He sat down and tried to look serious.

'I will continue to say that the man was the same one. I don't care how much you try to make me change my mind. But also, I heard that dreadful Wilde creature say something about a ghost. That's probably why I got so faint. I am, as you know, of an extremely sensitive disposition.' She looked at him with basilisk eyes, daring him to contradict her, but Matthew Grand was an officer of the Third Cavalry of the Potomac and, more than that, the son of a mother who brooked no argument, so he knew when to keep quiet.

'Yes, ma'am.' He shut his lips tight in a smile of sorts and she would get no more out of him until the tea arrived.

Under the influence of Darjeeling and crumpets, she began to thaw a little and allowed him to sit on the rug with his head in her lap. Smoothing his hair, she murmured, 'Are there such things as ghosts, Matthew, do you think?'

Matthew Grand had fought at Shiloh and had waded in mud and blood up to the knees. Part of him wanted to believe that those men so cruelly cut down had gone straight to a better place. But another wanted them to still be tied to earth, to be checking on their loved ones from whom they had been severed before their time. So, his answer in other company would have been equivocal. But here, there was only one answer.

'No, of course not, darling.'

This turned out to be not the right choice.

'I don't think you're right, Matthew. Mr Dunglas Home is very persuasive on the subject. Did you know, he can actually levitate out of one window and right back in in the room next door, having left his handkerchief on the roof as proof?'

Grand knew that name. 'Is that *Dan* Home?' he asked.

'His name is Daniel, yes.'

Grand's head was no longer in her lap and she brushed her skirts as if he was a shedding Pekingese.

'Do you know him?' she asked after a pause. 'For a big country, Americans seem to huddle together in just the one state, as far as I can tell. You all seem to know one another.'

'I can't say as I *know* him so much as know *of* him. He tried the levitation lay at one of the house parties my sister was at.'

She gave a little moue of distaste. 'I wish you wouldn't use low language, Matthew,' she murmured. 'What happened?'

'Well, he left the one room all right, then my brother-in-law took a pot-shot at him when he saw him hanging from the guttering. Thought he was a cat burglar. They get a lot of that in DC.'

'That's disgraceful! Shooting people!'

'Well, that's no worse than fleecing people, I suppose. Anyway, poor old Hamilton, he was in disgrace. Ruined the house party and they won't get invited back again in a hurry.'

Caroline sat back and thought. She was a sensible woman beneath the fashionable veneer and could see that Grand was probably right. Even so, she was not ready to give up ghosts just yet.

'Home notwithstanding, though,' she said after a pause, 'I think there must be something, mustn't there? We don't just' – she threw her arms wide – 'go?'

Something told him his head was welcome back in her lap and he snuggled up. 'No, Caro,' he said, reaching for her hand with his. 'No. We don't just go. But we don't wander round art galleries scaring beautiful women with paintings of dead women either. Let's not argue. Let's let this one be a draw, shall we?'

After a minute, she started to stroke his hair and, after two minutes, he knew he was forgiven.

The supper room over the Adelphi was not far from the premises of Messrs Grand and Batchelor, in the shadow of Nelson's Column and within a whistling piston's distance of Charing Cross Station. It was late into the night by the time the other customers had left, and Gan Martin and Oscar Wilde sat each side of the forlorn-looking fireplace, each with a very large brandy and each with a small cigar.

'I find your employers quite fascinating, Gan,' Wilde said, his eyes momentarily bothered by the smoke. 'Batchelor all Fleet Street and observation; Grand, a man of action trying to get out. You know he carries a gun, don't you?'

'Does he?' Martin was horrified. 'How do you know?'

'The bulge in his waistcoat,' Wilde said, 'under his left armpit.'

'How bizarre,' Martin said. 'Isn't that against the law?'

'No idea,' Wilde said, stretching and yawning. 'It's all to do with his past, of course.'

'His past?'

'Didn't you tell me he served in the American Civil War – Union army, and so on? I've never been to America, of course, and probably never will, but they are a different breed. Do you think you'll stay with them, in the private enquiry business, I mean?'

'Well, I've only just started,' Martin pointed out, 'so it's rather too early to tell. Some of their work can be quite humdrum if the files are anything to go by.'

'You've read their files?'

'My dear boy,' Martin beamed, 'I *am* their files. Remember old Bunbury at Magdalen? He'd have left soon after your first Tripos. Mind like a razor.'

'Hmm,' Wilde nodded, blowing smoke out of the corner of his mouth as he had seen post office boys do. 'Had a thing for choirboys.'

'Yes, yes, that; but *apart* from that. What the professor didn't know about Euclid, you could engrave on a pinhead. I learned my categorization skills from him.'

'Hanged himself, didn't he?' Wilde asked. 'When it all came out?'

'He did,' Martin said. 'Damned shame, really.'

'Damned,' agreed Wilde. 'Tell me about Lady Caroline.'

'Don't know much about her, really. I believe her people know my people, but I'm keeping the details under wraps. People get a bit funny when they know one's old man is a duke. And anyway, surely it isn't quite done for someone in line for a title to be a sleuth.' Martin blew smoke rings to the ceiling. 'She's definitely out of the top drawer, but damned odd behaviour at the Grosvenor, though. Seeing ghosts and all.'

'What's odd about that?' Wilde asked.

Martin looked at him. 'Er . . . I'm not sure I follow, Oscar.'

Wilde laughed. 'Everyone follows Oscar – or they will, one day. Are you telling me you don't believe?'

'In what?'

Wilde whipped a box of lucifers from his pocket, struck one and held it under his chin, the shadow of his lips and nose thrown up onto his forehead. 'In things that go bump in the night,' he whispered.

'Don't be ridiculous. This is the age of reason. Look at that Alexander Bell chappie – a telephonic machine that links room to room, even house to house. That's not the supernatural, Oscar, that's science. And do put that match out, dear boy, you're beginning to scorch.'

Wilde shook the flame out and threw the stub into the fire, which flamed once and returned to its sulk. 'Tut, tut,' he said. 'And you a Greats man.'

'I think we have to accept,' Martin said, 'that either Lady Caroline is as drunk as a skunk from time to time, as I am sure Mr Grand would say if he wasn't engaged to the woman, or she is of a particularly nervous disposition.'

'Or,' Wilde's cigar had gone out and he relit it with a fresh match, 'she saw a ghost.'

'Oscar,' Martin threw his arms wide in exasperation, 'there is no such thing.'

Wilde looked at him, a strange, almost sad look on his face. 'You don't know the story, then?'

'What story?'

'Do you believe in coincidences, Gan?' Wilde asked.

'That depends,' Martin came back.

'Spoken like a true Oxford graduate,' Wilde smiled. 'The Grosvenor gallery – a new venue, yes?'

'Yes. I believe it was opened last year.'

'On the site of . . .?'

'Er . . .'

'A plague burial ground. Hundreds of poor, demented souls driven half mad by an incurable disease, wandering in limbo to the solemn tolling of a bell; thrown in miserable heaps to rot in the stench of death.'

'Dreadful,' was the best Martin could manage.

'It was, but what was more dreadful was what survived.'

'How do you mean?'

'No one is sure of his name,' Wilde said, dropping his voice and leaning forward, his forearms on his thighs, 'but he was an artist. Painted Cromwell before Lely got to him. He was buried there . . . or was he?'

'What?'

'He may have been taken on the dead cart. He may even have been dumped in the pit. But he wasn't dead. Not when they shovelled the earth over him. They built over the burial ground, of course,' Wilde went on, 'a rather handsome, late Carolingian house, much smaller than the Grosvenor of today. One man working on it went mad. He was there late one night, finishing a doorway, when he saw . . . well, who knows what he saw? He never spoke a word of sense thereafter.'

'So . . .?'

'But it didn't end there.' Wilde was now in full flow and the fire chose the moment to flare up, making mad shapes of his springing hair, thrown in dancing shadows on the wall. 'First, an architect fell ill with a mysterious disease that no one could identify. His flesh, they say, hung off him like cobwebs. A vicar staying on the premises went to bed one night – in a room in the west wing. When they found him in the morning, he was dead, his hair snowy white. He was thirty-three. And the look on his face . . .'

Wilde let the silence speak volumes.

'The present owner . . .'

'Sir Coutts Lindsay.' Martin, of course, filled in the missing detail. Wilde went on hurriedly before he could furnish date of birth and all living relations.

'He wasn't sure he should open the gallery because of what he himself had witnessed. He lost no less than seventeen servants in his first year of occupancy. They all refused to stay. Whatever lingers in that house is there still. Was that what Lady Caroline saw?' he asked Martin. 'Something that you and I did not see? The ghost of an artist, long dead, a soul lost in purgatory, buried before his time?'

The clock struck eleven and Gan Martin jumped out of his skin, gripping his glass and dropping his cigar. When he could compose himself, he said, 'Is that true, what you just told me?'

Wilde smiled. 'Of course not,' he said. 'Good heavens, Gan, what are you? Twelve? I just made it up.'

Martin shuddered and got up to leave, to the relief of the staff who were waiting to close up and go home.

Wilde got up too, brushing cigar ash from his waistcoat. 'Or at least,' he murmured to himself, 'most of it.'

Eventually, every building falls silent. The people leave. The traffic outside slows to a trickle and then stops altogether. The wood expands, contracts with a crack and then sleeps. The mice in the wainscoting, home from foraging for crumbs, settle down with their latest brood and mumble their way into sleep.

Midnight strikes.

Then one.

This is the time when everything is at its quietest, approaching that time of night when sick men die and babies turn and grizzle in their sleep. The Grosvenor gallery was different, though. After an hour of silence, after the bobby in the street outside had tried the door handle for the last time on his rounds, a door creaked open. It was a door few knew about, high up in the rafters, in the hidden space above the lofty rooms. The room it hid had no light of its own. In the day, should that door ever open, it would share the beams of the sun that came through the adjustable skylights high above the art that hung on the walls far below, the art that could – and often did – divide the chattering classes. At night, on such a night as this, faint moonbeams penetrated only a few feet into the room, showing stacked canvases, leaning on each other like dominoes arrested in flight. In the shadows, a faint flickering movement caught the moonbeams but, had there been an observer, there would have been no way to tell quite what it was.

The Grosvenor gallery didn't mind this movement in its terra incognita. If buildings can feel such things, it would have been disappointed if it didn't have a ghost. This was the Grosvenor gallery, where art was hung for art's sake alone, and anything that could happen, would happen.

A door below whispered shut. The soft slur of badger on canvas was audible to the keenest ear only. Then, a susurration of clothing, a hiss of breath, the sound of air compressing at the passage of a body; followed by silence.

Even the Grosvenor gallery must sleep a little. And it slept now, until the dawn.

SEVEN

'I am appalled.' James Whistler's hair was wilder than ever that morning. 'Absolutely appalled.'

Batchelor was alone in the office, wandering down the Memory Lane of cases past, now that he could, thanks to Alexander Martin's indefatigable filing system. He was still chuckling to himself over the malfeasance of the late Bishop of Bath and Wells when the whirlwind crashed through the door.

'A problem, Mr Whistler?' he asked.

The artist looked at the enquiry agent. 'More than you can ever imagine,' he smouldered.

Batchelor looked blank.

'What, Mr Batchelor, I ask you, is the worst thing that can happen to an artist?'

'Um . . .' Not being of that persuasion, Batchelor was stuck for an answer.

'To have his work vandalized!' Whistler answered his own question just as Matthew Grand arrived, slipping off his top coat and hanging it on a hook, freshly installed at an ergonomically designated height from the floor.

'Mr Whistler is appalled, Matthew,' Batchelor said.

'I can see that,' Grand said. He adopted his best family physician persona. 'What seems to be the trouble, Mr Whistler?'

'My *Nocturne*,' Whistler bellowed. 'The one in blue and gold. It's been ruined.'

'Slashed?' Grand asked.

'Added to, taken away, what you will.'

Grand and Batchelor looked at each other. 'I don't think I understand,' Batchelor said.

'Of course you don't!' Whistler snapped. 'Only true genius can see it. I *am* that painting. I spent hours, no, days – nights, that is – in the Cremorne. That canvas is part of my soul, the stars, the rushing noise when your breath ascends with the rockets, the gasp and release as it cascades and falls. The watchers, shadows on shadows, ghosts on ghosts, looking up at the sky . . .' He came out of his reverie. 'I didn't paint any of that by accident. Every brushstroke, every angle, every line and dab of colour – I did not create a vision of brilliance to have it trashed by Ruskin.'

'You think Ruskin's behind this vandalism?'

'Of course he is.' Whistler stared around the room, glaring at Grand, at Batchelor, at the kettle in the corner on its spirit burner. 'Who else could it be?'

The door opened and Gan Martin walked in. 'Sorry I'm late, dears,' he said, quickly swallowing his words when he saw they had clients in the room. He caught the fury on Whistler's face and regretted his breezy entry. 'Is something amiss?'

'Mr Whistler is appalled,' Grand told him.

'Somebody's been mucking about with one of his paintings,' Batchelor explained.

'No!' Martin looked horrified. 'At the Grosvenor? Unthinkable!'

Whistler looked around the room and back at Martin. 'Who *are* you?' he asked.

'This is Alexander Martin, our assistant,' Batchelor introduced them.

'Charmed,' Whistler growled, as if he'd just kicked the cat. 'Who's coming with me?' He turned to Grand and Batchelor. 'I've just come from the Grosvenor and now I'm going back with witnesses. Then we'll pay a visit to that asshole Ruskin. It's not a paint-pot I'll be throwing in his face, believe me.'

'Ah, I'm afraid there's a problem there,' Batchelor said. He looked at Grand. 'In the first post this morning, Matthew. We've been banned from the Grosvenor.' He held out the letter. 'It's from Saunders, written last night. You remember, he's the flunky at the gallery but it's counter-signed by the Lindsays, both of them.'

Grand looked at it. 'Sorry, Mr Whistler,' he shrugged. 'It looks like we're persona non grata at the moment.'

'What about you?' Whistler rounded on Martin. 'Can't you come with me?'

'What exactly has happened, Mr Whistler?' the lad asked.

Rather than have the artist fly into the realms of self-adulation again, Batchelor cut to the chase. 'Someone's altered Mr Whistler's *Nocturne in Blue and Gold*.'

'Altered?' Martin frowned. 'In what way?'

'Changed, destroyed, ruined, despoiled. One flick of a brush would do irreparable damage,' Whistler assured everybody.

'I should like to see that,' Martin said.

'Would you, sir?' Whistler stormed. 'Why? To gloat?'

'No. To see why someone would go to those lengths. I am intrigued, Mr Whistler.'

'And you are as banned as we are, Gan,' Grand reminded him.

'Not necessarily,' Martin said. He ferreted in the third drawer from the bottom, second from the right, turning his back for a moment on the others. When he turned back, he was wearing a pair of spectacles with bottle-bottom lenses, a false moustache and an enormous pair of front teeth.

'The False Face Case!' Grand and Batchelor chorused.

'Five years ago,' Batchelor went on.

'Six,' Martin corrected him. 'I found these exhibits in my tidying up,' he said, wrestling with the teeth as best he could. 'No doubt they were crucial evidence once, but they could come in handy now. If I just comb my hair so' – he parted it in the middle – 'and borrow a hat' – Batchelor handed him his – 'I don't think my own mother would recognize me.' He gave a twirl. 'What do you think?'

'I'm game,' Whistler said. And just about everybody had to work hard to resist the urge to shoot him.

Lady Caroline Wentworth was dressing to go out. This meant that she kept Eleanor on the run, taking clothes out of the wardrobe, finding something wrong with them, putting them back in. Finally, her ensemble was complete, down to the smart hat and toning boots. It would never do, she told Eleanor, to have boots that *matched*. That would show a frivolous disposition and also a tendency to spend money like water. As an engaged person, she must start to develop a reputation for sober behaviour and also as someone who could manage a house frugally.

Eleanor had known Lady Caroline since she had come to the London house as a tweeny. She was allowed to speak her mind more than some other servants. 'But Mr Grand isn't poor, though, Miss Caroline, surely? He always dresses so well and . . . he's an American. They're all rich, aren't they?'

Lady Caroline gave her Lillie Langtry laugh, down the scale, to avoid sounding shrill and common. 'Of *course* he isn't, Ellie,' she said. 'In fact, he is rather rich. He is one of *the* Grands of Boston, you know.' She smiled at her reflection in the mirror and adjusted her hat a sixteenth of an inch.

'Then why does he work at that detecting?' Eleanor asked. In her world, you worked if you had to, shirked if you didn't.

Lady Caroline sighed. 'Because he likes it, Eleanor,' she said. 'He has promised to do less when we're married and they have at least taken on some help. But I don't know . . .' She turned and grabbed the girl's hand. 'You have a young man, don't you, Ellie?'

Eleanor was in a bit of a cleft stick. Cook was very strict about followers, but Eleanor had red blood in her veins and didn't want to be a maid all her life. She was doing well with the grocer's boy. 'Umm . . .'

Her mistress smiled. 'I know you do, Ellie,' she said. 'I've seen you with that lad who delivers the . . . things, you know, to the kitchen.'

Eleanor smiled. It took more than toning boots to show a wife would be a good manager, but she liked Lady Caroline and she wouldn't dream of saying so. 'Yes, I suppose we have an understanding,' she admitted.

'Well, when you are' – the woman lowered her eyes and blushed becomingly – 'you know, well, you don't want to be disturbed by people knocking on the door, do you?'

Eleanor was shocked. She had no more done any 'you know' than she had flown to the moon. That was something for after marriage, if then. 'I don't know, madam,' she said. 'I think I can hear Cook.' And she fled into the corridor where she could hide her burning cheeks.

'So, Effie,' Lady Caroline said to her hostess as she sipped her tea, 'I'm afraid I quite shocked poor Eleanor.'

'Well, dear,' Effie Millais still retained her artist's model looks and had never quite shaken off the slightly raffish reputation of being twice married, her first husband having been John Ruskin, that well-known pubic-hair-phobe, 'you should know by now that the servant class is *terribly* correct about these things. Otherwise, we would be overrun by the offspring of every kitchen maid in the house. Poor dear John often says he can't keep up with all our children, let alone if the servants started breeding.'

Lady Caroline Wentworth was, of course, adept at gossip, and had gone to Effie Millais's Morning with every intention of probing into her brief and – she had always been led to believe – singularly uneventful life with Ruskin. But now she was here, in the bright and crowded room, she was suddenly a little shy. She had originally hoped that by telling the story of Eleanor's horror and the implication that she and Matthew Grand were at it like weasels whenever opportunity permitted, she would suddenly open the floodgates of Effie's memory and she would Tell All. But it had all been so long ago and far away and Effie liked to live in the present.

'I hadn't thought of that,' Caroline said. 'I do hope she doesn't give notice. She has never seemed to mind when . . .'

'They don't, dear,' Effie said, comfortably. 'It's like thinking of one's parents doing it. It simply isn't done.'

Lady Caroline Wentworth blenched just a little.

'So, how is the lovely Matthew?' the older woman continued. 'Handsome, rich, my dear, you have yourself a catch, there. The American in him doesn't really matter these days, so there's no need to worry. Yorktown, they tell me, was a long time ago.'

Caroline, who hadn't been worrying until that moment, decided to move the conversation along. 'We had a slight altercation last night about ghosts,' she said.

'My dear *girl!*' another woman whom Caroline didn't know had joined their little group, sitting herself cosily on the third low chair before the fire. 'One must believe in ghosts, one really must. John' – she turned to Effie Millais to explain – 'that's *my* John, of course, dear, not your lovely man . . . John, Teddy and Georgie had *such* an interesting conversation at dinner last night, on *exactly* that theme! Of course, after our dear little Mary died in Florence, we were *heart*-broken, but John' – she turned again to Effie, who waved aside the explanation – 'John *knew* she hadn't gone, merely moved to another plane. So we often chat.' All the while she was talking, her eyes were swivelling over her hostess's head, looking for someone more interesting to bore half to death. 'Oh!' she suddenly cried, interrupting herself. 'Is that . . .? Why, yes, I do believe it is . . .' And, to the best of her ability, she jumped up and sped away across the room.

Caroline sat back, feeling as if she had been run over by a fleet of growlers. She looked mutely at Mrs Millais. 'Who was that?' she murmured eventually.

Effie laughed. '*That*, my dear, was Mrs John Roddam Spencer Stanhope, to give her her full title. Elizabeth, to her friends, who are few. She is the worst name-dropper you could wish to meet. "Teddy" is Edward Burne-Jones, a lovely man who is actually friends with her husband. "Georgie", I would imagine, is G.F. Watts to the art-loving public, because as I recall he was once Stanhope's teacher. A funny chap, used to be married to Ellen Terry, you know, when the world was younger and so was she. Only lasted a year, but he painted some lovely things of her.'

Lady Caroline felt she could add something. She hated to be the only one in the room who didn't know what was going on. 'Isn't *Choosing* her?'

Effie smiled as if her pet dog had done a trick. 'That's right, dear. It is rather unfortunate around the chin, don't you think, but that's Ellen for you. We all know each other, as you are aware, but somehow, poor Lizzie likes to think she knows everyone just that touch better. She is very active in the psychic community, though. But it would drive you mad to get into her clique, I think. Who else can I recommend?' She scanned the crowd milling in her drawing room. 'If I had known, I would have invited Fanny Cornforth. She has . . . in deference to your Eleanor, shall we say "kept house" . . . with Rossetti until recently, so of course she had to share her roof with Lizzie Siddal. Do you know that story?'

Caroline shook her head, but said, 'A little.' She had only

been a child, but remembered her mother being upset; women in the far-off sixties couldn't afford to lose one of their number who was making such strides in a man's world.

'Well, she was a model – weren't we all, dear? – but also an artist, poet . . . the usual mixture, dear. Anyway, she married Rossetti – he was a bit obsessed, if you want my opinion, but there, that's just women's gossip – but she died soon after. She was John's *Ophelia*, you know.'

'Ah.' Caroline could now place the face.

'I won't say Rossetti has been a monk since then, hence Fanny, but he has made rather a cult of the perfect Lizzie. There was a rumour that she caught pneumonia when posing for *Ophelia*, but my John – listen to me, I sound like Mrs S! – is a proper painter, not like some I could mention, and he didn't need her to be lying in water to paint her as Ophelia.'

'I did hear that story,' Caroline remembered.

'Well, there you are. People are so silly. John has just painted the princes in the Tower, but he didn't kill the models. Though it was a close thing – children just don't know how to keep still for a minute! And, speaking as we were of Watts and models, there's one of his over there. I can't bring her name to mind at the moment, but she was in that thing of his, *Ariadne*, somewhere. Lounging, like all his women do. She wasn't Ariadne, she was the handmaiden woman. I don't know how she came to be invited, now I come to think . . . I must look at my guest list in my diary. It's getting a bit unwieldy.' She looked around. 'Where was I?'

'People who knew about ghosts.'

'Yes. Not many people believe in *ghosts*, per se. They believe in spirits. But why do you want to know about ghosts? Chilly, shivery things, I always think. We try and keep our house full of light and laughter and I suggest you try to do the same, when you marry the lovely Matthew.'

'We were at the Grosvenor yesterday, and I'm sure I . . .'

Effie patted Lady Caroline's knee and laughed. 'The Grosvenor? Why didn't you say so? Everyone knows the Grosvenor's haunted.'

* * *

'Twice in one day, Mr Whistler,' the doorman touched his peaked cap. 'We *are* honoured.'

'You certainly are,' the artist snapped. 'This way, Mr . . .' He'd already forgotten the alias that Gan Martin had dreamt up.

The doorman peered closely at Whistler's associate. He *had* seen odder-looking blokes, but not often and usually on canvases. He watched as the pair disappeared into the second gallery.

Terence Saunders was already on edge that lunchtime. He had not seen Whistler the first time he had called, but Joe, the caretaker, had, and he had warned Saunders that the American looked a little put out. Saunders refrained from telling Joe that that was exactly what he'd like to do with Whistler. There was nothing worse than artists coming to admire their own work, if only because they inevitably disparaged everyone else's, especially when that everyone in question at the time was in earshot. What had really got Saunders's goat today was the unannounced arrival of approximately twenty-three girls under the watchful eye of Miss Easter of the Ladies' Academy down the road. They usually visited, as Saunders knew, the more rarefied halls of the Royal Academy, with its Reubenses, Titians and Nice Subjects. The Grosvenor specialized in the works of the more avant-garde painters, the pre-Raphaelite tendency that outraged society on a weekly basis. There would be some awkward questions in biology this afternoon, if he was any judge.

And here they all were, prim and proper in their starched apron-fronted uniforms, walking in pairs like a crocodile of snobbery, averting their gazes from certain canvases at the click of Miss Easter's parasol on the floor. The whole idea of an art gallery, Terence Saunders knew, was that the great British public should not only gawp at great art but buy it too. Fat chance of that with Miss Easter's gels.

'Well?' Whistler stood in front of his own creation. 'Aren't you appalled?'

Martin crouched and peered closely at the lower frame. Checking that no one was looking, he lowered his less-than-sharp spectacles and noted the famous butterfly signature. Then he stood up. 'I am,' he said. 'There are four more stars from the rocket than there were, more light on the river. That parapet has been altered. Oh, and this figure in the foreground – it's gone.'

Whistler secretly kicked himself. The figure in the foreground, an old man he'd seen wandering when he'd painted the thing, was one of the most obvious objects of the lower canvas. But it wasn't there now, merely a vague silhouette, transparent, with the rocket's light behind it.

'Cleverly done,' Martin murmured.

'I have never denied that Ruskin is an adequate painter,' Whistler said. 'If he'd confine his work to his own canvases. Until now, I'd only taken umbrage over the man's infantile critique. But this, this is a new low, even for him.'

'There's no proof it's him, of course,' Martin said.

'Don't talk such bollocks, er . . . Of course it's him.'

There was a shriek from behind them and Miss Easter had passed her parasol to her head girl in order to shield the ears of her youngest charge. Then she regained the parasol and proceeded to poke Whistler with it. '*You,*' she screamed, 'are an oaf and bounder of the worst water! This is an art gallery, sir, a place of beauty and finesse. It is not a place to use vile, base language in front of innocent young girls, no matter how much a canvas may offend you.'

'Offend me?' Whistler was almost speechless. 'Do you know who I am, madam?'

Martin cut in, anxious to diffuse the situation. 'This is Mr James McNeill Whistler, madam,' he said.

Miss Easter looked the American up and down. 'Never heard of him,' she trilled. 'And who are you? His keeper?'

'Sebastian Melmoth,' Martin announced. 'Art critic to the *Telegraph.*'

'*Everyone* is a critic, Mr Melmoth,' she sneered.

'Mr Whistler is . . .' Martin started the sentence but never finished it.

'. . . a blot on the escutcheon of a fine establishment. Come, gels, Sir Coutts and Lady Blanche shall hear of this!' and she shepherded them away.

'Sanctimonious old besom!' Whistler snarled. 'Right . . .

um . . . Melmoth. Ruskin it is. I'm not even going to the police over this matter. I want his kneecaps – pure and simple.'

In the end, Gan Martin managed to talk James Whistler down from the deadly ledge onto which he had metaphorically climbed, and they went back to Grand and Batchelor's offices in the Strand.

'Why, though?' Batchelor asked. 'Not outright vandalism but careful alteration. What for, in God's name?'

'I don't know,' Martin confessed. He had stashed his disguise back in the relevant drawer and was writing a cross-reference to it now it had been used in the Whistler case. He sipped a cup of Grand's best coffee, which beat anything Maisie could rustle up by a country mile, being merely coffee and not a mix of any liquids on the stove. 'But – and I don't know if you noticed this, Mr Whistler, there were other anomalies. In "your" gallery, if I can call it that, there was a Rossetti – *La Ghirlandata*. It was his musical instrument period, usual plain girl with red hair. But the harp was wrong. Rossetti knows his strings. There weren't enough of them in the version I saw today.'

'Really?' Whistler leaned forward. 'How on earth do you know that?'

Martin was horrified that the man even had to ask. 'I know how many strings a Renaissance harp has, Mr Whistler,' he said in affronted tones. 'So does Rossetti. Whoever "doctored" *La Ghirlandata* doesn't.'

'That, and the fact that Gan here has a photographic memory, Mr Whistler,' Batchelor said.

'And in the first gallery,' Martin went on, 'I couldn't help but notice Burne-Jones's *Pygmalion and Galatea* – the new one, called *The Hand Refrains*, I believe.' He winked at Whistler. 'One of those naked-lady jobbies our friend the teacher would have steered her gels away from, no doubt.'

'I can't imagine why,' Whistler growled. 'I remember that one. The Aphrodite statue has no pudenda at all. Can't really see what the other gods saw in her.'

'That's as may be,' Martin nodded, 'but she has no brush,

either. There was one, bottom right of the canvas, the one used to sweep up the bits of marble. The mallet's still there, but the brush isn't.'

'Still think it's Ruskin?' Grand asked. 'Defacing all these paintings. Is there any kind of link, Gan? Rossetti? Burne-Jones? Common ground?'

'The Pre-Raphaelite Brotherhood,' Martin said, 'their work is very distinctive.'

Batchelor nodded. 'It is,' he agreed, 'but James McNeill Whistler isn't one of them; are you, Mr Whistler?'

'Er . . . excuse me!' The doorman at the Grosvenor became shrill at moments like this. He knew perfectly well that the visitors trying to enter his establishment had been banned by his boss, Mr Saunders.

'Yes?' Grand loomed over him. Establishments like the Grosvenor didn't hire first-class muscle, largely because it was not necessary. The odd overwrought dowager in a bath chair, the occasional gaggle of giggling girls didn't merit a heavy with shoulders like wardrobes. The doorman stared at Grand's tie-knot, but he stood his ground nevertheless.

'You gentlemen are not welcome here,' he trilled.

Grand looked down at him, picked him up by the shoulders and moved him to one side. The doorman gave a strangled cry and muttered something about assault, but by that time his face was pressed against a pretty awful Fantin-Latour and he wasn't particularly audible.

'Where's Saunders?' Batchelor asked.

The doorman was trying to extricate his nose from the canvas when the manager of that name turned up. 'What's going on?' he wanted to know, more than a little of his Stepney coming through as he spoke.

'I assume you have an office?' Batchelor said.

'Or would you like us to have a conversation out here?' Grand smiled at the horrified punters milling around. They would have liked to have scurried out before the obvious art thief and general miscreant set about them as well, but he was blocking their exit.

'This way,' Saunders said, sweeping to his left. Grand let

the doorman go to recover whatever was left of his dignity
and the pair followed the manager into his office.

'I specifically told you two . . .' Saunders began.

'You did,' Grand said. 'We've just come to thank you in
person for your letter.'

'And to lodge a complaint,' Batchelor added.

'Complaint?' Saunders grunted. 'Complaint?' His volume
increased. 'You've got a brass neck after your behaviour the
other day. Not to mention just now.'

'Ah,' Batchelor beamed, 'but this time, it's about *your*
behaviour, isn't it?'

'I beg your pardon?'

'We are here to protest at the laxity of your security,' Grand
told him.

'Do what?'

'On behalf of our client, Mr Whistler,' Batchelor explained.
'We have reason to believe that his work *Nocturne in Blue
and Gold* has been tampered with. Along with others . . . what
were they, Matthew?'

'Rossetti's *Ghirlandata* and Burne-Jones's *The Hand
Refrains* – both vandalized.'

'Impossible!' Saunders said.

'Oh dear,' Grand sighed.

'I did warn you, Matthew,' Batchelor wagged his finger at him.

'You did, James,' Grand said, sadly, 'you did.'

'Inspector Metcalfe, then?' Batchelor wondered. 'Or should
we go straight to Superintendent Williamson?'

Grand feigned uncertainty. 'I was wondering whether old
Howie Vincent might want in on this. I mean, the man who
created the CID deserves some credit in art felony cases.'

'You're right,' and the pair turned to go.

'Er . . . just a minute,' Saunders said, his whole world
collapsing. God alone knew what the Lindsays would say
about all this. 'I can increase security.'

'How?' Grand asked.

'Wait here.'

They did and weren't waiting long before Saunders was
back with a wizened old boy with white fuzz on his chin.
'This is Joe,' the manager said, 'in charge of security.'

Grand and Batchelor looked at each other.

'So,' Batchelor looked at Saunders, 'when you say you can *increase* security, you're what? Hiring ten young blokes to replace this old one?'

Joe peered up at him. 'Whaddya mean?' he snapped.

'Don't take offence, old-timer,' Grand said. 'It's just that . . . well, looking after valuable artworks is a full-time job.'

'So?' Joe blinked.

'At the moment,' Saunders said, 'Joe's only here until soon after the gallery closes, sweeping up, that kind of thing. How about . . . how about we get him to live in? There's storage space in the attic.'

'You're missing the point,' Grand said, 'Okay, let's suppose you get a room for Joe. Let's suppose he hears something in the night. Let's suppose he approaches someone – oh, I don't know, to pick a name at random, John Ruskin – what does he do? Assuming he can find his false teeth in time, of course.'

Only one person in the room was ready for what happened next. Joe grabbed Batchelor's arm and wrenched it behind his back. He swung the man so that he landed flat on his face on Saunders's desk, papers and pens flying in all directions. 'I seen that Mr Ruskin here from time to time,' Joe said, pinning Batchelor down. 'He's about the same build as this bloke here. *That's* what I'd do, sonny,' and he beamed at Grand, whose mouth was still hanging open.

Joe let Batchelor go and the ex-Fleet Street man brushed himself down. 'You're lucky I controlled myself there,' he said, but the bravado fooled no one.

'I've been lifting canvases for more years than you boys have been alive,' Joe grinned, 'and I grew up in Bermondsey. All right, I'm a bit slower than I used to be, but I can still handle myself, I reckon.'

'You reckon right,' Grand smiled. 'And you don't mind living in, Mr . . . er . . .?'

'Just Joe will do,' he said. 'That depends on whether Mr Saunders has it in him to up the porridge. Security don't come cheap.'

'Mr Saunders?' Batchelor raised an eyebrow.

'Very well,' he said, 'I'll talk to Sir Coutts and Lady Blanche. I'm sure we can come to some arrangement.'

'Then we'll bid you good afternoon, gentlemen,' Grand said. 'But, rest assured, we'll be in touch.'

'Sweeping,' Joe said to Saunders. 'North Gallery.'

'Yes, of course,' Saunders said. 'Thank you, Joe.'

As the three of them left together, Joe patted Batchelor's arm. 'Sorry about that, young feller,' he said. 'Had a bit of a point to make.'

'You surely did that,' Grand chuckled. 'Mr Saunders was well impressed.'

Joe snorted. 'He don't know his arse from his chiaroscuro, that bloke.'

EIGHT

After a fine spring day, the Cremorne Gardens were doing a brisk trade. The Chinese lanterns bobbed bravely on a little westerly wind, sneaking through the houses from outside the city and bringing some freshness with it. The grass was starred with fallen blossoms, the last to fall as the trees came into full leaf. Around the lake on the eastern side, the swans and geese were beginning to seek the safety of their nests in the reeds and the last carousers were making their way home, before the Underground stopped running. Cabs were lined up at the gates to bear the better-heeled walkers back to their homes. Some gentlemen, looking rather more satiated than might be explained by a simple walk in the park, adjusted their clothing and left the hansom blinds open to dissipate the smell of cheap perfume.

The groundskeepers made their way around the perimeter, starting at one gate and walking round to the next, widdershins, locking it from the outside when they reached it and going home, another long day over and all's well. The League for the Right to Wander could do their worst – sometimes, safety really did come first. Harry Brownthorne lived just across the road from the lake side of the park, in rooms above a grocer. Although he and his wife didn't have much money, they were as snug as bugs and he knew he had a lot to be thankful for; a simple job, with no worries, simple pleasures and . . .

Harry Brownthorne stopped in his measured walk. Somebody had done in one of the swans again; there it was, floating, caught in the branch of a willow leaning over the water. He bet he knew who it was, too. It was those boozy lads who had mistaken a very respectable lady for a lady of the night and had had to be seen off the park. He knew they were trouble, the moment he saw them. He was in a quandary about the swan, though. If he left it, it would have attracted all sorts of vermin by morning. If a dead swan was likely to give the

vapours to elderly ladies giving their lapdogs a morning consti-
tutional, that was nothing to the shock which a swan mauled
by foxes and displayed in its component parts over the path
could provide. He sighed. He didn't fancy wading in, but he
saw no real option. He unlaced his boots, rolled up his trousers
and left his jacket on a nearby bench, noting as he did so a
bit of lost property to deal with later. The pleasant day had
a bit of a sting in its tail.

Late walkers in Cheyne Walk were startled to see a man,
barefoot, bare-headed and with his trousers rolled up to the
knees, suddenly barrel out of the gates of the Cremorne, his
mouth working soundlessly as he waved his hands above
his head. Locals had got used to all sorts of things happening
in the Gardens, but, thus far, not too much that was untoward
had sullied their pavements. The majority of the passers-by
swept aside their skirts or coats according to their sex and
passed by, but a constable of B Division, strolling round the
corner at his usual steady pace, saw a madman rushing towards
him and leapt on him with no fear for life or limb. The madman
seemed quite lucid when he got his breath back, though, and
the constable slackened his grip on the man's throat so he
could speak.

'A body,' Brownthorne gasped. 'A body in the Gardens.'

The policeman clambered to his feet and dragged Brownthorne
upright. 'A body?' he asked, and took in the man properly for
the first time. He appeared to be soaking wet, was the first
thing he noticed, just before he noticed the clinging clumps
of duckweed on his uniform. He would get stick for that, he
knew. Then, looking even more closely, he recognized him as
one of the park keepers.

'Harry, is it?' he ventured.

'Yes, that's right.' Brownthorne shook himself to rearrange
such of his clothing as he had on. 'There's a body in the lake.'

'So you said,' the copper said. He took out his notebook
and a pencil. 'Now, let's see. Name?'

'For God's sake! There's a body . . .'

'*Name?*'

'Harold Brownthorne.'

'Address?'

'There's a body . . .' Brownthorne pointed desperately into the Gardens. 'I've left her on the bank. Anyone could find her. For God's sake . . .'

'Oh ho!' The policeman was triumphant. These criminals always gave themselves away in the end. 'You left her on the bank, did you? After you had done with your foul . . . doings.'

'I didn't *kill* her, you idiot!' Brownthorne was almost hysterical now. 'I thought she was a swan at first . . .'

'Yeah, yeah, I thought my little Lottie was a swan until the teacher told me she was actually a goose.' He wrote down, 'Suspect delusional.'

'But when I went in to get it in, so the foxes didn't get it, it wasn't a swan at all. It was a woman.'

'Dressed as a swan?' The policeman was not of the park persuasion, but he had heard stories. 'Like that Greek bloke.'

'*Greek bloke?*' Brownthorne's patience had snapped and he ran off up the street, hopping occasionally as something stuck in his bare foot. '*Greek bloke?*' he yelled in the face of an innocent gentleman walking his lady friend home after a night out. 'They're all *mad*!'

The policeman, giving chase, soon caught his quarry, hampered as he was by bare feet.

'That's enough of that, my lad,' he said, in his best police jargon. 'You're nicked.'

Matthew Grand was a gentleman but not particularly innocent. But he knew that it wasn't necessary to be an enquiry agent to find it odd when a man with pond weed all over him, trousers rolled up and no jacket suddenly yelled 'Greek bloke' in your face. He and Lady Caroline had had a fairly stressful evening with three of her bridesmaids, one a clear nymphomaniac, one with a face only a mother could love and the other an annoying bluestocking with a fixation on the breeding cycle of the newt; he couldn't remember which was which but hoped he would not see them often enough for that to matter. He knew that he had blotted his copybook in countless unknown ways and so didn't just drop her at her door and race back to the scene. He merely tucked her hand more tightly into the crook of his elbow and walked on.

Eleanor was waiting for them in the hall.

'Oh, Miss Caroline, Mr Grand. What was all that shouting?'

'Shouting?' Grand said, looking around. 'Was there shouting?'

Caroline pulled off her gloves and put them down on the console with a slap. 'Mr Grand is pretending he didn't notice, Ellie,' she said, with the mock calm that showed a storm was coming. 'A madman shouting about Aristotle or some such thing.'

Grand was amazed – and not for the first time – at how witnesses embroidered the simplest fact.

'But Mr Grand could see that there was nothing he could do to help and so here we are. Aren't we, Mr Grand?'

'We are indeed, Lady Caroline,' he said, with a bow.

Eleanor, with the storm-awareness of a petrel, bobbed a curtsy and bolted through the green baize door to safety.

'I daresay Eleanor has left a tray,' Caroline said, with deadly politeness. 'Would you like to join me?'

'Love to.' Grand opened the door to the drawing room and there, sure enough, was a small spring fire lit in the grate and a covered tray of sandwiches and a kettle simmering on its burner. He lifted the cloth. 'Ham. My favourite.' He helped himself to a couple and plonked down in what was fast becoming his usual chair.

Caroline made the tea and joined him by the fire. 'I think this evening went well,' she said, still on her dignity.

'Don't be crazy, Caro,' Grand said, his mouth full of sand-wich. 'They all hated me and you know it. And I can't say I was crazy about them. To be honest, I kept waiting for Hecate to turn up.'

She looked at him, an eyebrow arched in query.

'You know.' He clawed a hand and hunched his shoulders. '"When shall we three meet again . . .?"'

She was so pleased to hear him quote Shakespeare that she let her guard down and laughed. 'They are my dearest friends,' she said, but with a smile.

'Well, your pals don't have to be mine,' Grand said. 'And,'

he was now serious, 'my job doesn't have to be yours, though you mustn't mind when I do my job, Caro. Like tonight.'

'He wasn't a client,' she said, looking away.

'No. He wasn't. But we *are* investigating a case which seems to be linked to the Cremorne, and a half-dressed man just ran out of there and shouted in my face. You can't blame me for showing an interest.' He put on his most winning smile and waited. She always came round in the end. The only question was when the end would arrive. This evening, it didn't take long.

'Point taken,' she said. 'I actually did some sleuthing myself today.'

That stopped him in mid-chew. 'You did?'

'Effie Millais' – she saw his blank expression – 'wife of John Millais the painter, and previous wife of John Ruskin . . .' She was rewarded by a gleam of interest in his eyes. 'Effie Millais has Mornings and I went to one today.'

'And?' Grand was pretty sure that wasn't all.

'Well, I was asking about ghosts and things, really, but I met the strangest people.'

'There are no such things as . . .'

'Strange people?' she said with a laugh. 'There certainly are. Mrs Stanhope for one, but I don't think she would interest you much. So much name-dropping! Burne-Jones, Watts – his model was there, but that's as near as we got to anyone famous. But they are all living in each other's pockets all the time. It's a bit like incest.'

'My word!' Grand was a little taken aback. 'I must say, when it comes to incest, I can take it or leave it alone.' He saw her face. 'Joke.'

'I had meant to do some sleuthing for you.'

He put an arm around her shoulders and gave her a manly hug. He had a choice of either condescending to her or treating her as one of the chaps, and the latter seemed the best course of action.

'But once I got there, it seemed a bit rude to ask her about Ruskin – it was a long time ago, of course – but it seems to me these artists do tend to marry young women very briefly; Ruskin, Watts, Rossetti. They've all done it in their day. So I don't think we could really make that a black mark against him.'

'I suppose young women are more beautiful.' He heard the words leave his mouth but didn't seem to have the power to stop them. Lady Caroline was twenty-seven but carried it with style and grace. He looked at her from under his lashes. She seemed to be taking it in the spirit in which it was meant.

'So,' she continued as if he hadn't spoken, 'I'm not sure I found out much, except that everyone knows the Grosvenor is haunted.'

He slid out of his chair, brushing crumbs from his vest, and went across to her on his knees. He put his arms around her waist and kissed her. 'Do you fancy making my spine tingle?' he whispered in her ear.

And her reply would have made Eleanor run for cover.

'So . . .' Inspector Metcalfe, called in specially, steepled his fingers as he leaned his elbows on his desk and stared with gimlet eyes at the constable standing to attention in front of him. 'So . . . a known Gardens employee, who you agree you recognized, comes running up to you – make a note of that, Barnes, because it is an important clue – and says there is a body in the lake.'

The constable snapped his heels together and barked, 'Yessir!'

Metcalfe closed his eyes. 'Just a simple "yes" would do,' he murmured. He had been fast asleep in the bosom of Mrs Metcalfe when the hammering at the door had come to waken him and he wasn't happy. It wasn't often he got an early night. 'So, you manhandled him here and threw him in a cell.'

'Yes, sir.' The constable remembered in the nick of time to keep his voice down. 'He was wet, sir, and partially clothed . . .'

'Having dragged a body from the lake.' Metcalfe still was moderately patient, but Barnes knew this wouldn't last much longer.

'Well, yes, but . . .'

Metcalfe decided to jump a stage or two. 'So, as you were in the station, filling out the form to explain why you have arrested a perfectly innocent – nay, I would go further, unusually altruistic – member of the public, a Mrs Penrose of Cheyne Walk, finding the gate of the Gardens inexplicably unlocked, decided to go for a late-night stroll to ameliorate her incipient indigestion, stumbled upon – and I use the phrase advisedly, you understand – a dead body lying halfway across the path around the lake.'

Barnes looked with sympathy on the bobby standing there. When Metcalfe's sentences became as involved as this, with long words thrown in for good measure, someone's head was going to roll.

'Well?'

The policeman had forgotten the question, but was pretty sure what answer was expected. 'Yes, sir.'

'Right.' Metcalfe relaxed his fingers and flexed his elbows. 'Now bugger off and ruin someone else's night.' He sighed. 'Barnes, is anyone there with the body?'

'Sergeant Simmons, sir.'

'Of course. Does that man never sleep?'

'He likes the overtime, sir, as I understand it.'

'Overtime?' Metcalfe did a double take which would have got a round of applause in any music hall in the city. 'We get overtime?'

And reaching for his hat, he left the room with Barnes in hot pursuit.

Sergeant Simmons was standing like an ox in the furrow on the path by the body. Harry Brownthorne was sitting on the nearby bench, soaked from the waist down but now at least reunited with his coat, socks and shoes. He was shivering in the little wind which he had welcomed earlier but now wished in Hell. Simmons was rocking back and forth, toes to heels, and was humming a little tune to himself under his breath. He actually didn't like bodies very much, but they seemed to be everywhere he went just lately.

'So,' he turned his head towards the park keeper, 'you just found her, then. On the bank.'

'No, I did not!' snapped Brownthorne. 'She was in the water, wasn't she? Thought she was a swan, didn't I?' He was getting tired of telling it and the knowledge that his bubble

and squeak would now be just a fragrant memory – eaten by
his wife as vengeance for his late arrival home – only added
to his annoyance.

'So, you dragged her to the bank?'

'Of course I did. Look.' Brownthorne was as fed up as a
soaking-wet park keeper still at work four hours after he
clocked off could possibly be. 'I'm not saying another word
until a proper policeman gets here.'

Simmons had no argument with that. He did his job, put in
his time and had an eye on a nice little pub somewhere in the
country when it was all done and dusted. Mrs Simmons's dad
had one, out in Kent, and that would do nicely. He carried on
rocking back and forth and could have gone on all night, had
Metcalfe and Barnes not loomed out of the dusk.

'Simmons.' Metcalfe didn't waste much time on subordinates.
'What have we got here, then?'

'A body.' Simmons didn't waste much time either. 'Sir.'

Metcalfe narrowed his eyes, a wasted gesture in the almost
total dark. 'Anyone we know?'

Simmons shuffled his feet. 'She does look a bit familiar,
sir, but it's hard to tell, with the wet and the duckweed and
all. I was wondering . . . the Halls, perhaps?'

'Well, with the Cremorne's reputation, I would say she is
a tart, surely?' Barnes was getting quite au fait with the jargon.
'Have you checked for . . .' He paused. He would never forget
what he found up the victim's skirt last time.

'I have,' Simmons said. 'All present and correct and nothing
up there that shouldn't be up there, if you follow. Her clothes
are a bit' – he waved a hand – 'a bit arty. A bit farty, know
what I mean? Not what you'd find on a lady of the night, nor
a lady either. Just a bit . . .'

'Calico,' Brownthorne said. 'Her dress is calico. And the
lace is home-made. Tatting.'

'You're very well informed on ladies' fashions,' Barnes put
in quickly. He was alert for this kind of thing now.

'My missus works in Debenhams, sir,' the park keeper said.
'She works in the alterations department, but she sometimes
brings work home when they're busy. Calico and cotton tatting
is all the rage, apparently, with what you might call the "arty

set". Some of them make their own, but them as can't, well, my missus and the other girls at Debenhams does it for them.'

'I see,' Metcalfe said. 'The arty set, you say. Not tarts, then?'

'I wouldn't say so, sir. It comes a bit expensive; bespoke, you know. And I wouldn't say that your average tart could be doing with all those frills and layers, would you?' He gestured to where the body lay, in a positive tangle of fabric. 'Not much chance of a quick over the head and do your business, is there?'

Metcalfe looked at him suspiciously. 'You sound a bit of an expert, lad,' he remarked.

'I haven't always been married to Mrs Brownthorne,' he said, drawing himself up. 'I was quite active, back in the day.' He looked at Simmons. 'He knows,' he said. 'Perks.'

Metcalfe and Barnes looked at Simmons, who examined the dark horizon with great concentration.

'And another thing,' Brownthorne continued, 'I reckon I know her as well. I've seen her face somewhere and if you give me a while, I'll remember it, I'm sure. Got that kind of memory. Well, you have to, working the Gardens, keeping an eye out for troublemakers, that sort of thing. She's not a tart, though, that I do know.'

'You said.' Metcalfe was bending over the body, looking at her with his head turned this way and that.

'Because this is her book, I reckon.'

Metcalfe got up slowly and turned, with Barnes and Simmons, to look at the man holding the volume out to them.

'Book?'

'Yes.' Brownthorne looked from one face to the other. 'Why? What?'

'Where was it?'

'Here, on this bench. It's got a hankie in it, same tatting as on the bodice.'

'I don't know,' Simmons said to no one in particular. 'I think they should bring in a law. Everybody finding a body ought to be an expert on tatting.'

'That's enough, Simmons.' Metcalfe reached out for the book. He turned it into the beam of Simmons's bullseye. '*King of the Golden . . .'* He peered closer. 'I can't read this last word. The writing's all curly.'

'*King of the Golden River,*' Barnes said. 'I had a copy when I was very young.'

Simmons thought to himself that that could have been as recently as last week.

'It's a children's book, but quite hard to understand. My sister liked it more than I did.'

Metcalfe was leafing through the book, peering at the rather scratchy illustrations. 'Who's it by?' he asked.

Simmons tried to look intelligent, but Barnes beat him to the tape.

'John Ruskin,' he said.

'But I still don't know why you've sent for me, Tom.' Inspector Daddy Bliss wasn't often to be found on dry land. The experience unnerved him.

'Surely, I don't have to paint you a picture, Dad.' Metcalfe topped up Bliss's rum toddy, early though it was. 'The deceased was found in the water. Drowned. So naturally, I thought of you.'

'Naturally.' Bliss circled the body again, squinting down at the serene face before folding back the shroud. 'But there are two things wrong with that. One, I am an inspector of the *River* Police, there being no such thing as the Lake Police. And two, she didn't drown.'

Metcalfe frowned. 'She didn't? What have I missed?'

Bliss yawned. He didn't know how long Metcalfe had got, so he came straight to the point. 'Look at the hands,' he said. 'No cadaveric spasm. No weed between the fingers or under the nails. When and if a doctor ever gets here, he'll be able to check her lungs, but I'd be prepared to bet there'll be no water in them.'

'Oh.' The nice little scenario that Inspector Tom Metcalfe had invented to explain away the latest problem had just floated out of the nick window and was, even now, drifting all the way down Walton Street. 'What, then?'

Daddy Bliss waggled his toddy glass to show that it was empty and Metcalfe did the honours. He checked the eyes, peeling back the lids and looked into the mouth. He ran his fingers through the hair. 'No obvious signs of strangulation,' he said. 'At least not by ligature. The neck is bruise-free, although of course the water does funny things.'

'How long had she been in the lake, would you say?' Metcalfe asked.

'About an hour, give or take.' He lifted up the dead woman's left arm. 'Starting to stiffen,' he noted. 'Allowing for the action of the water, which interferes with the cooling and also the rigor mortis, she could have died as early as nine or ten last night. Or four hours ago. Whatever fits with the facts, really.' Time of death was never an exact science, and Daddy always used to tell his rookies that the only way you could ever be sure when someone died was if you had shot them in the head yourself and then checked your watch immediately. He peered at the head again, lit as it was by Metcalfe's desk lamp, brought down to the makeshift mortuary for the purpose. 'No contusions. So, no ubiquitous blunt object.' He turned the girl over onto her side. 'Bruising here,' he pointed to her ribs. 'Where was she found, again?'

'In the big lake at the Cremorne.'

'The one with the jetty, pond yachts for the use of?'

'That's right.'

'That's a squarish bruise. I'd say she hit the jetty on her way in.'

'Still alive?' Metcalfe checked.

'Marginally,' Bliss said. 'But I doubt she gulped any water. As I said, the doctor can tell you.' He rolled the woman back on the table that doubled as a makeshift mortuary slab and, as gently as he could, prised open her legs. 'Nothing obviously untoward down there,' he said. 'So, not a sex fiend.'

'Could be poison, then?' Matcalfe queried.

'Could be,' Bliss nodded. 'Not exactly my area of expertise. Have you had others, then?'

'We have,' Metcalfe told him. 'Cyanide, to be exact.'

Bliss nodded.

'What do you make of this, Dad?' Metcalfe passed Bliss a piece of paper with three book titles written on it in Barnes's best copperplate.

Bliss looked at it and handed it back. 'What is it?' he wanted to know.

'Book titles,' Metcalfe said. 'One was found near bodies in the Cremorne recently – the first one eighteen months ago, the second just the other week and the final one last night, near this poor girl.'

Bliss read them aloud. '*Moby Dick*, *Fruits of Philosophy*, *King of the Golden River.*'

'Do you know them?'

'Nah,' Bliss shrugged. 'To be honest, Tom, if it's not tides and wind velocity, I'm not that interested. Let me have another look.'

Metcalfe passed it back.

'First one's about a whale, isn't it?'

Metcalfe nodded.

'Mrs Bliss gave me a copy, now I remember, one Christmas. I suppose she thought I would be interested, what with there being boats and all. But I couldn't get on with it.'

Metcalfe had tried a few pages with the same effect. 'Somebody's sending a message, Daddy – I just don't know what.'

'It's a mystery all right,' Bliss agreed. 'Funny it's her, though.'

'What is?' Metcalfe blinked. 'Who is?'

'The deceased,' Bliss said, as though to the village idiot. 'The lady in question.'

Metcalfe still looked nonplussed.

'*This* one,' Bliss pointed at her. 'She's that woman – you know, off of the soap advertisement.'

Mrs Rackstraw sometimes wondered where it would all end. One thing she had always been able to say about her gentlemen was that they always made a good breakfast. She had always maintained that it was the most important meal of the day and she made sure it was substantial; kedgeree, kippers, kidneys – all the kays were the secret of a happy day. And now, twice in a few days, they had gone out without so much as a kup of koffee. She wouldn't mind, were it not for one thing; her hatred of waste meant that nothing went in the swill bin that could be eaten. And so, she and Maisie sat forcing down a breakfast meant for two working gentlemen. As Maisie ate approximately enough to keep a very slender sparrow alive, Mrs Rackstraw was finding the going tough. She had already had to let her stays out a notch; this couldn't go on. She would either have to cut down on the breakfast comestibles – and something deep in her soul made that next to impossible – or she would have to speak to her gentlemen. They needed to be told.

Speaking for herself, Maisie blamed that Lady Caroline, stuck-up madam. When Mr Matthew saw sense and recognized Maisie's inner beauty and married her, then all would be well. Until then, she picked at a kipper and wished the entire Arbroath fishing fleet to hell.

Grand and Batchelor had just turned the corner into Walton Street when they almost collided with a very large policeman they thought they knew.

'Mr Grand. Mr Batchelor.' He tipped his hat.

The pair did likewise. 'Inspector Bliss,' Grand said, 'You're a long way from the river.'

'Ah, no one's ever *that* far from the river,' Bliss smiled. 'Not in London.'

'What brings you to Chelsea?' Batchelor asked.

Bliss looked at him. The simple answer was a cab. The complex answer was that his old mucker Tom Metcalfe had called him in to discuss nefarious activities in the Cremorne. Neither of these concerned Grand and Batchelor, enquiry agents of the private persuasion as they were.

'Nefarious activities in the Cremorne,' Bliss said. To his dying day, he didn't know why he had blurted that out, but he did.

'Told you,' Grand said to Batchelor. 'Wouldn't have anything to do with a potential madman running around barefoot, would it?'

Bliss narrowed his eyes. 'What do you boys know?' he asked.

'Buy us breakfast and we'll tell you,' Batchelor said.

'No,' Bliss insisted. '*You* buy *me* breakfast and *I'll* tell *you*.'

So, the Inglenook it was, an elderly chophouse off the King's Road that had seen better days, but their bacon and sausages were to die for. Because of their differences over scrambled eggs, Grand and Batchelor opted for the poached. The aproned waitress who served them was fairly appalled that Bliss had both, with a hard-boiled one on the side for afters.

'You first,' Bliss said, piling sugar into his tea.

Grand and Batchelor looked at each other. Then Batchelor shrugged and took up the tale. After all, the agents knew no more than the reporters who had covered the crimes and probably a great deal less than the average London bobby.

'Two women and a man,' he said, 'all found dead in the Cremorne, one eighteen months ago, the others in less than two weeks.'

'So I believe.' Bliss was dunking his toast into the poached egg.

'The women were ladies of the night. The man was . . .'

'. . . also a lady of the night,' Bliss finished the sentence for him.

'In a manner of speaking,' Grand said, sipping his coffee.

'Cause of death, we're not sure at the moment, but it looks like cyanide poisoning.'

'Is that it?' Bliss had waited for more, but nothing was forthcoming.

'More or less,' Batchelor said. 'Except that the man – Anstruther Peebles – obviously doesn't fit the pattern, being of the male persuasion, I mean.'

'Dressed as a harlot, though,' Bliss commented. 'Why was that, do you reckon?'

'Peculiar,' said Batchelor.

'Not as other night-walkers, that's for sure,' Grand nodded.

'So, was he killed as a case of mistaken identity?' Bliss asked.

'Unlikely.' Grand chewed his toast. 'If the modus operandi was different – if our boy, if it *is* a boy – struck from behind with a knife or a blunt instrument, I'd say, yes, maybe. But poison . . . that takes a little while, if only to be administered.'

'So the motive's different,' Bliss ventured.

'We'd say so.' Batchelor called the waitress for more tea.

Again, Bliss was waiting for more information. There wasn't any. 'What is it, then?' he felt obliged to ask.

Grand leaned forward. 'What if . . . what if our friend is some sort of glorified park attendant, cleaning the Gardens up, not of litter or leaf mould but what he sees as human detritus?'

'Funny you should bring up park attendants,' Bliss said. 'When we met half an hour ago, Mr Grand, you mentioned a barefoot lunatic. I assume you saw such a person.'

'I did,' Grand assured him. 'I was, as you guys say, walking in an easterly direction when he came hurtling out of the Cremorne. Rattled the lady I was with.'

'No doubt,' Bliss said. 'Metcalfe tells me his name is Brownthorne and he's one of the Cremorne groundsmen.'

'What was his problem?'

'Touch of arthritis, I shouldn't wonder.' Daddy Bliss knew all about the risks of working in a damp environment. 'Scooping up leaves in all weathers. But specifically, in this instance, he'd found a body.'

'Aha!' Batchelor clicked his fingers.

'It'll be in the papers tomorrow. In the case of the *Standard*, this evening.'

'Come on, Daddy,' Batchelor growled. 'We haven't forked out a small fortune on your breakfast to get the fob-off. You'll be telling us next you couldn't possibly divulge.'

Bliss laughed, a rare sound for him as it turned out. 'All right,' he said. 'To quote what I suspect will be the *Standard*'s headline "There's been another one".'

'A harlot?' Grand asked.

'Not exactly. But a body in the Cremorne, certainly.'

'Same modus operandi?' Batchelor asked.

Bliss chewed his toast. The tea had arrived.

'Very likely,' he said, when the floozy had gone. 'She was found in the lake, though.'

'Very Arthurian,' Batchelor said. 'Not drowned, though?'

'Definitely not. Metcalfe thought so – but, old mate though he is, poor old Tom isn't the brightest apple. That's why he called me in, because of my familiarity with water-borne malfeasance.'

'Do we know who she was yet?' Grand asked.

'Tom didn't,' Bliss said. 'But I do.'

'Who?' Grand and Batchelor chorused.

'Funnily enough,' Bliss said, 'she's over there.'

Both men turned. Through the dingy window, across the street from the Inglenook, a large poster covered a brick wall. It was faded and peeling, but the girl at her toilette with the radiant smile and the bunches of honeysuckle was still recognizable enough.

'The Pears soap girl?' Batchelor couldn't see anybody else.

'The same,' Bliss said, wiping the last of his toast around his plate. 'To be more precise, Miss Evangeline French, artists' model extraordinaire. Tell me, Mr Grand, are you going to eat that sausage?'

'Er . . . no,' Grand said, still taking in what Bliss had just told them. 'Feel free.'

Bliss stabbed it with alacrity, chewing contentedly. 'Nothing like the full American, is there?' He chomped his way through the last of the marmalade. 'By the way,' he said, as well as the sticky orange stuff would allow, 'you know you're being followed, you two, don't you?'

NINE

They parted company at the end of the King's Road. Grand hailed a cab rattling east; Batchelor took an omnibus, one of Mr Shillibeer's finest. As for Bliss, he did what he always did, travelled by boat along the river, putting the fear of God into the boatman by his very presence.

Whoever it was that Bliss had spotted watching the detectives now had a straight choice. He could either hail a cab too and stick like glue to Grand, or he could catch another omnibus behind Batchelor. They always come in pairs and sometimes three after an interminable wait, all of them following the same route and ending up in the same place.

Batchelor saw him briefly, waving his arm in the air as a gig lurched to a halt alongside him. He was tall and broad, wearing an appalling check suit, and Batchelor thought he looked quite familiar. Then, as suddenly as he had appeared, he had gone, vanished into the body of the cabriolet. Batchelor was sitting on the open top of the omnibus, at the back where he could watch his entire surroundings. In the end, his neck gave out as he was trying to twist in every direction, but there was no doubt that the cab *was* following the omnibus.

He deliberately got off at Charing Cross and made the rest of the way on foot, knowing that his shadow would have to do the same. He paused at the copy of the Eleanor Cross, admiring its Gothic symmetry. Then he bought a flower from a seller and placed it in his lapel. From there, he ducked down towards the river, under the arches at the Adelphi. Whenever he glanced back, his shadow was there, always with his head turned or his bowler tilted forward. At one point, he had his nose pressed up against the glass of a window displaying ladies' unmentionables. The next moment, he was risking life and limb walking along reading a newspaper, the *Morning Advertiser* in front of his face.

This was the Maryanne's Mile, where men were often followed by other men and nobody turned a hair. Batchelor nipped to his left, up the Embankment garden and back to the Strand. He let himself into the office and glanced down from the first-floor window. There he was, lounging against a tree. And he was sure of it now. He knew who his follower was.

Meanwhile, Matthew Grand had arrived at the Wentworth London residence without seeing anyone behind him. He had deliberately stopped his cab two streets away and had ducked and dived through gardens and at one point through a cab parked at the side of the road, to the consternation and surprise of the paying passenger. Arriving at the front door, he tapped on the knocker without turning his back on the street, no mean feat.

The door swung open and he slid inside, closing it behind him. Turning, he saw a startled Eleanor standing there, eyes wide.

'Morning, Ellie,' he said, breezily. 'Lady Caroline in?'

'I'll see if Her Ladyship is At Home,' Eleanor said in rather more formal tones than usual.

'Don't worry,' Grand said, heading for the drawing room, 'I'll show myself in,' and he threw open the door.

The wind that blew between the rooms cut him to the bone. On one side of the fireplace sat his fiancée. On the other, her mother, looking as though she were in the process of being thawed after long years in the permafrost.

'Mr Grand,' she said, offering a hand wrapped in a wisp of black lace. 'How lovely to see you at this early hour. Lady Caroline and I are not At Home at the moment.'

Caroline's eyes were on his face, filled with mute appeal. This was not the first time he had been in this predicament. It was almost – but not quite – as bad as the time he had waltzed into a dining room one morning in his dressing gown to find his current light o' love's grandfather sitting at the head of the table, reading *The Times*. That would take some beating, but this called for some quick thinking.

He stepped forward and took her hand, kissing it extravagantly. 'Lady Wentworth,' he said, hoping he had it right. If he lived to a hundred he would never get English titles worked out. 'How lovely to see you. I hope I haven't interrupted you and Lady Caroline, but I have a question to ask her, concerning a case.'

He had been doing well enough until he used the 'c' word.

'Lady Caroline is involved in a *case*?' Her mother's voice could have etched glass.

'Not involved, Mama, no, of course not.' Caroline always tended to regress to the nursery when her mother was about. 'But I was unfortunate enough yesterday to be taken by a friend to an artists' soirée and . . . I believe Matthew . . . Mr Grand, might need some information I gleaned in conversation.'

Her mother swivelled to face her as if on castors. 'You *conversed* with artists, Caroline?' she asked, aghast.

'No, no, Mama, not at all. I conversed with . . . Mrs Millais, mainly.'

Her mother's eyes narrowed and her mind clicked through a filing system that made Gan Martin's look like a pile of torn paper. 'Would that be Euphemia Gray, as was?'

Caroline shrugged. 'Possibly,' she ventured.

'The trollop who was married to John Ruskin?'

'I believe so, yes.' Caroline felt herself to be on safe ground. She knew her mother was a great believer in Ruskin's opinion.

'Then you should be ashamed of yourself!' The woman drew herself up in a scream of whalebone. 'You have no idea the distress that woman caused to that sainted man. He worshipped her, literally *worshipped* her, Mr Grand,' the implied inference that he would never reach those giddy heights vis-à-vis her daughter was written in capitals over her head, 'and she let him down. Just because . . .' She remembered she was in the presence of an unmarried woman and stayed her tongue. She sighed and let herself collapse into the embrace of her corset again, 'I digress. I merely say, for what it's worth, that I never want to hear you say you have met with this woman again. It is time I returned to London as your chaper-one, Caroline. I had no idea you were living this rackety sort of life.' She swivelled to Grand again. 'What was your question, Mr Grand?'

'Umm . . .' Grand wasn't sure how to couch it now. 'Caro . . .'

He saw the warning in her eyes. '. . . line,' he said. 'Could you tell me if the mod . . . person you met yesterday at Mrs Millais's Morning was the girl in the Pears soap advertisement.'

Caroline screwed up her nose. 'I'm not sure,' she said. 'Which one?'

Grand was stuck. He didn't know there *was* more than one.

She helped him out. 'Do you mean the one where she is looking in the mirror, or the lounging back one.'

'The second.'

'Then, yes,' she said. 'She is.'

Grand stood irresolute. At this point, he usually kissed his fiancée, but wasn't sure whether his mother-in-law-to-be would approve. Caroline saved the problem by standing up and offering him her forehead. He dropped a chaste kiss somewhere near her hairline, bowed to her mother and beat a retreat.

In the hall, Eleanor was dusting ostentatiously.

'You could have warned me, Eleanor!' Grand hissed.

Eleanor rolled her eyes and shrugged. She wanted the old besom to clear off as much as Grand did. When she was in residence, she made a point of going round with a pair of white gloves on, checking for dust on a daily basis. When the grocer's boy next arrived with an order, Eleanor was going to give him the treat of his life. Moral stands were all very good, but it was time she got this young man to the altar, and the quicker the better.

'No harm done, Ellie,' he muttered. 'Just don't let the old bat eat anyone. Especially Miss Caroline. I've heard that sows often eat their young.'

Eleanor was still giggling when Lady Wentworth swept out into the hall. 'You!' she said. 'Eleanor, isn't it?'

The maid bobbed a curtsy.

'Any more laughing and you can take your month's notice. I will not have laughing under my roof.'

In the drawing room, Caroline let her head fall back onto the antimacassar. Bugger the bridesmaids' dresses. She was going to have to get this wedding organized as soon as possible.

Grand was still feeling the chill in his bones when he got to the office. Batchelor was standing in the window, but pressed against the side of his elaborate desk-cum-bookcase, which was still tidy as he hadn't actually sat at it yet. He was looking down into the street.

'Well?' Grand asked him, using his elite detective skills to deduce that he was looking for the man supposed to be following them. 'I didn't see anybody behind me.'

'No,' Batchelor said. 'That's because he was behind me. It's . . .'

The door clicked open and Martin swept in, his friend Wilde in tow. 'Good morning, sirs,' he said. 'You're early.'

'What kept you, Wilde?' Batchelor snapped.

The younger Oxford man looked at him. 'I beg your pardon?' he said.

'Lovely gardenia in your buttonhole.' Batchelor was acid itself. 'Did you get that from the flower girl at the Adelphi?'

'The Adelphi?' Wilde frowned. 'Good Lord, no. When I'm in town, I get them from Bloomgard's, St James's.' He looked at the rest of the company. 'Doesn't everyone?'

'What about the ladies' whatsits in the window of Eulalie Lingerie? See anything there to fit you?'

'I must beg your pardon again.' Wilde was fuming.

'Not like you to repeat yourself, Oscar,' Martin said, smiling and trying to bring down the temperature. 'What's going on, Mr Batchelor?'

'What indeed, James?' Grand felt obliged to ask.

'Ask Fingal O'Flaherty here,' Batchelor said. 'Who has been following Grand and I for days now.'

'Grand and me,' Wilde corrected him.

'So you admit it!' Batchelor crossed to Wilde and stared at his cravat.

'No, I don't,' Wilde retorted. 'I was merely trying to preserve the beauty of the English language as best I might.'

'Explain yourself, Wilde,' Grand said.

But there was no time for that. There was a thunderous knocking at the door and Grand ran to answer it. The other three stood there, fuming still for different reasons. Then Grand was back, dragging a street urchin by the sleeve.

'Say that again,' he said. 'You'd think I'd be used to Cockney sparrer by now, but I'd rather have a second opinion.'

'Out with it, young feller.' Batchelor was London born and bred; he'd have no difficulty.

'This geezer,' the out-of-breath lad wheezed, 'bloke wiv a stick, looks like somefink out of the Bible. Artist, he said he was. Or a cricket – I'm not sure which.'

'John Ruskin?' Batchelor interpreted for the boy.

'That's 'im. 'E's round the corner in the Aldwych, gettin' the shit kicked out of 'im by anuvver bloke. Funny accent 'e's got, mad hair.'

'Funny accent like mine?' Grand asked.

'Yeah!' The lad clicked his fingers. 'Blimey, they're all at it.'

'Why are you here?' Batchelor asked.

'This geezer, the bloke with the stick said, "Get round the corner. Go to the hoffices of Mr Grand and Mr Batchelor, tell 'em to give you a quid."'

'How much?' Batchelor's eyebrows threatened to reach his hairline.

'Two bob,' the lad said.

Batchelor narrowed his eyes at the boy.

'All right, a tanner,' he said.

'I assume he needs our help?' Grand asked.

'S'pose so,' the boy said. 'What wiv the gammy leg and all. I don't know why 'e didn't ask a p'liceman.'

'No point,' said Batchelor, snapping up his hat. 'They don't even know what time it is.'

It was scarcely a battlefield, but quite a crowd had gathered at the Aldwych to watch two pensioners, as Grand might put it, slug it out.

'It's outrageous, Ruskin,' Whistler was shouting, 'and I won't put up with it!'

'For the last time, Whistler,' the Old Testament prophet was saying, 'I haven't touched your blasted painting. Nothing would induce me.'

'Liar!' Whistler screamed.

'Gentlemen, gentlemen,' Batchelor arrived, the others in tow. 'This isn't very seemly, is it?'

'Mr Whistler,' Grand murmured in the man's ear. 'Not exactly West Point, huh?'

Actually, it was *exactly* West Point, and both men knew it. Grand had long ago lost count of the altercations he'd had back in the day, on the banks of the Hudson. If Grand and Batchelor were determined to be peacemakers, much to the disappointment of the raucous crowd, Oscar Wilde was not. He assessed the situation, saw a sixty year old with a stick being bullied by a man in his mid-forties. It was no contest. He brought his right arm back and drove his fist into Whistler's chin. The man went down like a ton of bricks, much to the crowd's delight; here and there, money changed hands.

Martin saw the horrified looks on the faces of Grand and Batchelor. 'He boxes at Oxford,' he said, by way of explanation for Wilde's behaviour.

From nowhere, there was the cacophony of a police rattle and four boys in blue were forcing their way through the crowd, elbowing people aside, generally making their presence felt.

'He swung the first one, Sarge,' one of them said to the man with stripes on his sleeve. The two others grabbed Wilde, one to each arm.

'And he didn't swing at all,' the observant one pointed to the fallen Whistler.

'Never mind,' the sergeant said. 'Bring 'im in too.'

'This does add a whole new dimension, James.' Grand was lighting his cigar.

'What does?'

'The identity of the lady in the lake.'

'Yes, indeed,' Batchelor agreed, picking his way through a box of chocolates. 'Makes you wonder about the others, doesn't it? Mabel and Clara, I mean.'

'What, were they models as well, you mean?'

'Yes. I've no idea what an artists' model earns, but it's got to be safer than lying on your back under the stars.'

'That's very poetic, James,' Grand smiled. 'You've been spending too long in the company of Mr Wilde.'

'Heaven forfend.' Batchelor pulled a face.

'Coffee cream?' Grand asked.

'Strawberry delight.' Batchelor winced as it went down.

'No, when the boys in blue see fit to let that man go, I want to continue my conversation with him.'

'You still think he was following you? Us?'

'I do,' Batchelor said. 'Consider this, Matthew. We take on Gan Martin – all right, he was my contact initially. Then, lo and behold, Gan Martin turns out to have a friend – a year his junior, mind you – still at Oxford; a man who, despite being a student, seems to have all the time in the world. A man who is always there, like Banquo's ghost. I would expect to have met the man once, not stuck to Martin like glue.'

'But why would he follow us?' Grand was playing devil's advocate.

'I don't know,' Batchelor said. 'I only know he didn't turn up until the bodies began to do the same in the Cremorne.'

'What do we know about Evangeline French?' Grand pinched the hazelnut heaven just before Batchelor got there. He needed to get him off the vexed subject of Oscar Wilde.

'Worked for G.F. Watts.'

'Is that it?' Grand said. 'I thought you went to the Royal Academy this afternoon?'

'I did and I spoke to the curator chappie.'

'Helpful?'

'No. Had rather a smell under his nose. I made the mistake of mentioning the Grosvenor, after which he treated me like shit on his shoe. He didn't know much about Evangeline. Knew an awful lot more about Elizabeth Siddal, was the impression I got. Seemed to think her hair wasn't really auburn – or, as he called it, "spun copper".'

Grand snorted.

'He found Burne-Jones's work decadent – what he would expect, apparently, from the son of a frame-maker. Did I mention that he mentioned that Elizabeth Siddal worked in a milliners'?'

'You didn't.'

'Well, he did – and she did. Evangeline, on the other hand, began her working life as a seamstress. She doesn't seem to have been anybody's regular model.'

'You mean, she put it about a bit?' Grand wanted to be sure.

'In the nicest possible way, yes. Rather than assume that the other victims could have posed too, I think we should assume our murderer has changed direction. Could he have mistaken Evangeline for a tart?'

Grand shrugged. 'Not having seen her alive – or dead, come to that – it's hard to say.'

'G.F. Watts,' Batchelor made a lunge for the Turkish delight and beat Grand to it by a country mile, 'exhibits at the Grosvenor, doesn't he?'

'He does.' Grand got up and wandered to the fireplace; his cigar had gone out. 'Time we paid the man a visit,' he said. 'James.'

'Hmm?' Batchelor was not impressed with what was left on the top layer; he may have to break the gentleman's code and rummage in what lay beneath.

'You know that Oscar Wilde's been following us?'

'Yes.' Batchelor did.

'Who's that, then?' Grand was looking out of the window, down to the street, where a large man in a loud check suit was lounging against a lamppost.

Detective Constable Alfred Twisleton checked his half-hunter. Nearly eight o'clock. His shift had ended over an hour ago. Surely, those two amateurs wouldn't be going out again tonight? The American might call on that tart he was knocking off. The Englishman didn't have any friends at all. Time to call it a night. And he didn't notice his current charges staring at him out of the window.

There was nothing like a night in the cells for forging new friendships. On the other hand, how do you say sorry for having knocked out a doyen of the art world when you yourself had not yet graduated from Oxford and your whole life lay before you?

'I can only apologize, Mr Whistler,' Wilde said. He had long ago lost all feeling in his left buttock and his throat was bricky dry. 'Again.'

'Yes.' Whistler was resting his throbbing head against the cool iron of the cell door. 'I heard you the first time.'

Wilde buried his head in his hands and Whistler took pity on him. 'You'll agree, however,' the artist said, 'that I am the wronged party.'

'Indubitably,' Wilde nodded. 'If Ruskin is responsible . . .'

'*If*, sir? *If?*' Whistler sat bolt upright and held on to the edge of the bunk as the room swam. 'Don't speak to me of "ifs". Even if Ruskin hasn't been despoiling my painting, he is still guilty of the most appalling slander. Tell me, Mr Wilde, when you leave Oxford, what do you intend to do with your life?'

'Oh, I don't know.' Wilde leaned back on the impossibly hard, narrow bed. 'The fact is that *Literae Humaniores* doesn't exactly qualify a chap for the nineteenth century. I thought perhaps, writing poetry? Plays? Even children's stories pay good money these days, I'm told.'

'Good luck with that,' Whistler grunted. 'Whatever you heard, there's no money in any of it. Two hundred guineas per canvas is what I get. What would you make for a play? Ten pounds? Something like that?'

'I have no idea,' Wilde said. 'But can we really put a price on art, Mr Whistler? Art of any kind. What, for example, would you say this is worth? Umm . . . let me think . . . Yes, I have it.' He cleared his throat and struck a rather less lacklustre attitude. 'Like two doomed ships that pass in storm, We had crossed each other's way: But we made no sign, we said no word, We had no word to say; For we did not meet in the holy night, But in the shameful day . . . Let me see, now . . . Yes . . . A prison wall was round us both, Two outcast men were we: The world had thrust us from its heart, And God from out His care: And the iron gin that waits for Sin, Had caught us in its snare.'

Wilde relaxed from his declaiming and looked across at Whistler. 'So, how much?'

'Who's it by?'

Wilde was puzzled. 'Well . . . me. I just made it up. It's about us, you see. In prison.'

'Hmm.' Whistler was not immediately impressed. 'Tell me it again. I wasn't really listening.'

Wilde turned his back to the artist and looked fixedly at the wall.

Whistler was not a sensitive man when it came to other humans but he could see he had hurt the man's feelings. 'It sounded very good,' he said, placatingly. 'Very . . . very' – he didn't mix much with poets – 'tumpty. Something you could easily remember.'

Wilde was implacable.

Whistler gave him a while. He seemed like a nice enough lad, just a bit hot tempered. And sure enough, eventually, mainly because the bed was so hard, he turned over and sat up.

Whistler decided to try and make a fresh start. 'So,' he said, brightly, 'you work for Grand and Batchelor do you?'

'No,' Wilde said, a little sulkily. 'I am kicking my heels for a couple of weeks before my final examinations. Hanging around, as we have it in Oxford these days, with my friend, Ganymede Martin. *He* works for them.'

'Ah.'

'Actually, I thought I might actually enjoy sleuthing – ah, there I go, repeating myself again. But I don't. Do you know, Batchelor actually seemed to be accusing me of following him yesterday morning?'

'Did he? Were you?'

'Of course not!' Wilde was outraged. 'I can only assume that the more you delve into other people's private lives, the more paranoid you become. I think we're a lot safer with painting and poetry, don't you, Mr Whistler?'

There was a crash of locks and a rattle of keys.

'Visitor, Whistler,' the turnkey grunted. He was one of Nature's gentlefolk.

'My dear fellow,' the visitor said, extending a hand. 'I just heard. Are you all right?'

Whistler bounced to his feet. 'Keen,' he seized the man's hand. 'Thank God – and about time. Can you get me out of here? I *am* a celebrity.'

'Of course,' the QC said. 'My clerk has the paperwork.'

'Oh, Wilde,' Whistler turned to his cellmate. 'This is Perceval Keen, QC, my attorney . . . lawyer.'

'Thank you, Mr Keen,' Wilde said, picking up his hat.

'What for, young man?' Keen looked the reprobate up and

down. 'Hell will freeze over before I represent people like you.'

The keys rattled and the locks crashed. And Oscar Wilde was alone.

TEN

Mrs Rackstraw had been more vigilant that morning and had managed to get some breakfast down her gentlemen. They had no idea that giving them the food of champions before nine in the morning had become her main aim in life, and ate it with their usual mix of relish and total lack of concentration that was their typical morning mood. She stood at the baize door, her hands folded serenely in front of her apron as they bustled out into the street, leaving a wrecked table in their wake, the melange of kipper bones, eggshells and crumbs that made her so happy.

'Is it me?' Grand said as he hailed a cab on the corner, 'or is Mrs Rackstraw getting a bit peculiar?'

Batchelor looked nonplussed. '*Getting* a bit peculiar?' he asked.

Grand chuckled as he climbed into the hansom. 'Nightingale Lane,' he told the driver, and with a flick of a whip they were trundling west. 'That's true, but she watches us like a hawk these days. It's getting a bit creepy.'

'I suppose she's worrying about what will happen when you marry Lady Caroline,' Batchelor suggested. And she wasn't the only one.

'Why?' Grand was the nonplussed one now.

'Well . . . you'll have your own establishment. I can't afford to keep myself the way you have been keeping us. On my share of the business, I'll need to take rooms somewhere. And we have the added expense of Martin now.' He hadn't meant to have this conversation yet, and certainly not above the rattle of a hansom through the morning traffic, but here he was.

'I suppose I had never really thought about it. I know Caro has been looking at places. And dresses. And honeymoon destinations. And bridesmaids . . .' His voice died away. 'It looks as if this marriage might actually happen, James.'

'Isn't that the idea of an engagement?' Batchelor was wryly amused. His friend and colleague had swum around the edges of marriage often enough, but now he was caught in the vortex and circling the drain.

'I met her mother last night.' Grand couldn't suppress a small shudder.

'You've met the woman before, surely?' Batchelor said. Even he, who had never even contemplated marriage, had met enough mothers to give him nightmares till doomsday.

'Of course, of course. But only when there are other people there. Her pa is a nice enough old cuss. Quiet, sits by himself a lot, drinking port.'

Both men were silent for a moment, taking in the import of that thought.

'But the mother. Oh, my land!' It must have been talk of mothers that made Grand temporarily regress; the phrase was pure Boston.

That seemed to be all there was, so Batchelor prompted him a little. 'Difficult lady?'

'Difficult doesn't even begin to describe her,' Grand said. 'She's . . . she's . . . impossible. That's all.' He sank his chin on his chest and contemplated his toes.

'And you're afraid Lady Caroline is going to be like her?' Batchelor said, gently.

Grand looked at him with eyes hollow with worry. 'Is she?' he asked, grabbing Batchelor's sleeve.

'Don't ask me,' Batchelor said, shaking him off. 'You're the expert where women are concerned. I know you love Lady Caroline, or at least, I assume you do. She has lasted longer than any woman you've ever known; she's beautiful, she's clever, she's well-connected . . .'

'She is a bit of a harridan,' Grand said, gloomily.

Batchelor nodded and patted his friend's arm. 'She can be, I admit. But also, surely, she has a softer side?'

A slow smile crept across Grand's face. 'Oh, has she! Oh, yes, James. She can be . . .' He became aware of the cabbie leaning in to listen and turned his face upwards. 'Oi!' he shouted. 'Are we there yet?'

'Sorry, sir,' the cabbie said. He loved a bit of upper-crust tittle-tattle; it gave him something to tell the wife when he got home.

Grand subsided into his seat. 'So, the long and short of it, James, is I'm not at all sure. Do I want to become a quiet old geezer drinking myself to death on port? Or do I get out while the going's good?'

'It's never too late, these days,' Batchelor said. 'There's always divorce.'

'I'm too long in the tooth to look at it like that,' Grand said. 'And Lady Caroline's no spring chicken. If we want little uns, that is.' He sighed. 'I'll work it out, never you fear.'

'Nearly there, guv,' the cabbie called from above.

'So, enough about me. What about this Watts guy?'

'Well, he was married to Ellen Terry for less than a year—'

'Got to interrupt there, guv,' the cabbie leaned forward. 'My missus is a bit of a follower of the theay-ter, you know what I mean. She knows all the wossname, gossip. And the gossip is, he's only just got his decree thingummy.'

'Nisi?' Batchelor suggested.

'Prob'ly. And it's been ten years since she buggered off wiv that bloke.'

'Godwin.' Batchelor wasn't as good as Martin, but he wasn't bad.

'Thass him.'

That seemed to be the sum total of the cabbie's knowledge, and they had arrived at their destination. To show his displeasure at being eavesdropped on, Grand didn't give him a tip. To show his gratitude for a bit of gossip, Batchelor slipped the man sixpence.

The hansom rattled away and they looked at the house, set back behind a shrubbery from the pavement. To their right, a portion of the building was glass-roofed like an orangery and was obviously a studio. The rest was simply a large London residence for a gentleman of comfortable means. Behind it, the trees of Frederic Leighton's estate were coming into full leaf and brought light and movement to a rather dour pile of brick and tile.

'These tales of artists starving in garrets, James?' Grand ventured.

'What about them?'

'Do they? Ever starve in garrets?'

'I suppose so. But not as often as the stories would suggest, I imagine.' Batchelor looked along the impressive frontage of Watts' house. 'You could starve in here because you couldn't find your way out, but that would be the only reason, I would think. Anyway,' Batchelor extended a hand, 'your turn to knock?'

'I believe it is.' Grand opened the low, wrought-iron gate and walked up the tiled path. Windows looked blindly down at him from the first floor and the house seemed empty. He knew from experience that behind the scenes, servants of every level would be beavering away keeping everything spick and span – even an artist needs to have clean clothes and fires lit. And sure enough, on his knock, the door was flung open by a young man in the generic uniform of a footman who also brings the coal in and cleans the windows.

'Mr Watts?' Grand asked.

The footman looked at him dubiously. 'I'm not sure he's At Home,' he said, through his nose. He was obviously taking condescension lessons from a retired butler somewhere in the suburbs. He hadn't quite got it pat yet; he just sounded as if he had a heavy cold.

'Could you find out?' Batchelor said, leaning forward and proffering a card.

The footman took it as if it might have rabies and bore it away.

Grand said, rummaging in his pocket and coming out with a florin, 'Two bob says he comes back and tells us Mr Watts says he isn't here.'

Batchelor thought. The footman looked fairly dim, but that kind of thing was very much for the newly employed and he had noticed his uniform had wear around the buttons. 'You're on,' he said, checking he had a florin, just in case.

After a pause, the footman was back. 'Mr Watts says he isn't here,' he said.

Batchelor pressed the coin into Grand's hand, held behind his back for the purpose.

It was time to lean. 'Did you not see what's on the card,

boy?' Grand said, ratcheting up the hard-boiled American. 'Enquiry agents?'

'I seen . . . I mean, I *saw* it, sir,' the footman said, nasal as ever.

'That means we work with the police,' Grand said, putting a lot of emphasis on the 'p' word.

'They've just left,' the footman said, in the tones of one scoring a point.

'Precisely,' Grand added smoothly. 'We're here to just clear up a few questions. They're busy men, the police. They can't keep on coming back for nothing.'

The footman was undecided. Nothing in his *Instructions for Footmen by a Gentleman's Gentleman* told him how to cope with this eventuality. He chewed his lip and looked the enquiry agents up and down. They *seemed* to be respectable enough, pressed clothes, clean boots – he had just come up from boot boy, so knew you could tell a gent from his footwear – so he decided to go and make sure that Mr Watts realized who he was turning away. 'Mr Watts is painting,' he said in his normal voice, which was a little high and whining. 'He's got behind and—'

Batchelor realized the lad was unsure of his ground and reassured him. 'Mr Watts will be saved an awful lot of bother if he sees us today,' he said. 'Saves him having to go to the police station, give evidence, perhaps even go to court . . .'

The footman legged it and was back red-faced in a moment. 'Mr Watts will see you now,' he said, remembering to use his nose. 'Will you walk this way?'

The lad was noticeably pigeon-toed and Grand and Batchelor did their customary step or two in the same style, before reverting to their sober, grown-up selves to be ushered into the presence.

Watts was only just turned sixty but looked older. The Old Testament prophet look was definitely in vogue this year. The spring sunshine shone harshly on his balding head, the sparse hair springing up and looking almost like a halo. The old man was clearly in a towering temper and the footman disappeared back through the studio door like a jack rabbit.

'Mr Watts?' Grand began, politely.

'No, of course not!' the old man said, irritably. 'I am actually the bloody Akond of Swat. Why would George Frederic Watts, after all, be in the studio of George Frederic Watts, dressed in his painting garb and holding a paintbrush? It isn't as if – is it? – he is the foremost allegorical painter of the age or anything. Well? Don't just stand there like an idiot. Answer me.'

Batchelor butted in. 'Very amusing, Mr Watts,' he said, employing his best police speak. 'Not just an allegorical painter, but an extremely amusing raconteur, I can tell. But actually, your answers could be construed as perverting the course of justice, interfering with the police in the pursuance of their—'

'Don't give me that, Batchelor,' Watts snapped. 'I remember you when you were a bloody cub reporter on the *Telegraph*. I never forget a face. In fact, I think if you look in the background of one or two of my larger works, you may find yourself there. You have an interesting face, if a little weaselly. I was not taken in, gentlemen, by your threats of being connected with the police. I happen to know they wouldn't touch you with a bargepole. I merely find myself with time to spare because my goddamned model hasn't turned up. Again. Excuse my French.'

Grand and Batchelor looked meaningfully at each other.

'If it's Evangeline French you're waiting for . . .' Batchelor said.

'I'll wait for ever,' Watts said, dabbling his brush in some oil of turpentine and carefully drying it on his smock. 'She's dead as a nit, according to the policemen who have just left.'

'You don't seem . . . upset,' Grand ventured.

'Upset? Upset? Well, any man's death diminishes me, if I can quote John Donne for a moment there. But she was only a model, you know. Not the queen or anything. Not my wife.'

'Or your mistress?' Batchelor hinted.

'I think you must be confusing me with animals like Rossetti and his ilk. Excellent painter, don't get me wrong, but can't keep it in his trousers for love nor money. They're all the same, deep down. Marrying each other's wives, getting their models pregnant, there's no end to it. That's why I don't have much to do with them. I really can't be doing with it.

I keep up with Valentine Prinsep and John Stanhope, two of my students, you know, but that's about all. They are only second-rate, alas, but they make a living, as I understand it. But even those two I see less of these days – they do so love to hobnob.'

'What about your other students?' Grand asked. 'Do you see them? Do they use the same models as you?'

'I only ever had the three. And no, they don't use the same models. I hate to see the same faces over and over again. That woman with the face like a spoon, that generic pre-Raphaelite person – what's her name? Bound to be Jane or Lizzie, they all use the same names these days. Well, her; she's in all the paintings which are hung in any gallery. It's enough to give you the fits. I use models sparingly and then I don't always do their faces as they are.'

'But Evangeline was very recognizable . . .'

'Is it the *Ariadne* you're talking about?'

'Yes,' Grand said, assuming that was so.

'Well, it wasn't something I was particularly invested in, to be honest. I am more interested now in my allegorical works, proving that all emotion and all of the human condition can be shown through art. This one, for example,' he gestured to the huge canvas behind him, 'is the Angel of Death. My intention here is to show that death is not choosy. He – or she; you see I have made the angel androgynous and the face very vague – is not swayed by the human condition, but comes to all without fear nor favour.'

'If Evangeline had been in it,' Batchelor said, 'it would have made it worth more money.'

Watts looked at him as if he had passed wind in church. 'More money?' he said, horrified. 'What need have I of *more money*? Again, the other artists seek the gold of the buying public, whereas I' – he raised his chin and his beard stuck out like a bottle brush – 'I am above all that. I am G.F. Watts, after all. Do you know,' he lowered his chin again and spoke low, as if the walls had ears, 'when I go out, I have to wear a disguise, for fear I am recognized and mobbed.'

'My goodness.' Batchelor managed to think of something to say, though he had to agree it wasn't much.

'Yes. When I go out sketching, I wear a cape and a wide hat, pulled low. There are so very many peculiar people about.'

'I don't expect that makes you look like an artist,' Grand said, employing all his powers of irony.

'Well spotted!' Watts agreed. 'Indeed it does not. With a cane in my hand, I look like any gentleman out for a stroll. And then, when I see a pretty girl, or an interesting face or figure, I whip out my notebook and charcoal and sketch a likeness. Parks are a good place. Gardens in squares. Public houses, at a pinch.'

'I see.' Batchelor tried not to sound excited. 'Do you use the Cremorne?'

'I do, sometimes. But that idiot Whistler has rather spoiled the Cremorne for me. That thing of his in Purple and Dun or whatever it's called.'

'*Nocturne in Blue and Gold*,' Batchelor said.

'If you say so.'

Grand decided to move on. 'So what model hasn't turned up?' he asked.

'This one.' Watts gestured to the bottom left of the painting to where a figure was roughly sketched in. 'It's a cripple, showing death has no mercy. He is in supplication. See, can you see the head twisted towards Death, but to no avail.'

'A man?' Batchelor asked.

'Yes,' Watts said, with acid sarcasm. 'Not all paintings are full of nude women, you know, Mr Batchelor – except all of Leighton's, of course – though that may be all you are interested in, of course.'

'Not at all,' Batchelor replied, hotly. 'I think . . . well, our minds are rather more on female models just now.'

Watts had the grace to look a little shamefaced. 'I apologize,' he said. 'I was very flippant about poor Evangeline earlier and that was wrong of me. A nice enough girl in her way and a good model. She could adopt the oddest poses for hours without complaint. The best models for that are soldiers, oddly enough. If that ghastly Butler woman hasn't collared them all. This one,' and he pointed to the painting again, 'was to have been a private from the Twenty-First Hussars. They have barracks just—'

'Yes,' Grand said, with a sidelong look at Batchelor, 'we know where their barracks are.'

'I use their chaps a lot. I have to watch them; they are a bit light-fingered, some of them. But isn't everyone, these days? And, I say these days . . .'

Grand could smell an old man's rant coming on. His father was much the same.

'I gave up taking students because things kept going missing. They denied it, of course, and I suppose it could have been the servants, but I had had enough. And I didn't need the money, as I may have said.'

Grand and Batchelor nodded in solemn agreement.

'So I just got rid of them. We're friends now, I suppose. But mostly, I keep to myself.' Watts suddenly and rather disconcertingly closed one eye and put his hands out in front of his face, the thumbs and forefingers making a frame. He lined Grand up and turned his head this way and that. 'Do you have muscles under that coat?' he asked, suddenly.

'Well,' Grand was suddenly bashful. 'I guess I'm not what I was . . .'

'But still, muscles in all the right places?'

Batchelor could see what was coming but Grand could not. 'I guess so.'

'Perfect.' Watts started to undo Grand's coat. 'Let's get you stripped off and down on your knees. Look, I have a crutch and everything. There's a robe, somewhere, but I could manage without if you'd rather be naked.' Watts cocked his head like a robin spying a worm. 'Well, come on. Sooner you're done, sooner you're done.'

'But . . . I . . .' An idea occurred to Grand and he snatched his coat out of the old man's hands and started to do the buttons back up. 'You said that character is a cripple, right?'

'Right.' Watts couldn't see where this was leading.

'Well, you said did I have muscles, and I do. So, you don't want me for a cripple, do you? You want . . . well, you want a cripple.'

Watts looked at him in horror and made another assault on his coat. 'Nonsense! Whoever heard of anything so bloody ridiculous. Who wants a cripple up on their wall?' He had managed to get the coat half off Grand's shoulders. He was surprisingly strong. 'You'll be perfect.'

Grand wrenched himself free. 'No, I will *not* be perfect,' he said. 'I don't have the time and, anyway, I am subject to cramp if I stay in one position. Mr Batchelor here will bear me out.'

'Come, Matthew,' Batchelor said, helping Watts divest Grand of his coat. 'Just drop the kecks and let Mr Watts drape you in this toga thing here. That's it. On your knees . . .' Batchelor pushed him down. 'What else, Mr Watts?'

'Oh, oh,' Watts was scurrying around gathering his paints, 'if you can just lean on the knuckles of one hand . . . no, no, not that, the left. That's it. And lean on the crutch under the other arm. Careful . . .'

'God almighty!' Grand said. 'What the hell was that?'

'There might be a few splinters. There. Now, lean over to the left. Not on the knuckles, no, leave those there. Just lean. Now, turn your head around and look up. At that point on the skylight, if you will. Perfect.'

Batchelor looked down at Grand and knew he would not be forgiven for this for a good long while. But it was worth it.

'You'll pay for this,' Grand muttered.

'Yes, yes. Usual rates,' Watts said. 'Now, no talking. Genius is happening over here. And that's all that matters, after all, isn't it, gentlemen?'

'Ah.' Moses Metcalfe was waiting for the kettle to boil. The Walton Street nick wasn't exactly state of the art, but the occasional mod con had crept in; a kettle was one example. 'How's the surveillance business, Twisleton?'

'I think they're on to me, guv.' The constable was grateful to put his feet up. At least the weather was half decent – if it was raining it would be ten times worse.

'What makes you think that?' Metcalfe was lolling back in his chair, resting his clasped hands across his ample paunch.

'They split up,' Twisleton told him. 'One on a bus, the other in a cab.'

'Who did you follow?'

'Batchelor. I figured I could watch the comings and goings off a bus easier than trailing a cab. I mean, they're all so bloody alike, aren't they?'

'Seen one, seen 'em all,' Metcalfe concurred. 'Well, don't make me suffer. Where'd they go?'

Twisleton passed his notebook to his chief. Barnes arrived with two chipped cups. 'Oh, didn't see you there, Twis,' he said. 'Cuppa?'

'Thanks. I'm parched.'

'Hold that thought, Barnes.' Metcalfe stopped the man in his tracks. 'What's this, Twisleton? Grand and Batchelor had breakfast with Daddy Bliss?'

'Yessir,' the tail said. 'In the Inglenook as per my notes. Couldn't quite make out what they had.'

'Bugger what they *had*, Twisleton!' Metcalfe snapped. 'I want to know what they *said*. Next time, I'll send somebody who can lip-read. Never mind, they won't have got much out of Daddy; tight as a gnat's arse, that one. Who's this?' Twisleton may not have been able to read lips, but he could read upside down, especially when the writing was his own.

'G.F. Watts, guv,' Twisleton said. 'Painter.'

'Yes, I know who he is, Constable, thank you. Young Barnes and I could only have left there half an hour before – if that – if your timings are correct.'

'So he's part of the Cremorne case?' Twisleton asked.

Metcalfe slurped his tea and looked at the man narrowly. 'I've been telling everybody you're a university graduate, Twisleton – Oxford. Is that true?'

'Yessir.' Twisleton sat upright.

'Did you actually pass?' the inspector asked. 'Do you have a degree?'

'No, sir,' Twisleton acknowledged. 'I went down.'

'Went, or were sent?' Metcalfe queried.

'Er . . . technically, the former.'

'Oh, *now* he comes out with the long words!' Metcalfe was rummaging among his papers, looking for his pipe. 'You'll forgive me for saying this, Twisleton, but for an Oxford man, you sound very much like Walthamstow.'

Twisleton shrugged. 'It's a persona I adopted,' his accent was suddenly cut-glass, 'so as to blend with the hoi polloi.'

Metcalfe looked at him. 'Stick to Walthamstow,' he advised the man, 'for fear I may have to start looking up to you. Why did you "go down", as you snobby boys apparently say?'

'There was a bit of a misunderstanding with a bedder – er, maid, sir. Put it about that I was the father of her child.'

'And were you?'

'Probably.'

'Well, that's something, at least,' Metcalfe said. 'I thought all you Oxford types were Maryannes.'

'I didn't go to Merton, Inspector!' Twisleton reminded him.

'Right,' Metcalfe sighed. 'So, Grand and Batchelor are half an hour behind us. But *they* don't have' – he slid a piece of paper across the table – 'this.'

Barnes had come back with Twisleton's tea. He pulled up a chair and read the contents of the paper. 'So, it *was* cyanide,' he said, 'Evangeline French.'

'They don't muck about at Tommy's,' Metcalfe said. 'If St Thomas's Hospital says "cyanide", who are we to query it?'

'So, why the lake, guv?' Barnes asked. 'It fits the pattern of the others, and yet . . .'

'He's experimenting,' Twisleton said.

'Do what?' Metcalfe frowned.

'The murderer. He's trying out new ideas, a bit like a painter, talking of G.F. Watts. First he'll try gouache, then oils, turn his canvas to landscape or portrait, try reds and blues or greens and browns, searching for just the right milieu.'

'Walthamstow,' Metcalfe reminded Twisleton quietly.

'What suits him best,' Twisleton lapsed effortlessly into his East London alter ego again.

'So,' Metcalfe was thinking it through, 'he didn't like leaving his corpses on dry land, so he dunks this one in the water.'

Barnes was trying to piece things together. 'First one, eighteen months ago, mind you, lying on the grass.'

'Posed?' Metcalfe asked.

Barnes looked at him oddly.

'Were her parts on display, Constable?' Metcalfe had to spell it out.

'No note of that, sir,' he said, more than a little horrified.

'What about the second one?' Metcalfe asked. 'The first in the current series.'

'Sitting on a bench,' Barnes reminded him.

'And the fourth in the lake.'

'What happened to the third?' Had Twisleton left the bedder alone, he would have gained a BSc in Advanced Mathematics, so he couldn't let that go. As he was usually on surveillance duty, he was not all that au fait with the Cremorne case.

'Bloke,' Metcalfe said. 'Some sort of peculiar Maryanne.'

'Found half-hidden under a bush,' Barnes told him.

'So, he's different, then?' Twisleton said.

'Bravo, Constable.' Metcalfe had at last found his pipe. Now the search was on for the tobacco. 'I can see all those weeks at Oxford weren't totally wasted.'

'No, I mean, apart from the gender issue . . . er . . . the fact that he was a bloke. *Hiding* the body isn't what our friend does, is it? He's proud of his work, wants us all to see it.'

'And there was no book,' Barnes nodded.

'Book?' This was the first that Twisleton had heard of any books being involved.

'Books were found near the deceased in the cases of all three women but not the man. These.' He passed the list to Twisleton, miraculously to hand given the chaos of his desk.

'Well, look at that!' Twisleton chuckled.

'What?' Metcalfe was losing his grip on the conversation.

'*King of the Golden River* by John Ruskin.'

'So?' Metcalfe snapped.

'I don't think you got to the end of my report, guv,' Twisleton said. 'Altercation . . . um . . . punch-up between two geezers in the Aldwych – Whistler and Ruskin.'

Metcalfe pursed his lips. These university men needed keeping in their place. 'Common enough name,' he said, tapping some papers into a neater pile and inadvertently finding his tobacco. 'I had an old teacher called Ruskin.' This was a lie, but it needed saying. Altogether too uppity, some of these youngsters.

'Well done, sir.' Twisleton realized he was letting his sarcasm show and carried on, more humbly. 'Be that as it may, though

– this was not just someone called Ruskin; this was *the* John Ruskin. Author of this book. And he was fighting with a client of Grand and Batchelor.'

Twisleton waited for the penny to drop and had the pleasure of seeing Metcalfe's eyes start out of his head. 'Do I still have to follow them, guv?' He realized as he spoke what the answer would be.

'Still have to follow them?' Metcalfe said. 'Keep on their trail even more, Constable Twisleton. Don't take your eyes off them.' He slammed his hand down on the desk and his tobacco pouch jumped off and scattered its contents on the floor. 'I *knew* there was something dodgy about those two. Enquiry agents, my arse. I'll have them in quod before this week is out, or my name's not Thomas Fazackerley Metcalfe.'

Batchelor looked at his friend with a smile on his face, but it wasn't unkind. He had always stood out among the reporters at the *Telegraph* as being reasonably fit, but next to Grand, he was a weakling. So to see the American hobble from the drinks tray, using the furniture for support, and then have to lower himself onto his chair with muted cries of pain did make rather a pleasant change.

Stifling an urge to laugh, he said, 'Are you all right, Matthew? Really, don't just grunt.' He'd had little else as response ever since the cabbie had helped him half carry the American in that evening. 'I will be the first to admit it didn't look very comfortable, but you didn't complain at the time.'

Grand took a huge swig of his bourbon and leaned carefully back in his chair. 'At the time,' he said, not moving his head, 'it didn't hurt. There were pins and needles for a while, but after that, nothing. I think the splinter in the armpit was the worst, but even that went away after a bit.'

'You should have said,' Batchelor said with exaggerated sympathy.

'Every time I opened my mouth to speak, that mad old bastard told me to be quiet.'

'You didn't *have* to stay,' Batchelor pointed out. 'You weren't doing it for the fee, after all. You could have just got up and walked away.'

Grand closed his eyes. 'I could,' he agreed, 'I could. Looking back now, I don't know why I didn't. But there's something about him, I don't know – he doesn't shout, and he isn't very big, but you don't want to cross him. Do you know what I mean?'

Batchelor did. He hadn't been half naked on his knees at the time, but even so, the strength of the man's personality had been very strong. He nodded, then realized that Grand couldn't turn his head to the right yet to get him in his eyeline, so added, 'Yes, I do.'

'I reckon he's our man,' Grand said, sipping his drink. He really wanted to knock it back in one, but just didn't have the neck muscles for it right then.

'No!' Batchelor laughed. 'Of course he isn't. Look at him – he's old.'

'He *looks* old,' Grand corrected him. 'Did you see him wrestle me out of my coat? And shinning up and down ladders all day for those big canvases. Moving the big canvases, if it comes to that. No, mark my words, he's our boy.'

'Why?' Batchelor thought that was a perfectly reasonable question.

'Why? When did "why" ever matter? Because he's bonkers. Because Evangeline French had something on him and so he wanted her dead.'

'And the others?'

'Time will tell,' Grand said, portentously, 'that they were also his models. As was,' he waggled his glass at Batchelor who took pity and refilled it for him, 'Anstruther Peebles.'

'Unlikely?' suggested Batchelor, handed him his glass.

'Why? His regiment supplies models to Watts. Why not him?'

'Well, he's a lieutenant. Surely, it's only the ranks who model for pocket money.'

'Or a lieutenant with an expensive prostitute habit. Men with his preferences don't get their pleasures cheap.'

Batchelor twirled his own glass round a few times, looking into the amber depths as though the truth was in there somewhere. 'I concede that, then,' he said, finally. 'But I don't think it's him, all the same. What about Clara Jenkins and Mabel Glossop? Did they have something on him too?'

'Why not? You've met Whistler and Ruskin. You know how weird these artists are.'

'I still think that if you let one model find out something about you, you make sure the rest don't do the same. Killing everybody who knows something about the skeletons in your closet is a bit . . . draconian.' Batchelor preferred an easy life and was pretty sure that murderers in the main felt the same.

'It could be that he killed Mabel Glossop to hide the murder of Evangeline French.'

'Eighteen months in advance? That's what I *call* planning ahead.' Batchelor was willing to push a point but that was really a step too far.

Grand sank his chin on his chest and gave a small scream of pain. 'James! James! Help me lift my head back up.'

'For heaven's sake, Matthew.' Batchelor put a hand under his friend's chin and one on the back of his head and eased him gently upright. 'You just posed for a while, that's all. Pity the poor souls who do it all the time.'

Grand would have nodded, but decided not to. 'They have training. They must do. I can hardly move a muscle. I'm all right in a few positions. It's getting between them that gives me gyp.'

'Do you want me to send round for Caroline?'

Grand rolled his eyes at him. 'Her mother might come. No, strike that. Her mother *would* come.'

'Or worse,' Batchelor laughed, 'her mother might come *instead.*'

Grand held his ribs and tried not to laugh. 'That hurts, James,' he moaned. 'Stop it.'

'Or,' Batchelor held up his finger as if he had suddenly had an epiphany, 'we could introduce her to Watts as a model and when she finds out something about him, he can try to kill her, but she gets him instead. How about that?'

'You're mocking me, James, and it's not fair. I'm not well.'

'You're perfectly well,' Batchelor said. 'Just a bit creaky. My old granny would have you in a hot bath full of mustard by now, and *that* would larn ya!'

'A bit odd, was she, your old granny?' Grand eased one buttock carefully and extended his leg. There was a crack and

Batchelor jumped. 'No, no, leave me. That was quite good as it happens.' He tried the other leg. 'I'll probably be able to blink without help by tomorrow.' He closed his eyes. 'If I never see another artist again as long as I live, James, it will be too soon.'

Batchelor thought it would be cruel to remind him that their main client was James McNeill Whistler, Nocturnist extraordinaire. When he ached a bit less would be soon enough.

ELEVEN

John Stanhope stood back from the canvas and looked at it first with one eye, then the other.

George Frederic Watts stood by his side, hands clasped complacently across the front of his smock. 'Well, John? What do you think of my angel of death?'

'Is it . . .' Stanhope knew he must be diplomatic. 'Is it . . . a trifle *gloomy*, George?'

Watts bridled slightly, but knew from sad experience that everyone was an idiot when it came to art. 'Not all angels can have pink wings, John,' he said, sniffily.

Stanhope knew he had got away lightly. 'Eros, George,' he said. 'My *Eros* has pink wings. But point taken, nonetheless. This is one of your allegories, I take it.'

Watts brightened up. 'Not finished yet, of course, dear chap. It's finding the models which is so tricky, don't you find? That one,' he pointed to the figure in the foreground, 'is an enquiry agent, if you would believe it.'

'Looks like one of your soldier chappies,' Stanhope remarked. He swept an eloquent finger down the line of a muscle. 'You don't think of enquiry agents needing musculature like that.'

'No, indeed,' Watts said. 'He kept as still as a rock, you know, for simply hours. I don't think he needs the money, though, so I doubt I will see him again.'

'That's too bad,' Stanhope said. He did feel for his old mentor – finding models was one of the most difficult things about being a painter, that was certain. 'I know Val had the most awful trouble getting those women for his *Linen-Gatherers*. Do you know,' and his eyes were wide, 'they objected to carrying wet clothes?'

Watts tutted. 'Really!' he said. 'Where is the verisimilitude?'

'Indeed.' Stanhope looked at the painting again. 'But, we

digress. How did you happen to end up with an almost nude enquiry agent in your studio – or shouldn't I ask?'

'It's all Evangeline's fault,' Watts said, grumpily, 'though I suppose one shouldn't speak ill of the dead.'

'Dead?' Stanhope was horrified. 'But Lizzie was at a Morning at Effie Millais's the other day and Evangeline was there. She was looking quite well, Lizzie said.'

'Murdered, dear boy,' Watts said, suddenly leaning forward and dabbing at Grand's right thigh with a dry brush. 'Sorry. Fly caught in the paint.'

'Murdered? Do we know by whom?' Stanhope was not one to let his grammar lapse simply because someone he knew had been done to death.

'Yes to the first, no to the second. Although,' Watts chuckled drily, 'I think they may rather suspect me.'

Stanhope looked at his feet. Ever since Ellen Terry had walked out on him, Watts had been something of a hermit, or so his friends all thought. Could it be that his recent decree nisi had brought out the beast in him at last? Stanhope coughed delicately. 'You and she . . . weren't . . .?' He blushed almost purple.

Watts took pity. 'That's a rather interesting colour you've gone there, John,' he said, peering closer. 'Just what I need for my angel's shadows. Hold still while I make a note – I may be able to mix it from scratch.'

'Very amusing, George,' Stanhope snapped. 'I merely ask because we have all worried about you. Wondered, perhaps, more than worried. You are by no means an old man . . .'

'Thank you, John.' Watts patted his hand. 'No, Evangeline and I weren't whatever you were struggling to say. I can't say I have not had my moments in the last ten years, but they have not involved my models. I feel I have a duty of care towards them. I pay proper rates. I give them meals if they are here all day. Some sleep here when the job is a long one. But not by my side, I can assure you.'

Stanhope let out his breath. 'Sorry to ask,' he mumbled.

'I do understand,' Watts said, unscrewing the lids of small pots on a table under the window. 'I know people love to gossip. And I was fond of Evangeline, as it happens. But she was too . . . vain for my tastes. As you know, John, I am a simple man and don't like to put myself forward.'

It was as well he had his back to Stanhope so he couldn't see the wry grin on his face. Watts had been known to storm out of showings if he wasn't recognized in the first ten seconds.

'What are you doing?' Stanhope asked, taking a step forward.

Without turning round, Watts put an arm in the air. 'Don't approach, John, please. Some of these pigments contain poisons and I don't like mixing when people who are not used to exposure are nearby.'

Stanhope took the criticism well – he had heard it many times over the years. The painters who mixed their own pigments looked down on those who had them delivered by Messrs Winsor and Newton. But as far as Stanhope could see, what was good enough for John Constable was good enough for him and, in a couple of generations' time, it would be intriguing to be able to come back and see whose paintings still looked as good as new and whose had peeled off the canvas with a waft of rotten egg.

Watts added one more pinch from a final jar and turned, mixing a pot of brownish purple with a spatula. 'There!' he said, holding it up. 'The colour of your cheeks when you accuse me of philandering with models and, incidentally, perfect for the shadows of death.' He held it up to the light and grimaced. 'Have you seen your medical man lately, John?'

Stanhope was taken back to his student days when he and Valentine and Giuseppe had sat at the feet of the master, accepting his veiled – and not so veiled – insults and hoping that it would make them good artists. He knew Watts didn't think that they had made the grade and, indeed had thrown Giuseppe out bag and baggage when the man had dared to criticize one of Watts' own paintings. Watts had not been fair. He had lined up four works and asked them, one by one, to pick out the worst one and move it aside, the idea being that the best one would prevail. He had masked off the signatures and it really had been impossible to tell whose work each one was. Valentine Prinsep – Watts' favourite and the baby of the group – had gone first and had picked an un-hung Ruskin. It

was an easy pick, representing something of an off day for
the critic. With the odds still long, Stanhope had gone next
and had picked a Siddal. Lizzie had been a nice enough woman,
but was to painting what Queen Victoria was to tightrope
walking. Giuseppe had not worked out what he and Val had
done; that one of the works was by Watts himself. The signs
were there, the figures tending to lounge, the rather dour
subject, and they had avoided it like the plague. But now,
Giuseppe had a choice of only two, and the other was a rather
lovely study by Rossetti of a girl's head. It was streets ahead
of the Watts, but the muse of art was not smiling on Giuseppe
that day. Without even pausing, he picked up the Watts and
put it in the reject pile. He and his belongings were gone that
afternoon.

'Penny for your thoughts?' Watts said. He pulled a cord by
the fireplace. 'Shall we have some tea? Let's sit over here,
shall we?'

'Hmm?' Stanhope came back to the present. 'Tea would be
splendid. Shouldn't you wash your hands?'

Watts looked down at his paint-flecked fingers. 'Why?'

'Well, the poison and everything.'

Watts laughed. 'I am sure that's overdone, you know, John.
Just rumours put about by you ready-made chaps. I've never
felt any ill effects and I have been mixing paints since Adam
was in the militia. But, as I said, penny for your thoughts.'

Stanhope had forgotten this trait – Watts never gave up on
an idea once it was in his head. 'I was thinking about the old
days. Whatever happened to Giuseppe, do you know?'

Watts shrugged. 'I have no idea. I know he never paid his
last term's tuition fees, but after that, no, nothing. He was no
longer at his lodgings when I sent the bailiffs in, that I do
know.'

Stanhope couldn't help feeling a little shocked. Watts had
sacked the man, after all.

'I expect he got a job somewhere within his capabilities.
Illustrating cheap books for Mr Smith, perhaps, or newspaper
advertisements. That would be his level.'

Stanhope thought it was probably best not to mention Pears
soap.

'I often wondered, George. Was he actually of Italian extraction? Val and I asked him but he was always evasive.'

'I doubt it,' Watts said. 'I suppose his father may have had a barrel organ. Or an ice-cream parlour, perhaps. Further than that, I have no idea. The world is full of good artists, John. Let's not waste our time on bad ones. Now . . .'

He was interrupted by the arrival of the tea and Stanhope waited patiently as it was poured.

'Crumpet?' Watts asked. 'The cake is delicious; I can vouch for that, but the crumpets do go a bit greasy if left to grow cold.'

Stanhope took his cup and nodded yes to a crumpet. Nothing worse than a cold one, he would have to agree.

'Now . . .' Watts settled himself comfortably, putting the crumpets back under their lid to keep them warm and checking the spirit burner underneath.

Might it be possible, Stanhope thought, that this would be the day when George Frederic Watts asked about Lizzie and the children; how Stanhope's new work was coming on? He waited, a crumpet to his lip, oozing butter down his chin to soak into his cravat.

'Now . . .' Watts wiped his buttery fingers with a painty cloth. 'Really, John, what do you *honestly* think of my Angel of Death?'

Twisleton was back in position, watching Grand and Batchelor, but there had been no movement all day. They hadn't gone to the office and the office had not come to them. He knew there were men back at the station who would be delighted to be on special duty allowance just to lounge all day against some railings and occasionally wander to the end of the street to buy a pie from the vendor as he passed, but that wasn't really Twisleton's speed. He preferred to keep moving, keep wheeling, keep dealing, keep bucking for promotion. Although he had not got his degree, he was still a university man at heart. So leaning on a railing, even on a beautiful spring day in a rather nice part of London, was not really testing his brain overmuch.

Twisleton perked up as the front door swung open, but he

sagged again when he saw it was just the rather frightening-looking housekeeper, coming out with a basket over her arm. Why she ever went out shopping, he couldn't fathom. The house seemed to have more deliveries than any other he had ever known. The grocer. The butcher. The knife grinder seemed to be almost in residence. Flowers were delivered. Newspapers. A separate delivery for periodicals. No one could say the household didn't keep local businesses busy. But as for Grand and Batchelor, there was no sign. Even so, Twisleton pulled his hat down a little further as the woman turned in his direction. She didn't look like the noticing type, but even so, he had been there quite a lot over the last days and he didn't want to be spotted. She glanced in his direction, but no more than that as she marched off to her marketing.

A dog came up behind her and sniffed in a determined way at Twisleton's ankles but, apart from that, the afternoon wore its tedious way onwards.

Around the corner, Mrs Rackstraw was leaning forward eagerly and whispering to two men in mufflers and hats pulled, if possible, even lower than Twisleton's. One of them leaned on a gnarled stick, the other was quite upright, but they both nodded with equal enthusiasm at Mrs Rackstraw's news.

She pulled herself upright and walked off smartly in the direction of the butcher's. Mr Juniper had started to take an interest over and above her complaints about the quality of his chops. She had noticed he replaced his apron rather more often than had been his wont, and he clearly was no longer using dripping to keep his hair neat; there had definitely been a whiff of lavender last time she had visited. She had never seen herself as a butcher's wife, but with Mr Grand getting married any day, a person of her means and age had to think of herself. And Mrs Juniper had to be an improvement on Rackstraw.

The men watched her go and the one with the stick chuckled. 'I believe she's sweet on the butcher,' he said.

'She could do worse,' the other said. 'So could he. She's a dab hand with tripe.'

'True. Well, shall we do this thing?'

'Are you bringing the stick?'

'Have to. I'm still as stiff as could be and it might come in handy.'

'Right. After you.'

And the two crept round the corner, quiet as cats.

Alfred Twisleton didn't know quite what hit him for quite a while. And he only found that out when the two men responsible sat him down and explained. One minute, he was leaning on the railings, putting the weight on the other leg, because he was getting pins and needles. He had seen a curtain twitch on the first floor, but his keen eyes told him it was the maid, poor little soul. He had seen her once or twice and, in his opinion, she was about twelve ounces in the pound. He wondered whether anyone was ill indoors. She wasn't usually above the kitchen level after the shaving water had been taken round first thing. He stamped his foot. The pins and needles were developing into a horrible dead feeling. He hated that.

'Now!' A voice appeared to explode in his head and everything went dark. His head and shoulders were swathed in some thick material and his arms were pinioned to his side with something that felt like a thick leather belt. He was pushed over sideways but, before he hit the pavement, he was caught in strong arms and carried away. He heard one of his assailants give a howl of pain and his legs were briefly dropped lower, but soon he felt himself being carried up a short flight of stairs and then he was suddenly untethered and unrolled across a floor like Cleopatra being delivered to Julius Caesar.

Instead, however, of a bald Roman, all Twisleton could see, when his eyes stopped spinning, were two pairs of feet, one tapping a toe impatiently, the other pair clearly very reliant on an associated cane.

'James,' a voice came from over Twisleton's head. 'That isn't Oscar Wilde.'

'Umm . . . no, I can see that. There is a resemblance, though, surely?'

'He's wearing a loud check suit, I grant you.'

'And,' Twisleton said, struggling to his feet, 'I also attended Oxford, which I believe is where Mr Wilde is attempting to gain an education currently. Terrible oik. I remember him clearly.'

'You went to Oxford?' Batchelor said, surprised and more than a little dubious. 'You look a bit like a cheap bookie, no offence.'

Twisleton dusted off his suit. 'This is all the go, actually,' he said. 'But that aside, I am afraid I must arrest both of you gentlemen for assaulting a police officer.' He whipped out his tipstaff and waved it under Grand's nose.

'Police officer?' Grand was now sceptical and took the tipstaff to the window, limping a little. He turned to Batchelor. 'Seems genuine.'

'Of course it's genuine!' Twisleton snatched it back. 'I *am* a police officer. I am Detective Constable Alfred Twisleton, of B Division.'

'Why are you following us?' Batchelor said. 'I'm sure that's against the law.'

'I have been following you because I was told to,' Twisleton said, testily. 'And it isn't against the law.'

'Who told you?' Batchelor was feeling rather foolish now it wasn't Wilde, and that always made him a little testy.

'Inspector Metcalfe, as if it's any of your business,' Twisleton said.

'Idiot,' Batchelor spat and flung himself into a chair.

'So,' Twisleton continued, 'are you going to come quietly, or do I have to call for help?'

'Come quietly?' Batchelor was ready to leap on the man again.

Grand sat down more carefully and extended a hand to invite Twisleton to sit opposite. 'This has all been a misunderstanding,' he said. 'I assume you do admit you do tend to look a little like Oscar Wilde.'

'Not at all,' Twisleton blustered. 'He's . . . well, he's at least half an inch shorter than me. And fatter. And his hair is much more . . .' He quailed under Grand's stare. 'Yes, perhaps we do look a little alike. But why did you think he was following you?'

'We didn't,' Batchelor said. 'We saw you . . .'

'In fact, Daddy Bliss saw you,' Grand admitted. 'Until then, we had no idea.'

'Oh.' Twisleton brightened considerably. He had begun to worry whether he might be losing his touch.

'And then when we *did* spot you, we noticed you looked a lot like Oscar Wilde.'

'Who,' Batchelor added, 'seems to hang around our office a lot.'

Twisleton narrowed his eyes and then laughed. 'You've got Gan Martin working for you, haven't you?' he asked. 'I thought I saw him going into your offices.'

'We have,' Grand admitted.

'Well, that's why Wilde is always there,' Twisleton explained. 'His current mad passion is for Martin. It will soon pass.'

Grand looked puzzled, Batchelor suddenly saw the light.

'I suppose it was him who coined the nickname,' he said.

'Correct,' Twisleton said. 'He uses it all the time. Martin must be about the eighth or ninth Ganymede since Oscar went up. He'll get married or something and Oscar will move on. Happens all the time.'

'Does Martin know?' Batchelor wanted to be there when the penny dropped.

'Doubt it. Not the brightest apple in the barrel, is he?'

'He's amazing at filing,' Grand pointed out.

Twisleton shrugged. To him, that was his point well made.

'And he never forgets *anything*,' Batchelor thought it was only fair to say.

'Hmm. But he has to be told it, doesn't he?'

'Doesn't that apply to everything?' Grand wanted to know.

'No. Of course not. I for instance, have been making assumptions based on what I have seen while following you. They may not all be correct, though I do think your housekeeper has something going on with the butcher, if that's a good enough example.' Grand nodded. So he was right, then. 'But Martin needs to be *told* something. To read it, or see it as a fact, not a supposition. I'm surprised you've taken him on. He doesn't have a detecting sort of brain, I wouldn't have said.'

'He's been quite useful so far,' Batchelor said. 'He noticed some things at the . . . ow!'

'Sorry,' Grand said. 'Hit you on the ankle with my stick,

there. Let's not get too official, Detective Constable Twisleton,'
he said. 'You don't really need the paperwork, do you?'

'All right.' Twisleton came to a decision. 'I'll tell Inspector
Metcalfe you spotted me but that anyway there is nothing to
report. But if you take my advice, stay off the Cremorne case.
Metcalfe is taking it personally and he'll start making arrests
right and left any time soon, so make sure you're not in the
firing line.'

'How did you know we were working on the Cremorne
case?' Batchelor said.

'Well, I didn't,' Twisleton said, 'but I do now. And don't
worry about Wilde. He'll find someone else to batten onto
soon. Hold on – didn't he share a cell with Whistler after that
punch-up?'

'Yes. But surely, Whistler is hardly his type?'

'No,' Twisleton conceded. 'But he's famous. And that's
Oscar's other preoccupation. One day, he'll meet a man who
is famous and beautiful and then the sparks will fly. See if
I'm not right.' He gave a tug at his jacket and retrieved his
hat from where it had rolled under the table. 'I'll see myself
out. Good day, gentlemen.'

The urge came upon him again that night, that rising tension
that made his heart beat faster and the blood pound in his ears.
It was a fine night for a killing. No moon, just the pale glow
of the lanterns and the mist wreathing the river. The ducks
fidgeted in the bushes that ringed the lake and a dog barked
somewhere Battersea way.

There was talk they were going to close this place down.
As it was, he had to wait until the keepers had gone and he
had to use the hairpin he had taken from one of his models,
long ago. He had quite a little collection now: Mabel Glossop's
purse; Clara Jenkins's lucky coin; Evangeline French's
lorgnette. He even had Anstruther Peebles's cigar-cutter, and
he chuckled at that. They reminded him, alone in his little
room at night, of the thrill of the chase; they helped him to
relive it. He would make his selection carefully. The colour
of the hair, the sway of the body, the angle of the head –
everything was important, everything had to be just so. All

that, that wasn't true of Peebles; he was a mistake and – in the end – an interfering busybody who had to be silenced.

Then, there were the books, and he had one in his pocket now as he approached the Cremorne. *Little Women* by Louisa May Alcott. How many little women could he add to his collection before his luck ran out? But his luck would never run out, because luck had nothing to do with it. It was all carefully calculated, planned to the last minute. And the cake was in his bag, delicious and tempting.

He saw them before they saw him; two patrolling bobbies of B Division, the fading light glinting on their helmet plates and buttons.

'Evening, sir.' To run now would invite disaster. He'd have to brazen it out.

'Evening, Constable.'

'Out for a stroll?' one of them asked.

'I wish,' he said. 'I suppose the Gardens are still shut?'

'They are, I'm afraid,' the other copper told him. 'Some rather peculiar goings-on after dark these nights.'

'Tell me something I don't know,' he chuckled and they joined in the joke. The Cremorne had been peculiar for years.

'May we ask what's in the bag, sir?'

He felt his heart jump and his hands, as he gripped the leather handles, felt like lead. He had never been stopped before, let alone searched. Had the world gone mad?

'Of course,' he managed a smile.

'What's this?' One of the coppers held up the package.

'Cake,' he said. 'I'd offer you some, only it's the wife's birthday and I'm late already. Wouldn't do to arrive with half of it missing, would it?'

Both men were married. They understood.

'Well, then, sir,' one of them said, 'mind how you go. Oh, and wish the missus a happy one from us, won't you?'

'I certainly will, officer,' he said. 'Good night.'

He continued on his way, listening to their footfalls fade. He glanced back; they'd gone. Then he doubled back on himself, past the railings and the rhododendron bushes. Then he was at the gate, its wrought iron curling up into the night sky. He checked left and right, then the hairpin did its work and he was in.

He was not the only one who made light of the Cremorne's locks. He knew that most of the harlots whose patch this was had something similar in their folderols to gain entry. Gates had been locked before, but it had never seriously hampered progress, still less damaged business. Ahead of him the lawns stretched grey, dappled now as the cloud broke and the moon peeped through. There was one – tall, angular, not his type at all and he veered away, pulling down the brim of his hat.

'Feeling good-natured, dearie?' The words sliced through his brain like a knife. He must be getting old – he hadn't seen this one at all.

'Not tonight,' he said. She was squat and dark. They were all the same length lying down, of course, but he didn't want them lying down; at least, not in the way they meant.

'Suit yourself.' And she muttered something unpleasant as he moved away. The girls here may have had hatpins, but their customers didn't, and men in the Cremorne after dark were rarer than hens' teeth now. A girl couldn't afford to strike out too often.

There was a couple canoodling beyond the lake, an elderly gent who wouldn't last long. He couldn't wait because it was likely she would see the old boy off the premises and that would make his life very difficult. Another opportunity missed.

Another girl caught his eye as he rounded the corner, following the curve of the pagoda path. She couldn't have been more than twenty and he liked the way her breasts threatened to leave her bodice. She was walking slowly and he caught her eye too. She stopped and swayed, jutting out her right hip, and she undid her bonnet, letting her blonde hair cascade onto her shoulders.

'Are you feeling good-natured, dearie?' She was speaking the words, but not to him. A shady character sauntered out from the pagoda's arches. He was tall and dark and he reached out to touch her arm. Coins twinkled in the half-light and they moved away, a couple, if only for a few moments, the melody of her laughter stifled by a kiss.

Shit! He turned sharply and saw beyond the railings the

patrolling bobbies he'd met earlier. He ducked back into the bushes. The red mist had gone. He could no longer hear his heart. There would be other nights, other chances.

Time to go home.

'Joe!' Terence Saunders stood at the top of the basement stairs and shouted down into the depths. The morning post was still in his hand and he still wore his top coat. 'The gamekeeper's daughter!'

The old man jerked awake, the voice from on high not what he was expecting from the Last Trump. He let out an involuntary, incoherent shriek. Saunders clattered down the stairs and flung the door open onto Joe's small, frowsty room. 'The gamekeeper's daughter!' he yelled again.

'What about her?' Joe took a while for his eyes to focus.

'She's been defaced. It wasn't there yesterday and now it is. I don't know how I can face Valentine Prinsep.'

'Yes,' Joe grunted. 'I know how you feel.' Years on the edge of the art world had made him less than charitable.

'Get up. Then get up into the second gallery. We've got less than an hour before we open. The canvas will have to be moved. Come on!'

Joe struggled into his socks and threw on his shirt. Remembering that there might be the odd lady cleaner upstairs, the Lindsays being philanthropists, he wriggled into his trousers too. When he reached the second gallery, he found his boss staring at the Prinsep, shaking his head.

'I had my doubts about the others,' he said. 'The subtle changes to the Whistler and the Burne-Jones that Grand and Batchelor were talking about. But *this*; this is *so* obvious. Look!'

Joe did. 'What am I looking at?' he asked.

Saunders's collar stud chose that moment to ping off, clattering against the canvas before tinkling on the floor. The man had gone a nasty shade of puce. 'Isn't it obvious?'

Joe peered closer. 'Is it the number of sticks in the girl's brushwood?' he asked. 'Only I never counted 'em before, so I'm not the best person to ask.'

'Number of sticks, my arse!' Saunders let rip *à la* Stepney on the assumption that the pair were alone. 'Look behind her, man, behind the daughter. What do you see in the trees?'

'Er . . . lanterns,' Joe suggested.

'Lanterns!' Saunders folded his arms. 'Chinese lanterns. And where've you seen those before?'

'Um . . .?'

'For God's sake, man.' Saunders had now turned magenta. 'In the Cremorne. Some utter vandal has placed *The Gamekeeper's Daughter* in the Cremorne.'

'Are you sure?' Joe asked.

'Of course. You've been there . . .'

'No, sir,' Joe said. 'Not for years. The last time I was in the Cremorne, they was throwing a party for that Garibaldi bloke. And that *was* a while ago.'

Saunders turned to the caretaker. 'I employ you as a night-watchman,' he said, acidly, 'among other things.'

Joe looked at him bleakly.

'So what part of "night" and "watch" don't you understand?'

'Very Rembrandt,' Joe muttered.

'Last night,' Saunders bellowed. 'Where were you?'

Joe pointed silently to the basement. 'Except,' he guessed what Saunders's next line would be, 'every two hours, on the nose, when I did my rounds.'

'Every two hours,' Saunders repeated, 'so you visited *this* gallery, walking past *this* portrait at . . .'

'Nine o'clock, eleven o'clock, one o'clock. Which explains why I had to be woken a moment ago.'

He did his level best to stifle a yawn, but failed miserably.

'And there was nothing untoward on this painting – these lanterns weren't here?'

'I didn't see them,' Joe shrugged.

'Precisely,' Saunders fumed. 'So either you're as observant as that picture frame or you didn't do the rounds as you claim.'

'Perhaps it wuzzn't done last night!' Joe was fighting his corner and for his livelihood.

Saunders reached out a finger and wiped one of the lanterns that smeared across the canvas. 'The paint's still wet, man. This is all your fault!'

'I . . .' Joe was outraged.

'You're no use to me! I'll give you one hour to clear out whatever you have in that cellar of yours and then you're out. See me before you go and I'll make your wages up.' And he stormed off, stopping suddenly. 'And get rid of that canvas,' he said. 'I'll have to talk to Mr Prinsep.'

Joe watched him march away. 'I suppose a golden reference is out of the question?' he said.

TWELVE

Matthew Grand was feeling a little more limber and had ditched the stick but had a new respect for artists' models.

'I think we have underestimated these women – and Anstruther Peebles, I suppose – when we say they were models on the side. It's a real skill.'

'Matthew,' Batchelor could tell that this could soon get very boring, 'you stayed still for a while . . .'

'Six hours straight.'

'. . . which isn't actually a skill, is it? I've known reporters who stay so still at their desks there have been at least two examples where they died before ten in the morning and no one noticed until after the deadline that night.'

'Not the same. But the point I am making, James, is that I don't think Mabel Glossop and Clara Jenkins were moonlighting as models. They were pretty girls, true, but I don't think real artists pick girls off the street. Caro said that Evangeline French was at a soirée and no one was looking down on her at all – the wives and mistresses treated her just the same.'

'The fact that you say wives and mistresses like that shows we're not talking about normal people, though.' Batchelor, as a would-be novelist, wanted to be bohemian but wasn't proving to be very good at it – he had a Puritan streak a mile wide.

'We'll pop into the office, see what Martin has to say for himself. He's bound to have a list of models in his head.'

'Not if Twisleton is right. He wouldn't have extraneous information like that for no reason.'

'Well, we can but try.' Grand put his arm in the air to summon a cab.

'We could walk,' Batchelor observed.

Grand clutched his back. 'We artists' models prefer to ride,' he said, clambering aboard as the hansom clattered to the kerb. 'You can walk if you want to.'

Batchelor sighed in mock-exasperation and followed him into the cab. 'It's all right. If you insist.'

And the cabbie flicked his whip and they were off, whirled into the traffic towards the Strand.

'Sorry, sirs.' Martin was distraught. 'I'm afraid I don't know any artists' models, except Evangeline French, actual name Ethel Phipps.'

'How did you know that?' Batchelor was still impressed. 'That hasn't been in the papers.'

'I went round a few galleries this morning. We don't seem very busy in the office at the moment and with all the filing done . . .' He spread his arms. 'Miss Wolstenholme held the fort, didn't you, Phyllida?'

'Yes, Mr Martin,' she said over her shoulder. 'Look, Mr Batchelor, Mr Grand, I can type without looking. Now I use the right fingers, the keys don't lock or anything.'

'Good for you.' Grand was grateful that there wouldn't be the grinding noise every few minutes, and also the need to pay to have the keys unbent.

'I'm using the time I save to study Mr Pitman's shorthand method. Alexander . . . I beg your pardon, Mr Martin, is teaching me the rudiments.'

'Of course he is.' Batchelor's shorthand was rusty, but he was cross with himself for not having thought of it first.

'So, apart from finding out that Evangeline began as Ethel, do we have any more new information?' Grand looked around. 'There's something missing. What is it?'

'I threw that dead plant out,' Miss Wolstenholme suggested.

'No . . . bigger. Oh, I know. No Mr Wilde.'

'I haven't seen him since he came out after his night in prison,' Martin said. 'I think he may have gone back to Oxford. Or perhaps he and Mr Whistler have become friends.' He paused and seemed to think for a moment. 'Oscar tends to do that.'

'Perhaps that's it, then,' Grand said. 'I must say, it does leave the office feeling a little more roomy.'

'So,' Martin got back to the point, 'I'm afraid there was little to glean. Evangeline was a very sought-after model because she was incredibly good at keeping still, and also a genuinely nice girl, it seems. She made a good living, to the extent that she had her own suite of rooms and a maid and everything. Most of them have to share with other models or live at home.'

Batchelor narrowed his eyes. 'A good living from modelling, or . . .?' he left the rest open, in deference to Miss Wolstenholme.

Martin was quick to the dead woman's defence. 'Oh, just from modelling,' he said. 'The standard rate for one-off jobs is quite substantial, but regular models are also paid a retainer, so they can be available. It all adds up.'

Batchelor knew that Grand was about to share his experiences, so spoke quickly. 'Thank you, Alexander.' He somehow thought Gan was not appropriate now that Wilde had moved on to more famous climes. 'Well done.'

Martin beamed; he loved nothing so much as praise.

'I think we should perhaps go round to the Grosvenor one more time,' Grand said. 'I can't help wondering whether Saunders might know more than he's saying.'

Martin chimed in. 'When I was there with Mr Whistler,' he said, 'he struck me as a very short-tempered gentleman, but not one very au fait with art. He is a salesman more than an art aficionado, one might say.'

'*One* certainly might,' Grand said dryly. '*I* might say he is a barrow boy made good. The accent slips from time to time.'

Batchelor was surprised and impressed. 'How can you tell?' he asked. 'Don't we all sound the same to you?'

'James,' Grand said, patiently. 'You have known me, man and boy, for thirteen years now, and I know you love to think I am a Yankee in London who doesn't know his ass from a hole in the ground. But I can tell accents, just like you can. And a man trying to sound as if he comes from one side of the tracks when he is clearly from another is as clear to me as the next cuss. Also,' Grand smoothed an already perfect lapel, 'he doesn't have a tailor so much as a peg.'

Batchelor decided to swallow his confusion and get on with the plan. 'If he isn't any good at judging art, then how can he help us?'

'Just *because* he isn't in their world, he might see things that the artists don't. And also, I think he is a bit of a gossip. I would love to get inside that gallery out of hours, see what goes on.'

'You could hide,' Martin suggested. 'It's full of odd corners, stacks of canvases, packing cases, all that sort of thing.'

'How would we manage to stay there, though?' Batchelor wondered. 'They count you in and count you out.'

'Old Joe might be able to help,' Grand said. 'He isn't much as regards security, but he must know that place like the back of his hand. He must be able to find us a place to hide.'

'If he'll help,' Batchelor pointed out, remembering the drubbing he'd received at the man's hands. 'He does work for Saunders, after all.'

'We'll offer him a bribe,' Grand said, bluntly. 'Every man has his price. Let's go round now and see what Joe's is, shall we?' He reached for his hat. 'Coming, Alexander?'

'May I?' Martin was excited. This was real sleuthing, hiding and everything. Perhaps they would let him actually do the hiding. Though he wasn't that keen on the dark . . .

Grand and Batchelor had timed arrivals better in their careers. They got out of their cab outside the Grosvenor gallery as Joe stumbled out of the door carrying two bulging sacks, watched over by a very tight-lipped Terence Saunders, standing in the doorway with arms folded.

'Joe?' Batchelor held the man's shoulder. 'What's going on?'

'Sacked me, innee?' Joe choked on a laugh as he held his sacks up. 'Chucked me out on account of somebody messing with the gamekeeper's daughter.'

Batchelor blinked. He couldn't immediately see how that could involve Joe. And how many gamekeepers were there in London, let alone ones with daughters.

Martin helped him out. 'I would imagine,' he said, in the slightly automaton tones he affected when remembering something, 'that he is referring to the study of *The Gamekeeper's Daughter*, by Valentine Cameron Prinsep. It hangs in the Long Gallery here and is considered to be one of his best works.'

Grand and Batchelor looked at Joe, who nodded and coughed again, spitting out the dog-end which had been adhering to his lip. 'That's the girlie,' he said. 'Somebody got in and painted lanterns in the background. His Nibs,' he gestured with a thumb over his shoulder, 'got his rag out well and truly. Said it was my fault.'

Grand felt he must play devil's advocate on this one. 'Well, you *are* the nightwatchman,' he pointed out.

'Wuz,' Joe said, bitterly.

'You can see how he might be annoyed, though?'

'Well . . . yeah. But if he puts me down in the basement to sleep, it's no wonder I don't hear what's going on overhead.'

'But you patrolled, though?' Grand needed all his ducks in a row if he was going to plead with Saunders for Joe's reinstatement.

''Course. He's moanin' I didn't notice, but I can't notice everything, can I?'

Martin gasped slightly – the mere thought of that made him feel a little queasy.

'Stay here,' Grand said. 'I'll have a word.'

Grand walked steadily up to the doors of the Grosvenor, blocked as they were by the seemingly implacable Saunders. He pushed and Saunders had to step back or be knocked over. Batchelor, Martin and Joe watched as Grand worked his magic and Batchelor thought again what a good job it was that he was on the side of the good guys; the man could sell sand to Arabs.

Finally, Grand turned and waved Joe back inside.

'Mr Saunders has decided to give you another chance, Joe,' Grand said. 'He realizes that perhaps asking you to stay awake all day and then check hourly all night is just too much and so he will employ cleaners for your day duties and you can just do the night shift. Because that might take a day or two, he will be doing the sweeping himself until that can happen. So, if you would like to take your things back to your room, we'll say no more about it.' Grand beamed at Saunders. 'That's about it, Mr Saunders, isn't it?'

Saunders nodded; the smile on his face was like the silver plate on a coffin. 'That's right,' he said. 'I'm very sorry, Joe. I overreacted when I saw the damage to the painting.'

'Which . . .?' Grand prompted.

'Which is easily put right, I'm sure.'

'Thank you very much, guv'nor,' Joe said, touching the brim of his cap. 'And you, guv'nor,' to Grand. 'Come down and see me before you go. I'll make you a cuppa tea.'

'Thank you,' said Grand, with his typical New World courtesy. 'I believe I will.'

Martin was open-mouthed and even Batchelor couldn't have hoped for a better outcome. Grand had excelled himself.

Meanwhile, Saunders had regained his poise. 'And of course, gentlemen,' he said, 'I would be delighted if you would like to look around. *The Gamekeeper's Daughter* is with the restorer in the rear workroom, but otherwise, I believe we are all present and correct. Ha.' He ended with what at the moment was passing for a laugh. What he needed was a lie-down and a glass of something restorative. Then he would have to get on with the sweeping, he supposed. He turned an eye to the doorman, who read his mind.

'No, Mr Saunders,' he said, quickly. 'I don't do sweeping.' He lifted one foot then the other, 'Flat feet, see. Interferes with the bristles.'

It sounded unlikely, but Saunders was almost beyond caring. He went to his office behind the reception desk and took out the brandy from the drawer marked 'receipts' and poured a hefty snifter. He lay back in the chair, his eyes closed and the brandy clutched to his chest. When, oh Lord, he asked no one in particular, was this all going to end?

In the gallery, the three men wandered along the walls, looking at all the pictures with fresh eyes. Martin was murmuring to himself as he took notes. There were far more changes to the pictures – now he had his eye in – than he had seen before. Nothing huge and sometimes, he had to admit, the change was an improvement. Everyone knew Frederic Leighton was rubbish at feet, and yet here, in his painting of girls picking up shells, the one in the foreground actually had toes, instead of the fuzzy things on the ends of the other girls' feet. He pointed it out to Batchelor, who nodded agreement.

Batchelor waited for Grand to explain how he had achieved

the impossible, but it was obvious he would wait all day, so he asked outright.

'I just told him that if he didn't reinstate Joe, I would take his largest canvas and shove it up his ass, frame and all.'

'And there was me thinking you had sweet-talked him,' Batchelor said, disappointed.

Grand was surprised. He had thought he *had* sweet-talked him.

After they had walked the length and breadth of the gallery, Martin showed his employers a list of paintings which in his opinion had been adulterated. It was every one within easy reach of the floor, as simple as that.

'Alexander,' Batchelor said, having checked the list, 'is there anything else, apart from accessibility, that these painters have in common?'

Martin's eyes took on the rather glazed look the enquiry agents had begun to recognize. 'One is by Whistler, who is a client of yours. One is by Ruskin, who is . . . whatever the opposite of client is.'

'Anti-client?' Batchelor suggested, but was ignored.

'One is by a student of G.F. Watts, whose model was killed in the Cremorne, which also, by the way, links to Whistler, as his painting is set there. Umm . . .' Martin felt there were more links, but he needed to sit down and work them out in diagram form. In a perfect world, he would be able to liaise with his old mathematics mentor from Cambridge, Dr Venn, but he knew that wasn't possible this time. Even so, there was a pattern there, he knew.

'Don't worry,' Batchelor said. 'That there are any links at all is quite remarkable.'

Martin looked at him with pitying eyes – the man clearly had no idea.

'The thing is, how are we going to find out in the first place who is doing it; secondly, why; and thirdly . . .'

'The ghost of the Grosvenor!' Grand clicked his fingers.

'Are you serious?' Martin might be afraid of the dark, but without empirical evidence, he found it hard to believe in ghosts.

'No,' Grand said. 'But many people are.'

'Thirdly . . .' It upset Martin's psyche to leave a list incomplete.

'Sorry,' Batchelor said, kindly. 'Thirdly what?'

Martin's shoulders sagged. 'I can't remember. Perhaps there wasn't even a thirdly.' His eyes were haunted. 'This gallery is very odd. There is something about the dimensions, I don't know . . . it's lopsided, somehow.'

'Let's get you out of here,' Grand said, shepherding the lad towards the exit. 'I'll be along in a minute. All I need to do now is to ask Mr Saunders what would be the best night for a séance.'

Terence Saunders leaned on his broom and shook his head. 'Absolutely not!' he said. 'It is totally and categorically out of the question. Sir Coutts and Lady Blanche would never allow it.'

'What, not even if I told them that Lady Mary Wentworth would be of the party?'

'Is she? Of the party?'

'I have no idea. But as the affianced of her daughter, I have a certain amount of clout, wouldn't you say?'

Saunders risked a snort. 'As her daughter seems to be some kind of insane lush, I really wouldn't know.'

Grand closed to him and grabbed him so that his collar studs popped. 'I happen to love that insane lush dearly. And if I hear another word against her, you will find your head where the sun don't shine. So,' he dropped the gallery assistant back onto his feet and pulled his jacket straight, 'do I get my séance, or don't I?'

Saunders coughed. 'Would Thursday evening suit?'

'Thursday would be dandy. And by the way,' Grand pointed into a corner, 'you've missed a bit.'

'So the séance, again?' Batchelor and Martin were both fairly agog. It seemed to be counter-productive, to fill the gallery with people when all common sense pointed to the damage only happening when it was empty.

'At a séance,' Grand began, then had a sudden thought. 'Have you guys ever been to a séance?'

They both shook their heads. Miss Wolstenholme coughed lightly.

'Yes?' Grand looked at her as she sat, half turned from her spread page of practice Pitman's.

'We sometimes use a Ouija at my lodgings,' she said. 'We have found some *very* interesting things. Mostly about the Prince of Wales; our control is very in tune with the royal family. Apparently,' she leaned further back out of her chair so she could lower her voice to a conspiratorial husk, 'he likes to . . .'

'I think we all know that about the Prince of Wales, Miss Wolstenholme, but thank you all the same. At a séance,' Grand went on, 'people drop their guard. They get carried away with the proceedings and they let out all kinds of things that they would keep to themselves under other circumstances. My mother loves nothing better than turning the odd table, and she's been doing it since I can remember. My sister and I often had to make up numbers and I have to say, it's not always easy to explain what goes on.'

Martin rolled his eyes. 'Everything has an explanation, Mr Grand,' he said. 'Nothing on this earth is totally inexplicable.'

'I daresay you're right,' Grand agreed. 'But you have to allow for human nature, Alexander, and that is a many-headed monster. Many people when sitting in the dark come out with things they would never usually utter. They kinda forget that anyone else is there.'

Batchelor laughed. 'That's funny,' he said.

'What is?' Grand was confused.

'Well, isn't the usual question "Is there anybody there?"' Batchelor checked.

'Very funny,' Grand said. 'But, as I was saying, it's like when you lie in the dark next to someone, you say things you'd never say in the daylight.'

Miss Wolstenholme yelped. She had never heard anything so filthy in all her life.

'My first thought was to hide in the gallery, as you know. But I don't know whether Joe has the mental wherewithal to help us hide, and certainly not to carry on as normal with us hidden somewhere. He'd give us away, for sure. But if we hold a séance, with all the suspects and a few others for good measure around the table, we should be able to see – I say *should*, but with Alexander's computing skills and our knowledge of people and their expressions, James, I don't see why we wouldn't be able to find out who is the perpetrator of not only the art mutilations but the murders too.'

'Is it one and the same?' Martin asked. 'The crimes are very different.'

'I agree,' Grand said. 'And I am sure you have done this calculation already, Alexander, but I am prepared to bet that you won't find another single case in all these filing drawers where there are so many interlocking facts.'

Martin cast his eyes up till only the whites showed and muttered to himself.

'He'll be a natural at the séance,' Batchelor muttered in Grand's ear.

After a moment or two, Martin came back to earth. 'I believe you're right,' he said. 'Taking the criteria we have, there is no other case on the books which comes close. Always allowing that there is no such thing as coincidence.'

'And for these purposes, let's say just that,' Batchelor said. 'So, given that a séance is a good way to test our theory, who are we actually going to be watching?'

'Watts,' Grand and Martin said together.

'I would have said Whistler, myself,' Batchelor said.

'He came to us, though,' Grand pointed out.

'True. But then, that's not unknown. Hiding in plain sight.'

Grand shrugged. 'You could be right. And then there's Saunders, of course. He could be doing it.'

'Or Ruskin. He's as mad as a box of frogs and the stick could be just a prop.'

'Oscar Wilde's an odd one, too,' Grand added, 'no offence, Martin.'

'None taken.'

'It could be the Lindsays. Or one of them, anyway.'

Batchelor looked doubtful. 'Why?'

'Well,' Grand wasn't sure either but he preferred to leave no stone unturned, 'Their names naturally crop up whenever the Grosvenor is mentioned. I wondered whether perhaps they were planning some big press announcement. That's more in your province, James. Would that increase takings at the gallery?'

'It might,' Batchelor conceded. 'There are people who would want to own a piece which had been adjusted, if that's the word. A talking point. Rarer than an unsullied piece by the same artist. Yes, I could see that.'

'But surely,' Martin was the voice of reason, 'murder for a few more sales is going a bit far?'

Grand and Batchelor looked at him as if he was a favourite nephew who had suddenly learned to juggle.

'Shall I?' Batchelor asked.

'Be my guest,' Grand said.

'There is, quite literally, no limit to what people will do for gain,' Batchelor explained. 'Murder is only one on the list. Sorry, Alexander, but welcome to the world of the enquiry agent.'

Martin was stunned to silence. He had always known people could be cruel and unusual, but this was almost a learning curve too far.

'I could go on,' Grand said, 'with reasons for everyone linked to this case to have done it. And I don't exclude the police. Metcalfe put a tail on us. Why would he do that? No one has ever done that before. Might it be so he knows what we know, knows whether we are getting close?'

'And what about that soldier, the one with the odd name?' Batchelor asked.

'Willoughby Inverarity.' Martin inevitably filled in the missing information.

'That's the feller. He pretended to be someone else and then that someone else turns up dead. Oh – and the lawyer, Keen, he of Keen, Griswold; denying you know anything isn't exactly a defence.'

'All in all,' Grand said, 'I think we agree that the séance might be something that will work. So, shall we plan some strategies?' He pulled open his desk and invited Batchelor and Martin to gather round. 'Would you like to practise your shorthand, Miss Wolstenholme?' he said.

She leapt up immediately. Perhaps this could be the start

of her new career as a lady enquiry agent? But then, she thought again – she had never heard of such a thing in any of the books she read, so it was unlikely there could be such a thing.

'After you've made some tea, of course. I'm parched.'

As soon as Eleanor opened the door, Grand could tell that Lady Wentworth was still in residence. The girl looked exhausted but also on the alert; friends of Grand's back home had come back from visits to Haiti with stories of *zumbi*, the living dead, and he had always pooh-poohed it. Now, he wasn't so sure.

He raised his eyebrows and nodded towards the drawing room. Eleanor nodded and slumped back through the green baize door.

In the drawing room, Caroline and her mother sat decorously at either side of the fireplace, sewing. Caroline looked up and her eyes were not dissimilar to Eleanor's.

'Mr Grand.' Lady Wentworth extended her black-wisped claw for him to kiss. He wondered how many women in this year of their Lord 1878 sewed wearing gloves. He was willing to bet not that many. 'You are enjoying better fortune today. Lady Caroline and I are At Home.'

'Lucky me,' Grand smiled. 'My visit will not be a long one, Lady Wentworth. I am here to invite Lady Caroline out for the evening, this coming Thursday.'

'May one ask to where?'

'The Grosvenor gallery,' he said, with a smile and a re-assuring look at Caroline.

'I have gathered from my daughter that she is not really that fond of the Grosvenor,' the woman said, with a basilisk smile. 'So she will have to decline.'

'But, Mama . . .'

Lady Wentworth raised her chin and looked at her daughter through her lorgnette. 'Caroline,' she barked. 'You either dislike the Grosvenor or you do not. Or,' and she screwed up her mouth in distaste, 'you were indulging in your habit of hyperbole again, against which I have warned you time without number.'

'Perhaps an evening event, Mama,' Caroline ventured, 'may remove my antipathy.'

Her mother looked at her with sympathy. 'I am not a fool, Caroline,' she said, 'nor, and I think I may say this as you are not a child any longer, am I a stranger to the feelings you no doubt have for Mr Grand.'

Grand narrowed his eyes at Caroline and stuck his tongue out in the merest flicker. He doubted very much whether this shrivelled woman had ever had even a quarter of the feelings he knew Caroline harboured under her high-buttoned bodice.

'So,' the woman continued, 'I fear I must answer for you and say no. On the other hand, Mr Grand, if Caroline's absence will make an awkward number at the table, I will be happy to attend in her place. May I ask the occasion?'

Grand had little choice. It was fruitless to lie. Lady Wentworth was not exactly a vital member of stylish tables throughout London, but she did know people; if it got out that it was a séance and he told her something else, that would be the end of his engagement to her daughter, and he suddenly realized that he would dislike that very much. 'It's a séance, Lady Wentworth,' he said.

His future mother-in-law – unless he had blotted his copy-book irretrievably – gasped, closed her eyes and pressed a scandalized hand to her chest. 'A *séance*?' she whispered. 'You *dare* invite my daughter to a *séance*? Are you an *animal*, Mr Grand?'

'They are very popular, Mama,' Lady Caroline suggested, realizing as she spoke that she had used the wrong word. 'The very best people are seen at séances these days.'

'Frauds and charlatans the whole boiling of them,' Lady Wentworth announced. 'I shall go, Mr Grand, though it pains me to think of being in a room with such depravity. If, as I suspect, there is skulduggery to which you are all too keen to expose my daughter, then the engagement is off.'

'But Mama . . .' Caroline had tears in her eyes.

'Lady Wentworth . . .' Grand didn't take his eyes off Caroline.

'I have decided. At what time do I need to arrive, Mr Grand?'

'Nine o'clock.' Grand hung his head, defeated.

'An appalling hour. No wonder the whole of society is so effete, keeping to such times. But, I will spare nothing for my girl. I will be there. Good day, Mr Grand.'

Caroline started to get up for her ritual kiss.

'Stay in your seat, Caroline. I do not wish you to show Mr Grand any overt displays of affection. I am considering his position. Most carefully.' She looked up at Grand. 'I daresay you can see yourself out, Mr Grand.'

With a bow, Grand saw himself out of the room.

In the hall, he passed a note to a lacklustre Eleanor. 'Make sure Lady Caroline gets this. *Not* her mother. Promise me?'

The maid nodded and a small spark entered her eye. Mr Grand was fighting back. Perhaps the world wouldn't end, after all.

On his way home that afternoon, Grand put his head around the office door. Miss Wolstenholme had gone home, but Martin was sitting at his desk, sealing envelopes and putting them on a pile.

'How are the invitations coming along, Alexander?' Grand asked, though he knew the answer already. Perfectly, of course.

'This is the last one, Mr Grand,' Martin said. 'I will get them in the five o'clock post and, with luck, most of them will be there tonight; they're quite local. Worst case will be tomorrow morning.'

'And you've put emergency RSVP?'

'I certainly have, Mr Grand. We don't have much time. But I'm sure everybody will come – it's not every day you get an invitation to a séance in an art gallery. They'll be intrigued, if nothing else.'

'I hope so. See you tomorrow.'

'Well, Alexander?'

'Somewhat unprecedented, Mr Batchelor.' Martin sat at his desk with one full basket and one empty one in front of him. 'All the answers in, mostly hand delivered, and all are "yes".'

'Really?' Grand was surprised. 'Even Metcalfe?'

'His was the first in. Barnes brought it round.'

'Excellent. All we need now is a medium, and we'll be set.'

The door banged behind them and Grand barrelled in. 'I've been thinking about that, James,' he said. 'Do you think Miss Wolstenholme could carry it off?'

'Not a chance,' Batchelor said. 'She just doesn't have the . . .' He spread his arms in mute appeal to Martin.

'. . . charisma,' Martin suggested, and Batchelor nodded.

'Who, then?' Grand asked. 'It isn't as if we need a real one.'

Martin gave him an odd look. 'Is there such a thing?' he asked.

'Don't nitpick, Alexander,' Grand snapped.

'There was a medium in that case in '75,' Martin said. 'The one where that woman wanted to divorce her husband because she said he was having unnatural thoughts about . . .'

'I remember that one,' Grand said. 'Florence Cook, wasn't it?'

'Yes. She's in the papers from time to time, so she is still in business, if that's the word I mean.'

'She sounds ideal. Do we know her address? Of course we do.' Martin was already writing and passed the slip of paper to Grand. 'We'll go and see her, see what she'll do for money.'

'Almost anything, I would imagine,' Martin said, sourly, and watched his employers leave. He couldn't see, for the life of him, how this was going to end well.

THIRTEEN

Matthew Grand and James Batchelor were de facto hosts and had dressed the part. The invitations had not called for evening dress, but they knew that at least half of the guests would assume it was mandatory. So they had donned their best bibs and tuckers and waited to welcome the participants to the séance on the steps of the Grosvenor. Florence Cook – who would, indeed, do anything for money – was already ensconced in the Long Gallery. She was a tall woman, as pale as the spirits she summoned, and her large grey eyes were set deep to see into men's souls. The large circular table at which she sat had been cobbled together by Joe from various odd bits of timber from the packing room. His brief was simple. It had to have room for at least thirteen people to sit round it, but also be light enough to rock about, should the fit take it. He had not been keen to take on the task, until Grand had reminded him that, had it not been for his intervention, he wouldn't have a roof over his head, even, let alone a job. So, muttering, Joe had bent to his task and the end result was not at all bad.

'So, Caroline isn't coming?' Batchelor checked.

'Her mother wouldn't allow it,' Grand said shortly.

'Ah.' There seemed little more to say. Lady Wentworth appeared to be a fixture in London and the only person happy about it was Lord Wentworth, left to potter at will down at the country pile, as far away from the Season as good manners would allow.

Grand consulted his watch. 'They'll be arriving soon,' he said. 'I wonder who'll be the first to turn up.'

'Five bob says it'll be the police,' Batchelor said, holding out two half-crowns.

'My five bob says it will be the Lindsays,' Grand said. 'It is their gallery, after all.'

'Have you ever met them?' Batchelor asked. He knew his

partner mixed in some pretty exalted circles from time to time.

'Not as far as I know,' Grand said, as a carriage pulled up at the side of the road. 'This may be them now.'

Two people tumbled higgledy-piggledy out of the carriage. They were wearing what had possibly begun as evening dress, but splodges of paint could be seen on his shirt and her skirt and she had charcoal under her nails. They were bickering mildly together and she had her tiara caught in his tie. Eventually, they were separated by the footman sitting along-side the groom and they walked up the steps to greet Grand and Batchelor.

'Sir Coutts and Lady Blanche Lindsay,' the gentleman said, looking the two up and down. 'Are you the chaps causing chaos in our gallery?' He looked fiercely through his monocle at Grand.

'Well, not chaos, hopefully, Sir Coutts,' Grand said. 'We hope to lay the ghost tonight, that's for sure.'

'Never seen it!' the woman barked suddenly at Batchelor. 'Don't want to. Never mind. Nibbles?' she asked as the doorman did his job.

'In the foyer, Lady Blanche.' Saunders had appeared from nowhere, looking even more stuffed than usual in his tails.

'Who's payin'?'

'We are, Lady Blanche,' Grand called over his shoulder.

Sir Coutts Lindsay winked at the American. 'She'll enjoy them all the more for that,' he said. 'She likes to think of herself as an artist starving in a garret.'

Batchelor looked at Grand. 'So they do exist, then,' he chuckled.

The carriages were beginning to line up, and soon the people standing on the steps to be welcomed could officially be called a queue.

'Do you think they'll all come?' Batchelor asked.

'James, you sound like a debutante at her first party,' Grand laughed. 'Miss Cook says the perfect number is nine, but we're way over that. Perhaps it will be the more the merrier. Anyway, Florence Cook is a draw all by herself. You've heard the scandal, of course?'

'I never listen to idle gossip,' Batchelor lied. 'You seem very merry, anyway,' he said, looking at his friend rather askance. 'Do you have anything up your sleeve I should know about?'

'No, indeed. I leave that to Miss Cook.' Grand turned with his hand outstretched. 'Lady Wentworth. How good of you to come. And right on time.'

'Punctuality is the politeness of princes, Mr Grand,' the woman rapped out. She looked Batchelor up and down as if something the cat had dragged in and swept into the foyer, where she ignored the Lindsays and didn't even see Saunders.

Hard on her heels came the rest of the guests, Whistler being the next, with Oscar Wilde in anxious attendance. Having snagged his famous artist, he was unwilling to let go, and even Whistler, with an ego as big as the great outdoors, was beginning to find it wearing. And Wilde was wearing a huge gardenia in his buttonhole.

Barnes arrived on foot, in a shabby suit, an apology already on his lips. 'I'm sorry it's me,' he said. 'Inspector Metcalfe was going to come but he . . .' Here, his invention left him. He had no vocabulary to paraphrase the words that Metcalfe had used to describe what he felt about Grand and Batchelor. 'They'll be dressed up like a couple of sodding penguins' was the politest and, at least in that regard, he was right.

'Nothing to apologize for,' Grand said, politely. 'I know how hard you policemen have to work and we're happy to have you. A policeman's lot is not a happy one, after all.'

George Frederic Watts was alone. John Stanhope had offered to come along; Lizzie was a great adherent of table turning, and he thought he might be able to bring something to the table, so to speak. But his attempt at a pun had fallen on deaf ears and Watts was there, though unimpressed. 'Damn fool bloody thing, Grand,' he muttered. The man might be a good model, but that didn't make him intelligent. 'If this is all an attempt to contact poor Evangeline, it is in the worst possible taste. She didn't have much to say for herself when she was alive. I doubt that will have changed.'

'We are not trying to contact Evangeline,' Grand assured him. 'It's the ghost of the Grosvenor we are trying to lay.'

Alice Arbuthnot, the next in line, looking like a galleon in full sail with the sunset of middle age just gilding her canvas, nudged the gentleman by her side in the ribs. 'That sounds right up your street, Percy,' she whispered.

Perceval Keen, QC, looked her up and down. 'Unhand me, madam,' he said, with perfect accuracy. 'I don't know you and don't want to!' He passed his hat and scarf to the doorman.

Auntie Alice dropped a ghost of a wink to Batchelor as she swept past in a whisper of tulle and organdie. Keen stormed ahead, just snapping as he did so, 'Load of tommyrot!'

'Just two left, now,' Grand said, consulting his list. 'Ruskin and Inverarity.'

'And Martin,' Batchelor pointed out.

'True, but he wasn't exactly invited, was he? More a kind of staff do, I suppose, for him.'

'He does know to come, though?' Batchelor was suddenly worried that no one had asked him.

'Yes, yes. I've given him a few bits to do. Backstage, you know. Miss Cook needs . . .' He broke off as Willoughby Inverarity panted up the stairs, smart in his mess dress, the gold lace on his waistcoat gleaming in the lights streaming from the gallery windows.

'Sorry I'm late, gents,' he said, a hand to his chest as he gathered his breath. 'Not missed anything, have I? I say . . . we're not trying to get Peebles to speak, are we? Because, as you know, I had decided to cut the man from that moment on. Don't want to have to carry on the conversation from Beyond, as it were.'

'No, no,' Grand recited what was quickly becoming some-what of a mantra, 'we're attempting to lay the Grosvenor ghost.' He pointed into the foyer. 'Champagne inside.' And with a whoosh of conversation, cut off with the click of the door, he disappeared inside.

'So, just Ruskin now,' Batchelor said. 'I bet he doesn't come.'

'I bet he will,' Grand said. 'Men like him don't reply to invitations and then don't arrive, you know. It simply isn't done.'

'But what if he has found out Whistler will be here?'

'Then I would imagine he will be all the keener to come. If Whistler loses his temper again, Ruskin will win his case hands down.'

'He's late, though,' Batchelor pointed out.

Grand glanced at his watch. 'Just about fashionably late, I would say.'

A carriage rattled around the corner and drew up in front of the gallery. Ruskin alighted, leaning heavily on his cane.

'See. Five bob, was it?'

'Sorry to be tardy, gentlemen,' Ruskin said, making heavy weather of the few shallow steps. 'I hope I haven't kept you waiting.'

'Not at all.' Grand bowed and ushered him in. 'We will have to forgo champagne, though. It is time to begin.'

'Where's Martin, though?' Batchelor whispered to Grand.

'Don't worry. He'll be where I need him,' Grand said, then, louder, 'ladies, gentlemen, shall we go through? Mr Saunders, if you would lead the way.'

With a clink of glasses being replaced on trays and a murmur of low conversation, the guests moved through into the candle-specked darkness of the gallery.

Terence Saunders had seen the table being erected, but after that had not witnessed the transformation that had been wrought in the gallery. The pictures were hardly visible in the almost total darkness. Here and there, a candle guttered in the draught from the open door. In the middle of the round table, three fat candles burned low, grouped together on a mirror. A shrouded figure sat facing the door, her face lit in the flickering flame when she leaned forward, but otherwise hidden behind a lace veil she wore over her head. Her dress was white and almost glowed with a life of its own. The sleeves were loose and flowing, covering her hands. Saunders stopped in shock and the guests behind him cannoned into him and almost sent him flying. Lady Wentworth's skeletal forefinger in the small of his back soon got him moving again, and it was fortunate for his peace of mind that he didn't hear Lady Blanche whisper to her husband that the man really did have to go.

Grand weaselled his way to the front and shepherded everyone to their seats. There was a shortage of women, so it hadn't been possible to seat them alternately with the men, but Grand and Batchelor had done their best. Their main aim had been to make sure that no two people who absolutely hated each other were being asked to hold hands; in some cases, that might be a step too far.

In low tones, Grand sent them to their places. 'Ladies and gentlemen, please meet Miss Florence Cook, who many of you will know is a very accomplished and indeed acclaimed medium.'

The murmurs from the guests were mixed, but Florence was used to that. Speaking for herself, she really couldn't see why people were always so surprised when she was from time to time exposed as a fraud. What did they expect? That the dead would turn up on cue to talk to people about the other side? Why would Uncle Norman come back to a seedy scullery in Acton to tell his niece that it was all very lovely, he was at peace, and he'd been talking to Beethoven only the other day, who told him to tell little Bessie to carry on with her piano lessons? But, it was a living, and this evening – in nice surroundings, with champagne and a meat tea – was a pleasant bonus; as was the fee.

Batchelor sat people one by one, feeling as though he was dealing cards, a hand of which no one knew the outcome. He pulled the chair out next to Florence on her left and parked Ruskin there. Then Alice Arbuthnot. He and Grand were pretty sure that Ruskin wasn't a client of hers, present or past, so that seemed safe enough. Next to her came Whistler. Although that was quite close to Ruskin, the curve of the table meant that they wouldn't have to look at each other. Despite Wilde trying to muscle in, Batchelor put Lady Blanche next, followed by Barnes, who sat down looking like a rabbit in the gaze of a stoat. Next to Barnes, much to Grand's amusement, came Lady Wentworth, who sat with a loud cry of, '*Must* one?' Watts was next, so at least she knew that her left hand would be in the grip of genius. At this point, the women ran out, so Batchelor and Grand had employed some lateral thinking. Next to Watts came Wilde, who was in seventh

heaven, next to an artistic genius and still able to keep an eye
on Whistler across the table, to make sure he didn't get too
friendly with anyone else. After that, the choice was random,
simply making sure that Sir Coutts Lindsay didn't have to
hold hands with his staff, so it went Keen, Sir Coutts, Inverarity
and Saunders, closing the circle on Florence's right.

'Is everyone comfortable?' Grand asked, and got a mixed
response, with, as expected, the loudest complaints coming in
the strident tones of Lady Wentworth. Ignoring her, he smiled
and rubbed his hands together in the manner of a fairground
barker. 'In a moment, Mr Batchelor and I will be blowing
out all but a few of the candles, but there will still be residual
light so there is no need to worry. If anyone does get
distressed or concerned, please try not to break the circle,
but instead just say either my name or Mr Batchelor's and
we will attend you immediately. We will be in the background, but watching and listening, so there is no need for
concern. Does anyone have any questions?'

Grand looked round the table. One hand went up.

'Yes, Mr Keen.'

'Before we go on with this farce,' the QC said, 'may I
enquire whether this is some misguided attempt at self-
publicity for the gallery? As if the doubtful subjects of many
of the paintings is not enough.'

'No,' Sir Coutts Lindsay was quick to reply. 'This is no doing
of ours. And if this show isn't soon on the road, Blanche and
I are going home. We don't keep late hours and certainly don't
sit around in the dark with a lot of strange people waiting for
absolutely nothing to happen. We have watercolours to complete.'

'Here, here,' came from various parts of the table.

'In that case,' Grand said, 'let's get this show on the road.'
He was rather enjoying his showman persona.

He and Batchelor flitted around the room, blowing out all
the candles except those in the extreme corners. Someone had
lit one candle on the high mezzanine, which was a nuisance,
because he hadn't meant there to be light up there, but it was
too far away to blow out now and he wasn't even sure how
to get there.

*   *   *

In the small gallery beyond, Lady Caroline Wentworth was having her clothing adjusted by Alexander Martin. In the few candles which Grand had allowed, he looked positively ethereal, the flames glancing off the perfect planes of his face and glinting off his hair.

'You're very lovely,' she heard herself say.

Martin glanced up from where he was pinning up a layer of calico and lace. 'Tell me about it. It's a bugger.'

'Surely, you can't be ungrateful.' She could think of a dozen women who would kill to be in her position right now and two dozen who would sell their souls just to have his skin, his eyelashes, those *lips*!

'Not ungrateful, no,' he sighed. 'Just rather tired of it. I do have a personality, you know, things to say. But no one ever notices. That's why I have made such a thing about the filing, the photographic memory. Those things are nothing to do with how I look. I'm a bit of a slob at heart, but now it's second nature to put things in rows, to come out with unconsidered trifles.'

'Oh, poor you,' she said, and wondered if it was excuse enough for a kiss.

He stood up and she looked at him for a moment. He leaned forward and she lowered her lashes and licked her lips. This might be the moment when she threw caution to the winds.

Close to her ear, his voice murmured, 'Do we really need to blow these candles out? Because, to be honest, I am rather afraid of the dark.'

She unpuckered and opened her eyes. Beauty was all very well, but sometimes a girl needed someone to watch over her. And Gan Martin was clearly not that man.

'Are you ready?' he whispered, unaware of what he had missed.

'Ready,' she said, and they went and stood just inside the door, left just slightly ajar.

In the gallery, a pin dropping would have been deafening. Batchelor metaphorically doffed his hat to Florence Cook; even when not moving or making a sound, she completely dominated the room. Even Lady Wentworth was silent, possibly a world's first.

Under her thick veil, the medium looked around the table. Too many for her tastes, really, but the money was good and it didn't need much work from her. All that nonsense with locked cabinets and your hand in hot wax was getting a bit much. There must be simpler ways of making a living. Lowering her voice, she murmured, 'Will everyone please put your hands on the table, fingertips only. Arch your hands. That's right. Now, make sure your little fingers are touching. Just touching, lady in pink. No need to grab.' Ruskin and Whistler were for once united in their gratitude. Alice Arbuthnot gave in with good grace and just leant her little finger as provocatively as she could.

'There are thirteen at the table,' Florence went on, ignoring the cry of societal distress from Lady Wentworth, who had always gone to great lengths to avoid such a gaffe, 'so I am expecting rather wonderful things tonight. Also, Mr Grand and Mr Batchelor tell me there are artists present, so the sensitive vibrations will be very strong.'

Watts, Whistler and Ruskin preened themselves, joined to their surprise by Wilde.

'Now, if everyone is comfortable, please be silent and wait. The spirits are near, I can feel them.'

Soon the room was filled with a crushing silence, broken only by Wilde's tendency to catarrh.

A noise began to infiltrate the room. It was impossible to tell from where it emanated; it seemed to begin in each listener's head, deep in the hind brain, where all fears begin. Even Grand and Batchelor, who had been told to expect it, shook their heads like a puppy with a fly in its ear. The great building took up the sound and magnified it, moaning from the high roof and making the pictures hum on their wires. The sound grew and grew, almost to the point of pain. Ruskin, who was a little deaf in his left ear, inclined his head to the right, closing his eyes to prevent the candle-glowing dark from disorienting him further.

'Is there anybody there?' Batchelor had always thought it a cliché, but now, cutting through the hum which was turning his bones to water, it carried a threat, that whatever was there was not an any*body* any more, but an any*thing*.

The table gave a lurch and Lady Wentworth suppressed a scream. This had never happened in the table-turning evenings at Lady Fortescue's.

At the head of the table, facing down the gallery, the medium appeared to have changed shape. Ruskin and Saunders both looked down to check that her fingers were still in contact with theirs; it seemed hardly possible, as the woman had grown to a massive height. Her voice, like the hum, came from everywhere, and Barnes shut his eyes tight and in a high, small voice in his head called for his mummy.

The table lurched again and this time continued to rock back and forth, in a mesmerizing rhythm. Florence's voice was sharp. 'Stop that!' she said, and the table was still. 'Who are you?'

Points of light flickered into life along the gallery high above.

Batchelor leaned in and whispered in Grand's ear. 'That's clever. How is she doing that?'

Grand shrugged. 'I don't know. Perhaps she arranged it with Martin.'

'Oh.' Batchelor hoped so, because the lights were getting more and more, just little pinpricks against the distant ceiling, like stars on a frosty night.

'Who *are* you?' Florence demanded. 'Do you want someone here?'

'Yes!' The voice roared from all corners. It was impossible to tell the sex or age. It was just a voice, echoing and dead.

Florence shrank back to her normal size. It wasn't easy to balance on a concealed stepladder and be frightened out of your wits at the same time. The voice was none of her doing and she had never experienced such a thing in her years of fleecing the great and good at séances.

Behind their door, Caroline and Martin looked at one another.

'Is that in the script?' she asked him, in an anxious whisper.

'Umm . . . no,' he murmured. He didn't like it when life left the script. 'Perhaps she's improvising. Wait and see, and if she doesn't get back on track soon, you'll have to go in anyway.'

She nodded and pressed closer. He may not be as powerful as Matthew, but he was male, here, and between her and whatever was happening in the gallery. And for now, that would have to do.

'Who do you want?' Florence asked, when she had controlled the tremble in her throat.

The answer was not so much a word as a scream, visceral and with the pain of the fires of hell in it.

'This is very good,' Batchelor muttered to Grand. 'I can see why she's quite pricey.'

Grand kept his counsel. He had a sneaking suspicion that this was not the work of Florence Cook, Medium to the Gentry.

When the echoes had died away, Florence spoke again. 'I will ask the souls gathered around this table to speak their names and, as they do, I would ask you to let us know if they are the person you wish to speak to. Can you do that?'

Everyone braced themselves for the scream, but none came.

'Can you do that?' Florence raised her voice and waited.

'Yesssssssssss.' The sound filled the great room, a sibilant full of menace and hatred.

She turned her head to Ruskin. 'Just speak your name, sir,' she said. 'Then go round the table, leaving time for an answer.'

Ruskin went to speak, but found his lips were dry and his tongue somehow had cleaved to the roof of his mouth. He tried to raise his right hand to wipe his face, but Florence, feeling the movement, held on tight. 'Do not break the circle,' she begged them. 'It will keep us safe.' She was out of her depth, but rules were rules. She had a feeling that nothing was a guarantee any more, and promised herself that, after tonight, she would find a safer profession.

Ruskin coughed and somehow got enough saliva to speak. 'John Ruskin,' he said.

The voice, which sounded like the voice of the gallery, the echo making it sound as if all the frozen faces of all the models on all the paintings spoke in grotesque chorus, came again. 'Who?' it said and, even in his fear, Whistler could hardly suppress a chuckle.

And so they went, one by one, around the circle, the voice muttering and hissing quietly as each one spoke. Some were not worried and spoke their names clearly. Mrs Arbuthnot knew that she had been personally responsible for the deaths of at least three gentlemen, but as they had all died with smiles on their faces, she felt sure that this terrible voice was not here for her. The Lindsays, likewise, had consciences as clear as the day. Barnes was too terrified for coherent thought, but was sure that being a policeman made a person invincible. He had read it somewhere in the rule book.

'Lady Wentworth!' The woman's voice rang out and Grand had to admit to a grudging sense of pride. She was totally fearless. Or as stupid as an owl. But she talked the talk, all right.

'George Frederic Watts.' The old man lifted his chin and his Old Testament beard stood out defiantly.

The voice was silent. There was not even a hiss.

'Say it again,' Florence urged.

Again, the voice said nothing, but there was a sound like a rushing wind along the topmost gallery.

Behind the door, Martin turned to Caroline. 'It sounds as if something has gone wrong with her special effects. I think you should go on now.'

'But . . . I haven't heard my cue.'

'What are you?' Martin snapped. 'Sarah Bloody Bernhardt.' He reached round and pulled her into the doorway and gave her a push in the small of her back. 'You're on,' he said, uncovering a dark lantern he had ready for the purpose.

Into the silence, backlit by a sullen yellow light, an ethereal form floated into view. Its hair was long, its clothes diaphanous, its face white and melancholy. With it came the smell of water, of grass, of the outdoors. A low keening cry came from it as it wafted along the wall of the gallery, emerging from behind the medium to go round the table widdershins. As it passed, the guests around the table turned to watch, twisting their heads to see it go.

Batchelor grabbed Grand's arm. 'Who the hell is that? Is it Katie King?'

'Florence hasn't brought Katie tonight,' Grand told him. 'Use your eyes.'

Batchelor peered closer and shook his head.

'It's Caroline, you ass. I dressed her up as Evangeline French, but I don't know what she's doing. That wasn't her cue.'

There was a clatter of a chair as Watts leaped to his feet. 'Evangeline?' he said. 'Evangeline? Is that you?'

The spectre turned hollow eyes on him and extended an arm. A white hand emerged from the calico sleeve and a finger pointed at him.

'Good girl,' Grand breathed. 'I told her she might have to improvise.'

'Spirit,' Florence said, relieved to be almost back in the plot. 'What do you want of us?'

Watts was standing open-mouthed, his hands spread at his side. 'She can't want me,' he said, desperately. 'I haven't done anything.'

Ruskin tutted. 'Really?' he said, in a stage whisper to the whole room. 'Except that crime against humanity you call Sir Galahad. That armour!'

Everyone ignored him. All eyes were on the spirit, who was backing into the shadows. It lurched and fell back.

'The spirit is losing its grasp on the earthly plane,' Florence cried. 'Everyone, join hands. Mr Watts, I beg you, join hands.'

Watts felt for the hands on either side of him, not taking his eyes off the spirit, which was almost invisible in the gloom under the *Nocturne in Blue and Gold*. The fireworks seemed to flash in the light of the few candles then, suddenly, all was dark, except for Martin's lantern at the far end of the room. There was a sudden blast of air with a hint of decay in it and the spirit was gone.

'Nice effect,' Batchelor muttered, but Grand wasn't there to hear.

'Martin,' the American was shouting, 'turn that bloody lantern up. Everyone, find a candle. Light it. There's something wrong here.'

Martin dropped the shutters from his lantern and the light shone on his face. He looked like an angel floating there in the dark and Whistler, Ruskin and Watts all drew in their breath. If only they had paints and canvas right here, right now, what a picture that would make.

'Where is she?' he called to Grand.

'I don't know. Did she say she had a grand exit planned?'

'No. We didn't know what was going on. Everything was different to what we had rehearsed.'

Wilde winced. To hear his Ganymede sunk so low as to mangle the English language caused him an almost physical pain.

Bit by bit, the gallery came alive as candles were lit. With Martin's lantern, every corner sprang to life, but of the spirit there was no sign.

Perceval Keen spoke up as the voice of reason. 'Of course, one knew that it wasn't a real spirit,' he said, 'and was one to be the person paying for this utter farce, one would be formulating one's complaint as one speaks.'

'For God's sake,' Barnes said, in the anger of the recently frightened. 'Speak English, can't you? You'll strangle yourself at this rate.'

'Well said,' Whistler chimed in. 'Speaking for myself, I was almost scared to death. But from Mr Grand's face, I would guess he was in on it and it is all a fraud. How it was done, God only knows . . .'

'You're right there,' Florence Cook threw back her veil. 'I think it was a real spirit at first, as someone who has never seen one but has seen a lot of fake ones. But I know that "Evangeline" was a real woman, and so where on earth has she gone?'

'Do you mean,' Lady Wentworth piped up, 'that this was a *fraud*?'

Lady Blanche Lindsay looked at her with disdain. 'You mad old trout,' she said. 'You must be more stupid even than you look.'

'Ladies, ladies.' Inverarity attempted to pour oil on troubled waters and got a parasol round the head for his pains.

Meanwhile, Grand had hauled Saunders out of the melee and was shaking him like a dog shakes a rat.

'Hidden doorways,' he yelled at him. 'Fake panels. Where are they?'

Saunders shook his head. 'There aren't any,' he whimpered. 'This is a bloody art gallery, not some castle in a ghost story. We don't have priest holes and secret passages here!'

Grand continued to shake him, for want of anything else to do.

Whistler watched with horror. They were very near his painting and, if they weren't careful, they'd have it off the . . . he cried out in pain as it hit the floor, the frame splintering and the canvas cracking across his famous butterfly signature.

Ruskin laughed until it brought on a bout of coughing and he had to be ministered to by Alice Arbuthnot.

Wilde peered at the space where the portrait had hung. 'Gan?' he said, raising his voice over the general din. 'What's that?'

Martin looked closer. On the wall, where the painting had been, there was an irregularity in the panelling. Moving forward as if in slow motion, he reached out a hand and pressed it. On oiled and silent hinges, the panel slid away, leaving a black hole behind it.

'Good God,' Saunders said. 'So we *have* got a secret passageway.'

Martin stood back. 'So that's why everything seemed lopsided,' he said, half to himself.

Grand dropped Saunders, who sagged against the substantial bulk of Lady Blanche, who shook him off as if he were contagious. Staff just didn't know how to keep to their place, these days.

'Lopsided?' he asked.

Martin was looking around the enormous space of the gallery. 'Yes,' he said. 'When I was here before, I felt uncomfortable. There was something in the proportions, but I put it down to how the pictures were hung.'

Saunders gave an offended grunt.

'But now I realize it is because there are hidden rooms. This one, obviously, but not only that. There's something wrong with . . .' He looked up into the rafters. 'Look,' he said, pointing, 'there is a bit up there where the ceiling stops short.'

Everyone looked up, shielding their eyes against the candlelight.

'He's right,' Inverarity said. 'I see it.'

And that wasn't all there was to see. On the walkway above their heads, the spirit of Evangeline French was being dragged by an artist in full fig to a door which those with keener sight could now see clearly.

'Why did I never see that before?' Whistler said. 'I've spent hours in this gallery.'

'Because you can't see beyond your nose,' Ruskin muttered, and Perceval Keen smothered a laugh then turned it into a cough; he wasn't proud of being Whistler's brief, but it was money in the bank and there was no such thing as bad publicity.

'How the hell do we get up there?' Grand shouted at the crowd in general.

'Up those stairs, I would imagine,' Inverarity said, disentangling himself from the elderly titled ladies with pleasure. Heedless of his best mess dress, he dashed into the dark void and was soon back. 'There's no possible way up there for men of our build,' he said to Grand. 'Far too narrow.'

'How, then?' Grand shouted at Saunders. By now the artist and his captive had disappeared.

'Joe would know,' Saunders said.

'Fetch him, then,' Batchelor yelled. The man must be an idiot not to know his own building. Sir Coutts Lindsay was thinking the same and planning the advertisement for his replacement while he waited for developments.

'I gave him the evening off,' Saunders said. 'It seemed the perfect time, with all of us here.'

Grand felt ready to kill someone, and it might as well be Saunders. He wound his arm back for a killer right to the jaw, but Martin stopped him.

'No, Mr Grand, don't. You'll be sorry later. Look.' He pointed to a corner of the studio, the one where Caroline had seen her ghost and the phantom painting of a dead woman. 'That wall is shorter than it should be, look. It doesn't go in again after the door architrave. I bet there's a stair behind there. Hopefully, not as narrow.'

The crowd parted as Grand and Batchelor, with Inverarity, Barnes and Martin in hot pursuit, ran for the corner of the room. Barnes was not keen on small spaces, but when he thought of explaining to Metcalfe in the morning, squeezing up a narrow staircase seemed the sensible choice. Martin shouldered to the front and, after a little scuffling, a panel swung outward, revealing a perfectly normal-size flight of steps. The men disappeared into the cavity and, within moments, there was a cry from Florence, who was looking up at the gallery.

'There he is!'

And indeed, Grand had appeared on the balcony and was already shoulder-barging the door through which the artist and model had disappeared.

FOURTEEN

T he room beyond the door was in almost total darkness beyond the distant candlelight filtering in, but within the dark, something moved. It wasn't silent, though. Caroline's whimpers could be heard, begging the artist not to hurt her.

'Be quiet,' a low voice answered her. 'I won't hurt you. Models are too hard to come by.'

Caroline, her voice steadying now she could see that help might be at hand, replied. 'You did hurt some though, didn't you? The girls in the Cremorne.'

'You're alive, though,' the voice argued.

'Of course I'm not,' she said. 'You threw me in the lake.' She sounded as if it were the most normal thing in the world, and Grand's heart almost burst with love and pride.

'Only because I thought you were dead,' he said, also very reasonably. They could have been two friends chatting over the teacups.

'And you were right,' Caroline said, calmly. 'I'm here to find out why.'

Barnes whispered into Grand's ear. 'When all this is over, I think we should have that young lady in the police.'

'I saw her first,' Grand said, which was only the truth.

The scrape of a match made everyone jump and the room was suddenly filled with the golden light of an oil lamp. The canvases, stacked to the far end of the attic, looked almost like spectators, watching this battle of wits. Women's faces – for only women had been put down in paint – seemed to follow every nuance, the throbbing light giving them life which their indifferent painter had been unable to provide. Inverarity, though no judge of art, could tell that the execution was not of the first water. Possibly, their artist could have made a living making portraits of tradesmen wanting to go up in the world. But even Whistler looked accurate and meticulous by comparison.

'This is why,' he murmured. 'Every one of these women are my models. Some are dead. Some are living. But none of them brought me fame.' Still holding Caroline tightly to him, he marched her down the rows. 'This one, see, she came to me to have her portrait painted. She is no beauty, but I tried my best. She laughed when she saw it, said she couldn't give a thing like that to the man she loved. She asked for her money back.'

'What . . . what happened to her?' Caroline hardly dared ask.

'It's many years ago,' he said quietly. 'I think she died.'

'Died?'

'Yes. It was sad, I suppose. She . . . ate something that disagreed with her.'

Caroline was silent. 'I see.' She was dragged a little further along the row and another painting was pulled out into the light so she could see it better. 'And her?'

'She may be alive. She may be not. I . . . loved her, for a while.'

And on the *danse macabre* went. Some faces stared out without arousing a flicker of recognition. Others were brought out into the light, displayed for Caroline to look into their eyes. Was it her imagination, or was there fear in those dark pupils; did the lips look as if they were begging for their lives?

Inch by inch, the men in the doorway came closer, Grand at their head. Soon, they were all inside the low room, Inverarity and Grand having to stoop to accommodate the ceiling height.

The artist seemed stuck in a reverie looking at the next portrait.

'I know that face,' Barnes whispered. 'It's Ellen Terry.'

'I didn't have you down as a theatre-goer,' Batchelor said quietly.

'Just now and then,' Barnes said, and blushed. 'I quite like amateur dramatics.'

Grand turned, surprised. 'Don't you get enough in the police?' he asked. 'Drama, I mean, not amateurism.'

'I do just lately.'

While they had been speaking, the artist had dragged Caroline to a chaise longue, set up in front of an easel. He threw the painting propped there to the ground and replaced it with a fresh canvas. Caroline rolled her eyes at Grand, silhouetted in the doorway. The discarded painting was of a woman, clearly dead.

'I've always wanted to do a lounging study,' he said. 'I've tried everything to get those stupid girls to relax. I've provided them with reading matter. I used to take pillows and rugs, but they misunderstood. One-track minds, those Cremorne girls, that's their trouble.'

'That's not exactly a surprise,' Inverarity murmured, and Grand looked at him. The soldier shrugged. 'Needs must,' he said, with a disarming smile.

'Watts, he does lounging studies,' he was saying as he tied Caroline down with silken ropes. 'They all lounge for him, oh, yes. And he'd let us paint them too, sometimes. Then suddenly, it's "Giuseppe. You have the artistic insight of a camel. Get out." And that was it. I was twice the artist of all of them put together, Watts, Prinsep and Stanhope. But it's out I go.'

'Watts said he had three students,' Batchelor said in Grand's ear. 'This must be the third one.'

Grand nodded and crept an inch or two nearer.

The knots were tied to Giuseppe's satisfaction and he walked round to face the canvas. He turned it landscape and with an almost dry brush, began to sketch the basic shape.

'Was Watts in on this?' Barnes asked. 'I thought he was a bit dodgy.'

Grand shook his head. That seemed unlikely.

'And since then,' Giuseppe went on, 'I've lived hand to mouth, painting ugly women and trying to make them beautiful. And when I succeed, as often as not they don't recognize themselves. Or they laugh. And so here I am, caretaker at an art gallery – know what I mean, darlin'? – that only hangs the rubbish no one else will take.'

The changed voice helped the penny drop for Grand and Batchelor. Giuseppe. Joe the caretaker. The caretaker who didn't wake up when paintings were defaced because he was awake and doing the damage himself.

'I had a few close calls.' He was mixing flesh tint in a small jar. 'That mad soldier, the one who liked dressing up, he saw me one night. I can't remember which one I was doing; they've all run together in my mind, to be honest.'

Barnes's eyes nearly dropped out of his head. There were more?

'I thought it would be all right. After all, he had almost as much to lose as me if he came forward. But that idiot Whistler put him in the foreground of his daub and I had to paint him out. So then, I had to change other pictures as well, so no one would get suspicious. And so on and on and round and round I go. Murdering and painting, painting and murdering . . .' He suddenly put his brush down. 'I don't know about you, but I'm a bit peckish. Do you fancy a slice of cake?'

Martin leaned forward and pulled at Grand's sleeve. 'Cake,' he muttered urgently. 'Don't let her eat the cake. Almonds in the marzipan. Cyanide.'

Giuseppe heard the last word and spun round, leaving a gash of crimson lake across his embryonic painting.

'What are you doing here?' he asked, aghast. 'My oeuvre is by no means ready for viewing yet. I am still working on my masterpiece.'

'And what a masterpiece it is,' Batchelor said, stepping forward and reaching towards Caroline. 'But I think she needs to stretch her legs, don't you, Evangeline?' He popped the knots with ease. 'Can't overwork your model, you know.'

Grand wondered what Batchelor could possibly know about that.

Caroline got up from the chaise longue. The ties on her wrists and ankles hadn't hurt, but they had felt like chains of iron. Batchelor, keeping his body between her and Giuseppe, propelled her to the door, where she was caught expertly by Grand who held her to his heart with all his strength. Inverarity gently disentangled her and took her to safety.

Giuseppe watched her go. 'She'll come back, though?' he checked.

'Of course.' Batchelor sat down on the chaise longue and looked the artist in the eye. 'We know what you've done, Joe,' he said. 'You'll have to come with us.'

'Come with you where?' the man said, dragging off his

floppy beret and mopping his brow. Although he kept himself in trim, it had been quite the evening, what with running about lighting candles, and manhandling strapping young women. Even using the room's natural acoustic, making his voice boom out like that had been quite tiring. Being taken somewhere quiet for a while, where he could just get on with his painting, would be quite pleasant.

'I have a nice studio,' Grand began.

'And I have an even better cell,' Barnes said. It wasn't that he was insensitive and he could see quite well what Grand was trying to do, but he had Inspector Metcalfe to deal with, and if this loony was carted off to some nice bin somewhere, then he could kiss his promotion goodbye.

'Cell?' Joe's eyes were wide with shock and sorrow. 'Cell?' He looked at Batchelor. 'Do they let you paint in prison?'

The silence was the answer.

Joe's arms fell to his sides. 'Can I just sign my last work?' he asked and laughed, just a little. 'It might make it worth some money, one day.'

'I don't see why not,' Barnes said. He had his man; he could afford to be magnanimous. Batchelor raised a hand to stop him, but Grand shook his head.

Joe dipped his brush carefully into a pot of dark paint, then dipped it again. He looked at the end, which was splayed and useless for a signature. He put the brush to his lips and rolled it around, giving it a good, sharp point. Then, with a look in his eyes straight from his own, special circle of hell, he took one last gasp, and fell to the floor.

Barnes looked frantically about and finally his whirling brain recognized Grand. 'Is he . . . is he . . . dead?'

''Fraid so,' Grand said, kneeling beside the man and checking his pulse. 'Never mind, Constable Barnes. We'll make sure that Inspector Metcalfe knows you had your man, no matter how briefly.'

The next morning, no one felt like going to the office, so Martin joined Grand and Batchelor for breakfast. To his amazement, Lady Caroline Wentworth was there too, in a rather fetching peignoir of peach silk. Batchelor was also amazed, but had decided to stay out of it. Mrs Rackstraw was too busy to be amazed because Maisie had been taken silly having found Lady Caroline déshabillé in Mr Matthew's bedroom, so breakfast was a one-woman affair, though no one would have guessed it from the groaning table. But as she scuttled around, the housekeeper was hoping that Mr Juniper would soon step up and be counted; this was all too much for a woman of her years and sensibilities.

For quite a while, everyone chewed, slurped or nibbled according to their lights, but eventually, someone had to speak.

'So,' Martin said, 'all's well that ends well, eh?'

'That's it, is it?' Batchelor said, bitterly. 'A private school and then an Oxford degree and that's all you can come up with?'

Martin was crestfallen. He had thought that a Shakespeare quote was good enough for anyone.

'I don't call it ending well, Alexander,' Caroline said. Although she had, in the end, chosen brawn over beauty, she had a soft spot for the lad. 'So many people died.'

'People die all the time,' Grand said. 'But not usually so many for the sake of art, perhaps.'

'I felt a bit sorry for him,' Caroline said. 'He didn't really hurt me and he only did it at all last night because he was scared by the séance. He was muttering all the time as he dragged me upstairs. He could see all the women he had killed, in the air, he said. They were with him all the time, not just when he was in the attic with their paintings.'

'Oh, yes,' Martin said, 'talking of those. I understand the Lindsays are going to have a retrospective of Giuseppe's paintings.'

The three others were open mouthed. 'That's *horrible*,' Caroline said.

'Business is business, I suppose,' Batchelor said.

'Trade, Mama would call it,' Caroline said, with the usual smell under her nose. 'But it is still rather lacking in taste, James.'

Grand caught her eye. They had had a long talk, well into the small hours, about her tendency to turn into her mother.

'But of course, at the end of the day,' she said, with a smile, 'it is entirely up to them, dear.'

Grand nodded and smiled, lowering his lids in acknowledgement.

'So perhaps you won't find this gratuitous either,' Martin said. 'Oscar was rather taken with the idea of portraits in the attic. He thinks there might be a story in it.'

'Ooh,' Batchelor said, thinking of his Great British Novel lying unheeded upstairs. 'I doubt it, Alexander. I really, really do.'